SPIDER-MAN

JUMPING TO CONCLUSIONS

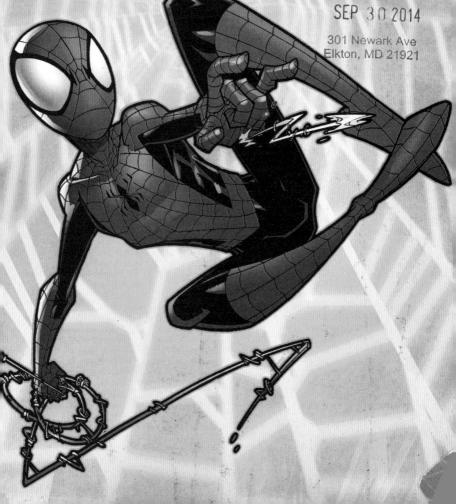

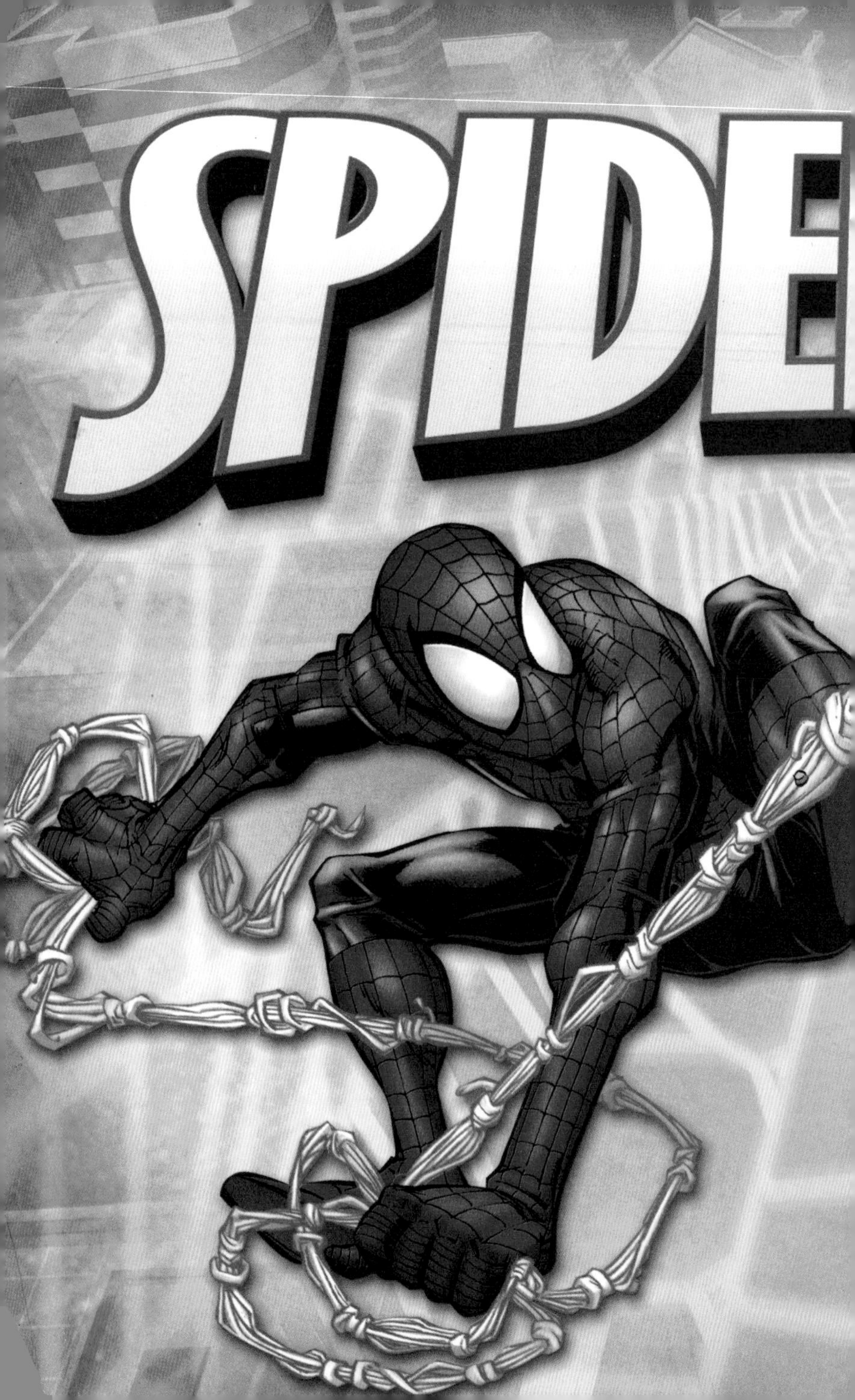
SPIDE

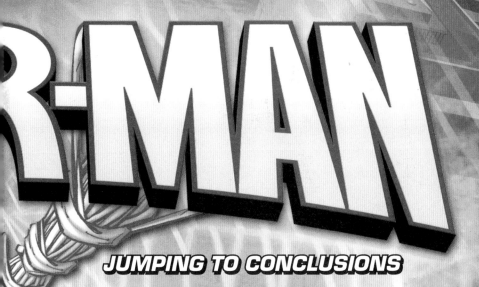

R-MAN

JUMPING TO CONCLUSIONS

Writer: **Todd DeZago**
Pencilers: **Zach Howard, Roberto Castro, Sanford Greene & Jonboy Meyers**
Inkers: **Zach Howard, Greg Adams, Kris Justice, Nathan Massengill & Jonboy Meyers**
Colors: **Sotocolor's A. Street**
Letters: **Dave Sharpe**
Cover Artists: **Zach Howard & Brad Anderson; Francis Tsai; and Sanford Greene, Nathan Massengill & Chris Sotomayor**
Assistant Editor: **Jordan D. White**
Consulting Editor: **Ralph Macchio**
Editors: **Mark Paniccia & Nathan Cosby**

Collection Editor: **Jennifer Grünwald**
Editorial Assistant: **Alex Starbuck**
Assistant Editors: **Cory Levine & John Denning**
Editor, Special Projects: **Mark D. Beazley**
Senior Editor, Special Projects: **Jeff Youngquist**
Senior Vice President of Sales: **David Gabriel**
Vice President of Creative: **Tom Marvelli**

Editor in Chief: **Joe Quesada**
Publisher: **Dan Buckley**
Executive Producer: **Alan Fine**

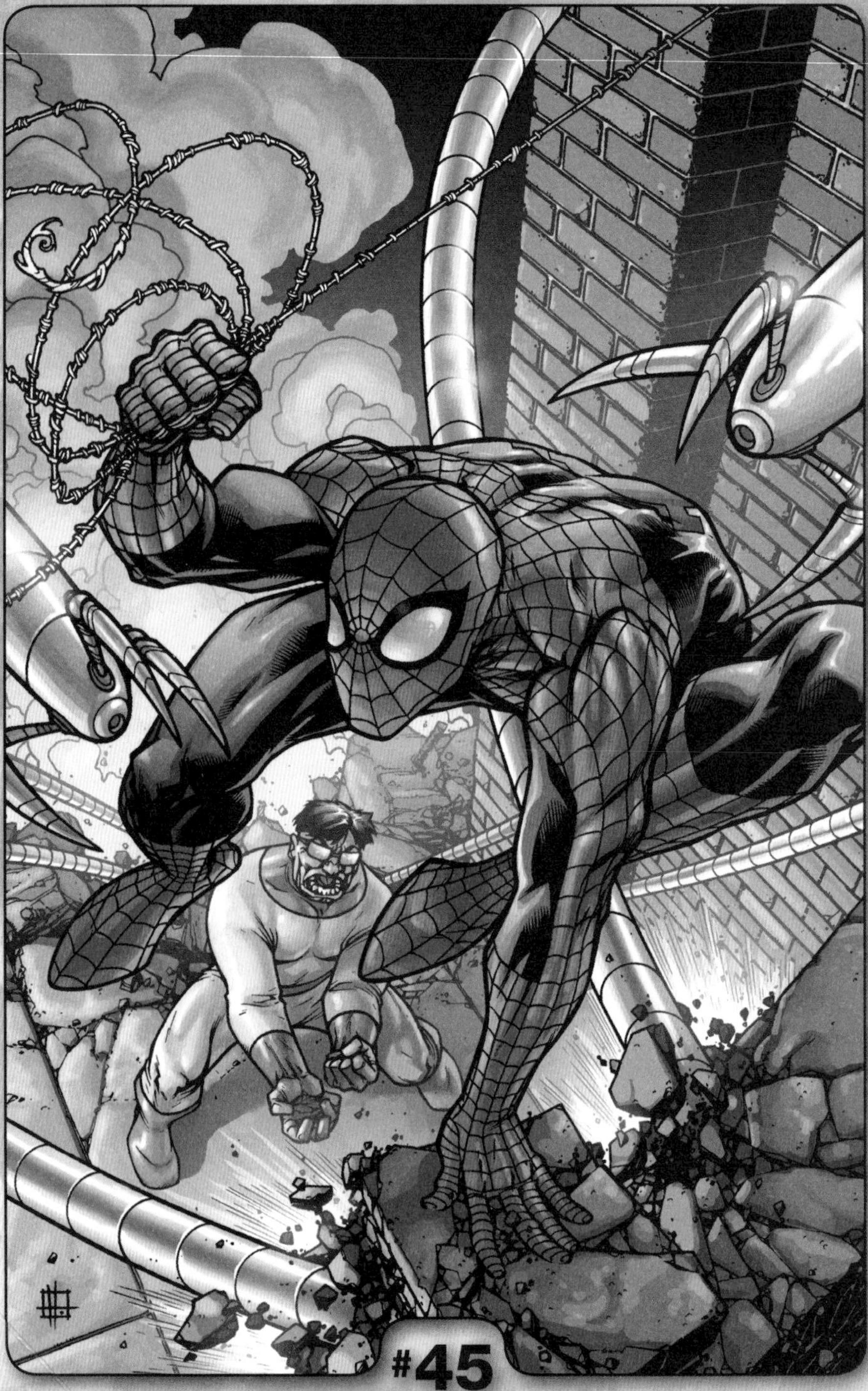
#45

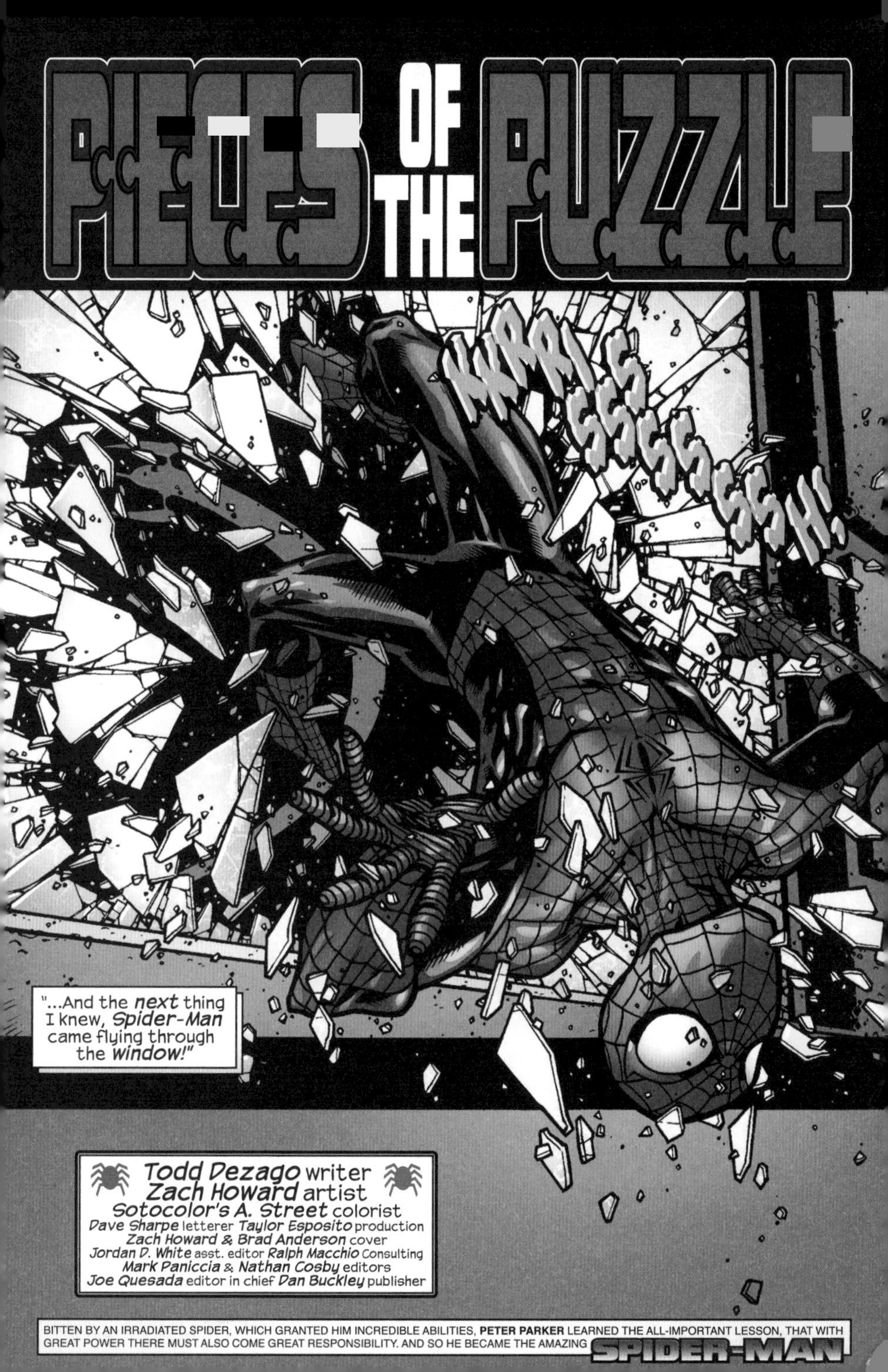
PIECES OF THE PUZZLE
KRRISSSSSSSSH!
"...And the next thing I knew, Spider-Man came flying through the window!"
Todd Dezago writer
Zach Howard artist
Sotocolor's A. Street colorist
Dave Sharpe letterer Taylor Esposito production
Zach Howard & Brad Anderson cover
Jordan D. White asst. editor Ralph Macchio Consulting
Mark Paniccia & Nathan Cosby editors
Joe Quesada editor in chief Dan Buckley publisher
BITTEN BY AN IRRADIATED SPIDER, WHICH GRANTED HIM INCREDIBLE ABILITIES, PETER PARKER LEARNED THE ALL-IMPORTANT LESSON, THAT WITH GREAT POWER THERE MUST ALSO COME GREAT RESPONSIBILITY. AND SO HE BECAME THE AMAZING SPIDER-MAN

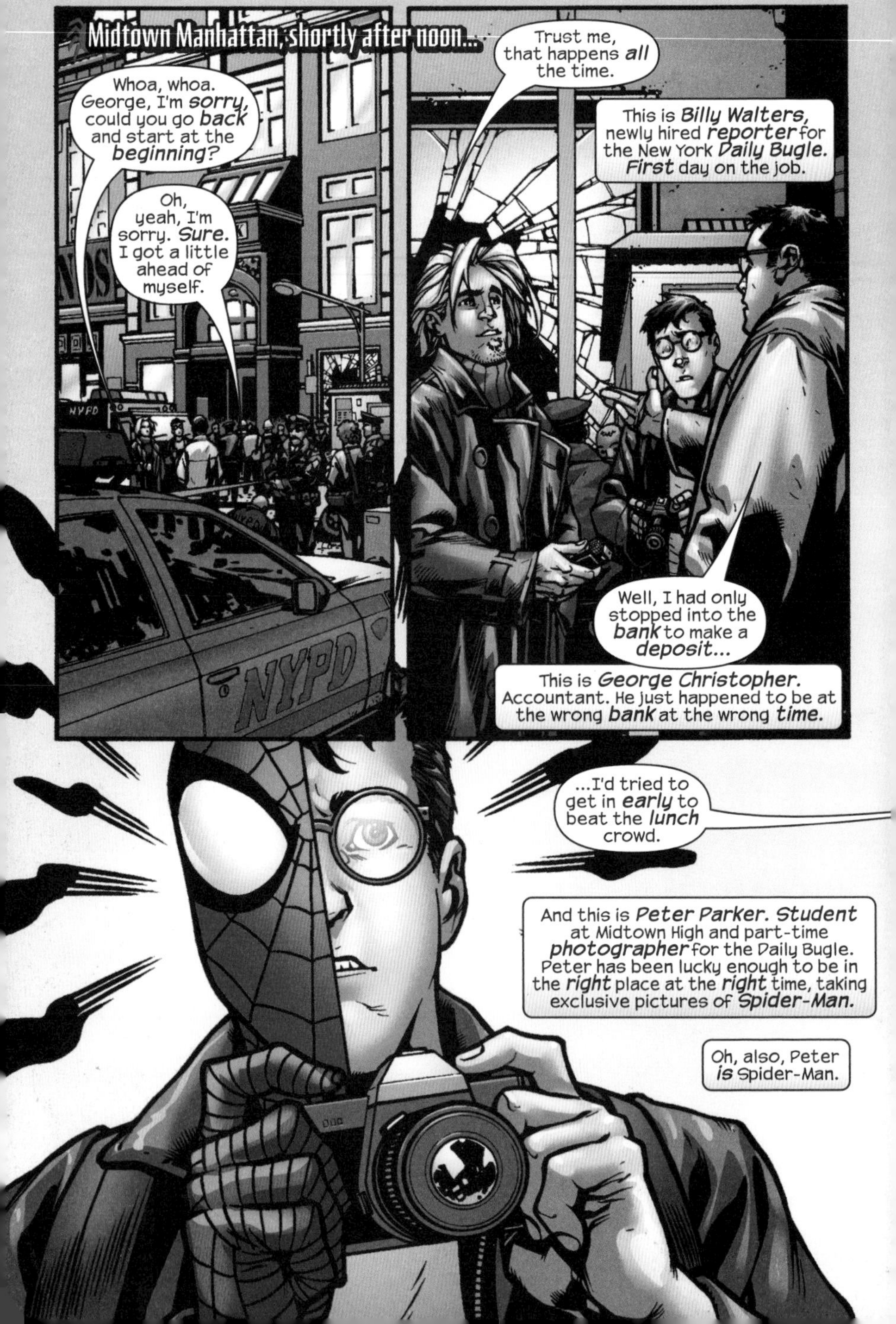
Midtown Manhattan, shortly after noon...
Whoa, whoa. George, I'm sorry, could you go back and start at the beginning?
Oh, yeah, I'm sorry. Sure. I got a little ahead of myself.
Trust me, that happens all the time.
This is Billy Walters, newly hired reporter for the New York Daily Bugle. First day on the job.
Well, I had only stopped into the bank to make a deposit...
This is George Christopher. Accountant. He just happened to be at the wrong bank at the wrong time.
NYPD
NYPD
...I'd tried to get in early to beat the lunch crowd.
And this is Peter Parker. Student at Midtown High and part-time photographer for the Daily Bugle. Peter has been lucky enough to be in the right place at the right time, taking exclusive pictures of Spider-Man.
Oh, also, Peter is Spider-Man.

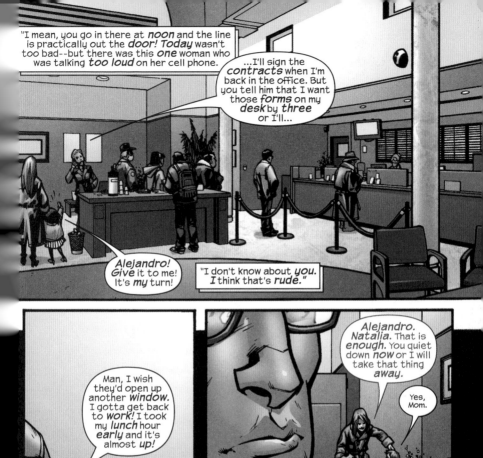

"I mean, you go in there at *noon* and the line is practically out the *door! Today* wasn't too bad--but there was this *one* woman who was talking *too loud* on her cell phone.

...I'll sign the *contracts* when I'm back in the office. But you tell him that I want those *forms* on my *desk* by *three* or I'll...

Alejandro! *Give* it to me! It's *my* turn!

"I don't know about *you.* I think that's *rude.*"

Man, I wish they'd open up another *window.* I gotta get back to *work!* I took my *lunch* hour *early* and it's almost *up!*

Alejandro. Natalia. That is *enough.* You quiet down *now* or I will take that thing *away.*

Yes, Mom.

"So, really, just a *quiet* day. Nothing out of the *ordinary.* So none of us were *expecting* what happened *next...*"

Attention, my fellow bank patrons!

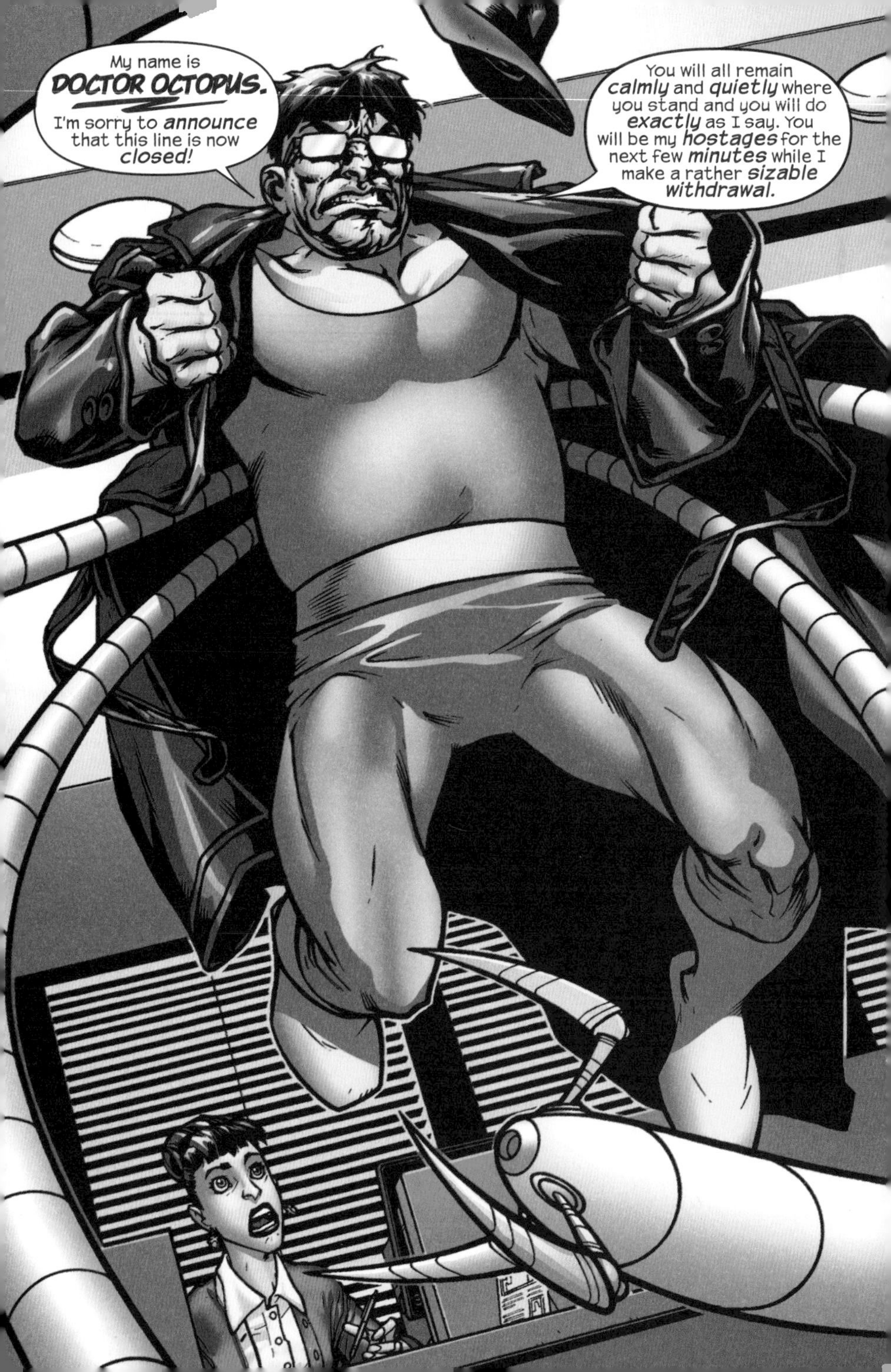
My name is DOCTOR OCTOPUS. I'm sorry to announce that this line is now closed!
You will all remain calmly and quietly where you stand and you will do exactly as I say. You will be my hostages for the next few minutes while I make a rather sizable withdrawal.

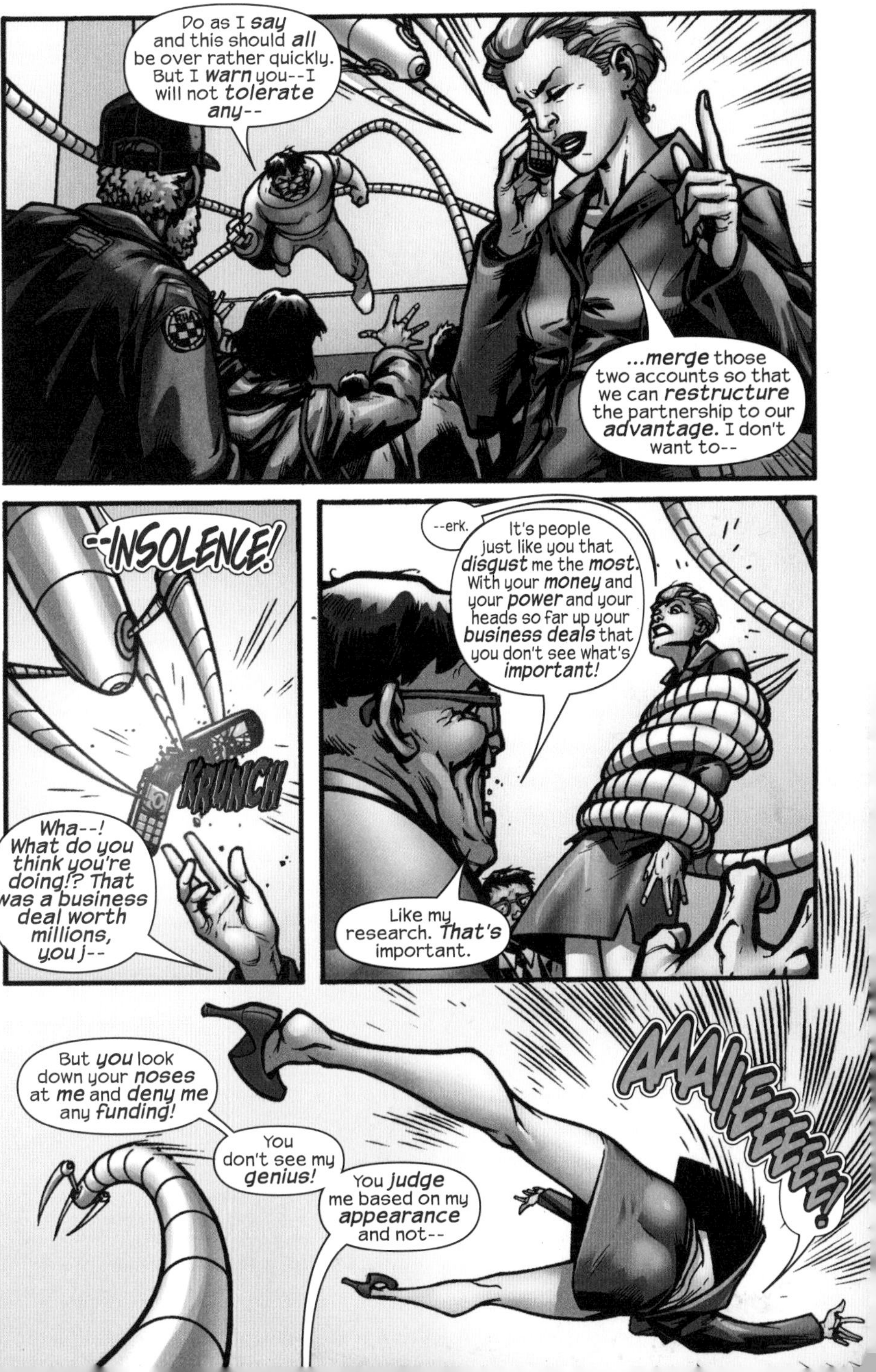

Do as I say and this should all be over rather quickly. But I warn you--I will not tolerate any--
...merge those two accounts so that we can restructure the partnership to our advantage. I don't want to--
--INSOLENCE!
KRUNCH
Wha--! What do you think you're doing!? That was a business deal worth millions, you j--
--erk.
It's people just like you that disgust me the most. With your money and your power and your heads so far up your business deals that you don't see what's important!
Like my research. That's important.
But you look down your noses at me and deny me any funding!
You don't see my genius!
You judge me based on my appearance and not--
AAAIIEEEEEE!

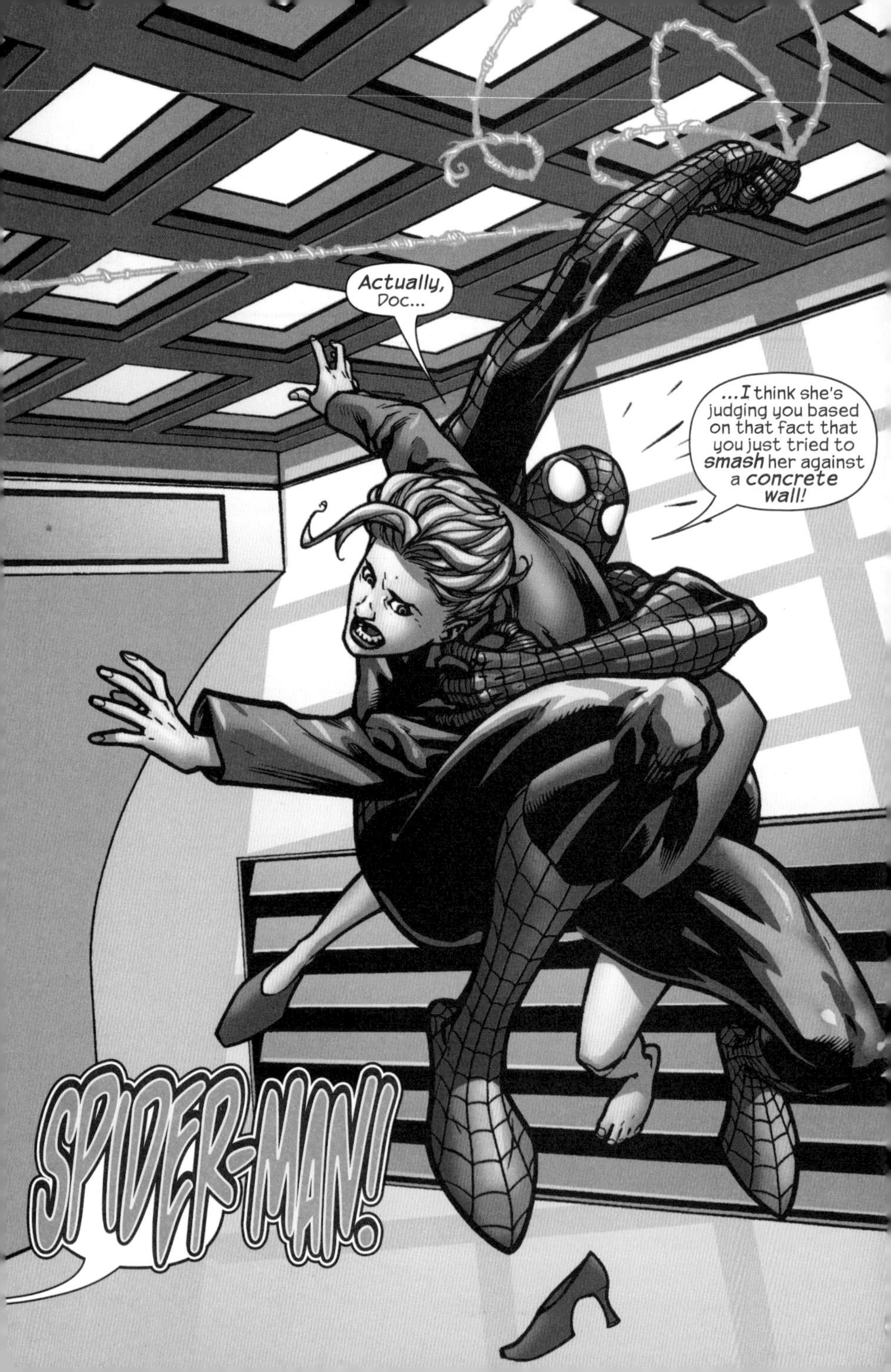
Actually, Doc...
...I think she's judging you based on that fact that you just tried to smash her against a concrete wall!
SPIDER-MAN!

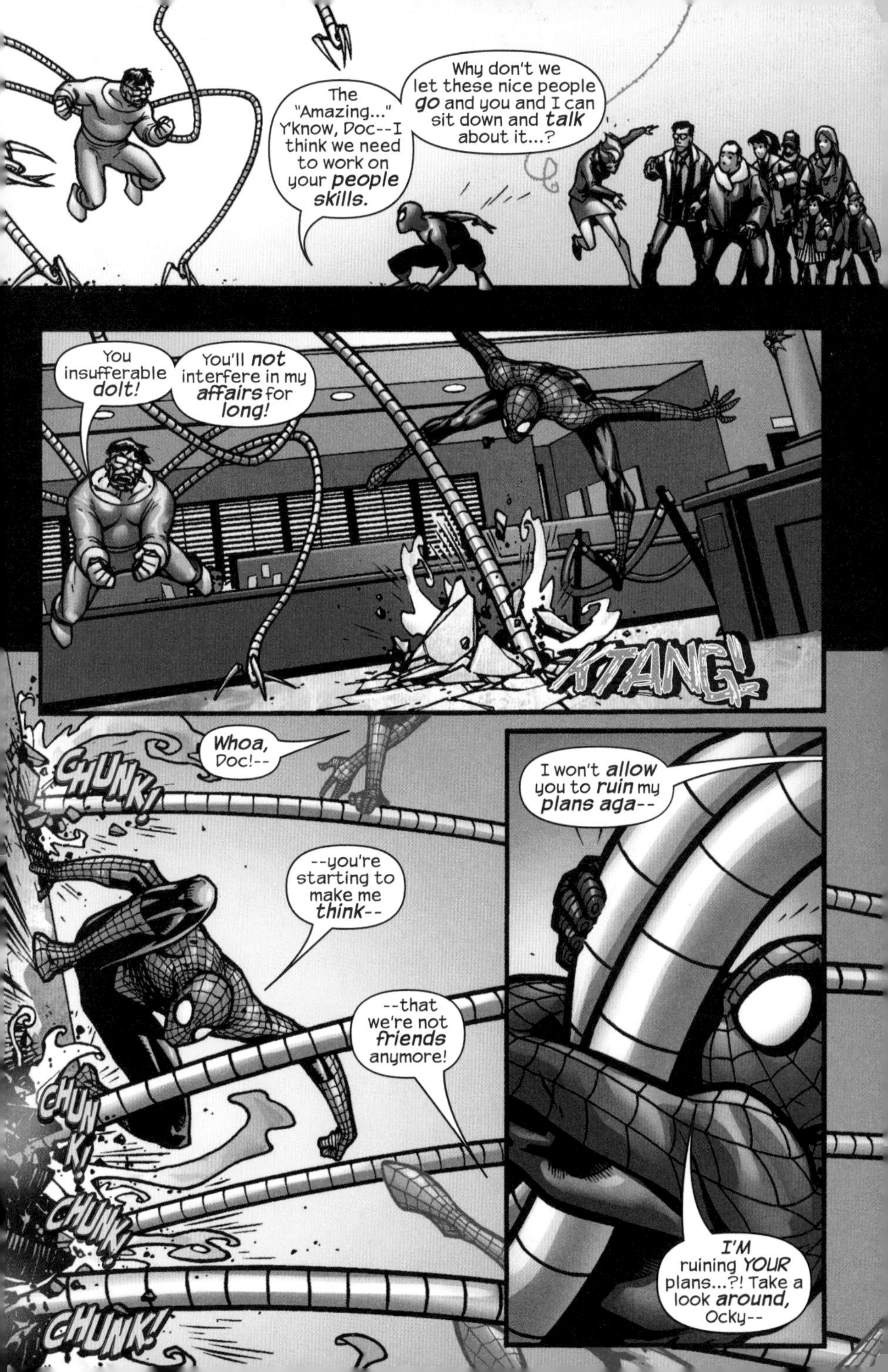

The "Amazing..." Y'know, Doc--I think we need to work on your people skills.
Why don't we let these nice people go and you and I can sit down and talk about it...?
You insufferable dolt!
You'll not interfere in my affairs for long!
KTANG!
Whoa, Doc!--
CHUNK!
--you're starting to make me think--
--that we're not friends anymore!
CHUNK!
CHUNK!
CHUNK!
I won't allow you to ruin my plans aga--
I'M ruining YOUR plans...?! Take a look around, Ocky--

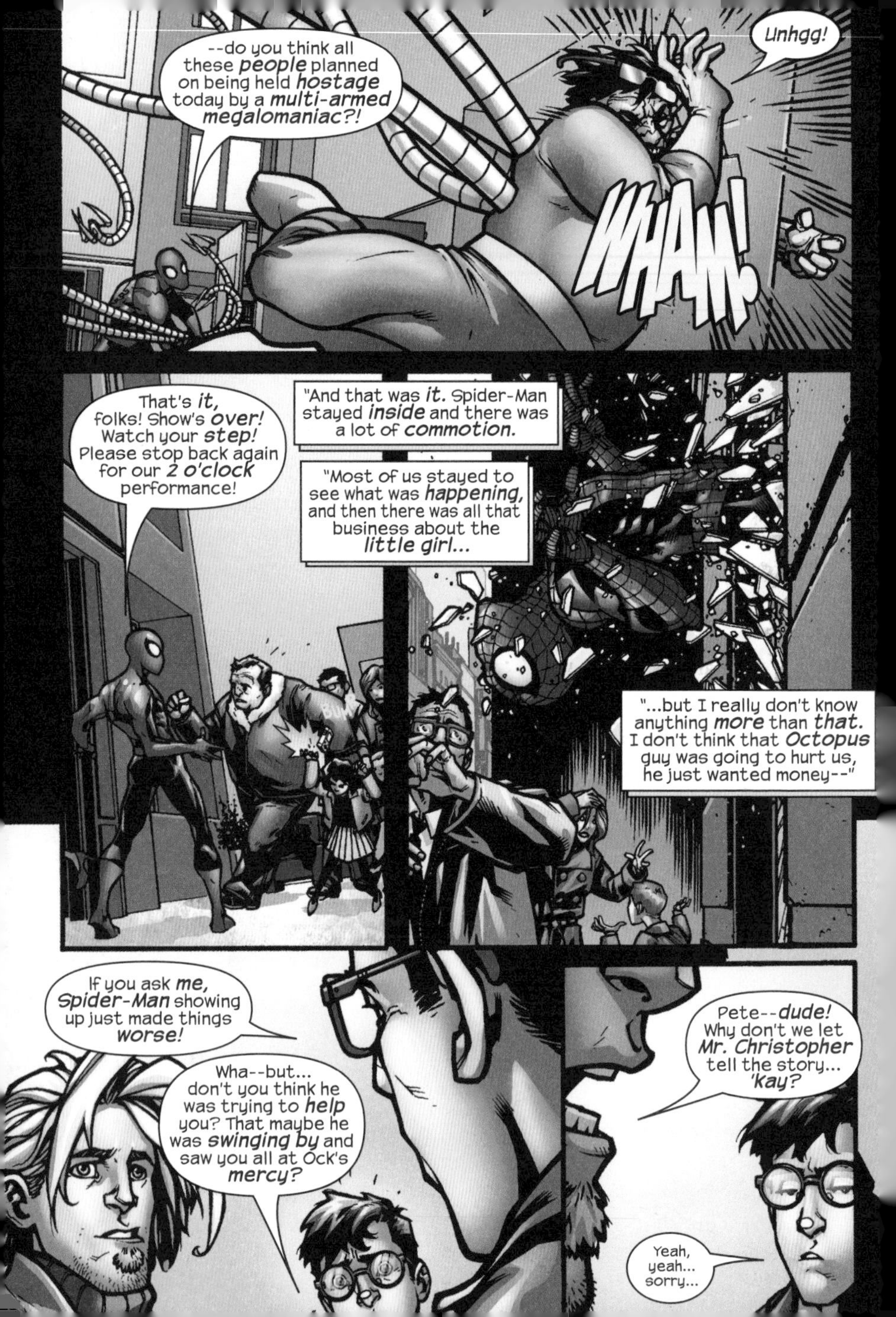
--do you think all these people planned on being held hostage today by a multi-armed megalomaniac?!
Unhgg!
WHAM!
That's it, folks! Show's over! Watch your step! Please stop back again for our 2 o'clock performance!
"And that was it. Spider-Man stayed inside and there was a lot of commotion.
"Most of us stayed to see what was happening, and then there was all that business about the little girl...
"...but I really don't know anything more than that. I don't think that Octopus guy was going to hurt us, he just wanted money--"
If you ask me, Spider-Man showing up just made things worse!
Wha--but... don't you think he was trying to help you? That maybe he was swinging by and saw you all at Ock's mercy?
Pete--dude! Why don't we let Mr. Christopher tell the story... 'kay?
Yeah, yeah... sorry...

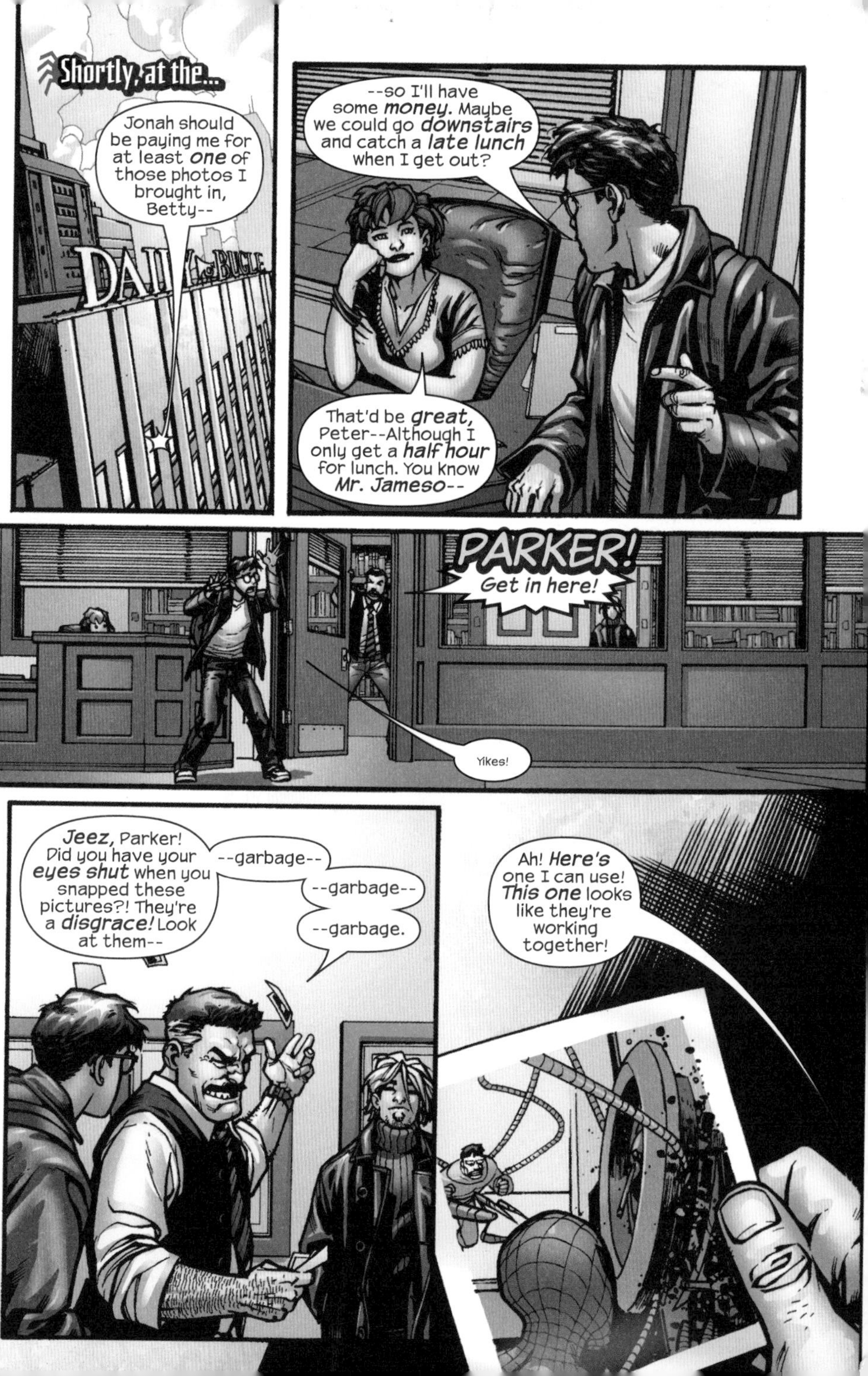
Shortly, at the...
Jonah should be paying me for at least one of those photos I brought in, Betty--
--so I'll have some money. Maybe we could go downstairs and catch a late lunch when I get out?
That'd be great, Peter--Although I only get a half hour for lunch. You know Mr. Jameso--
PARKER! Get in here!
Yikes!
Jeez, Parker! Did you have your eyes shut when you snapped these pictures?! They're a disgrace! Look at them--
--garbage--
--garbage--
--garbage.
Ah! Here's one I can use! This one looks like they're working together!

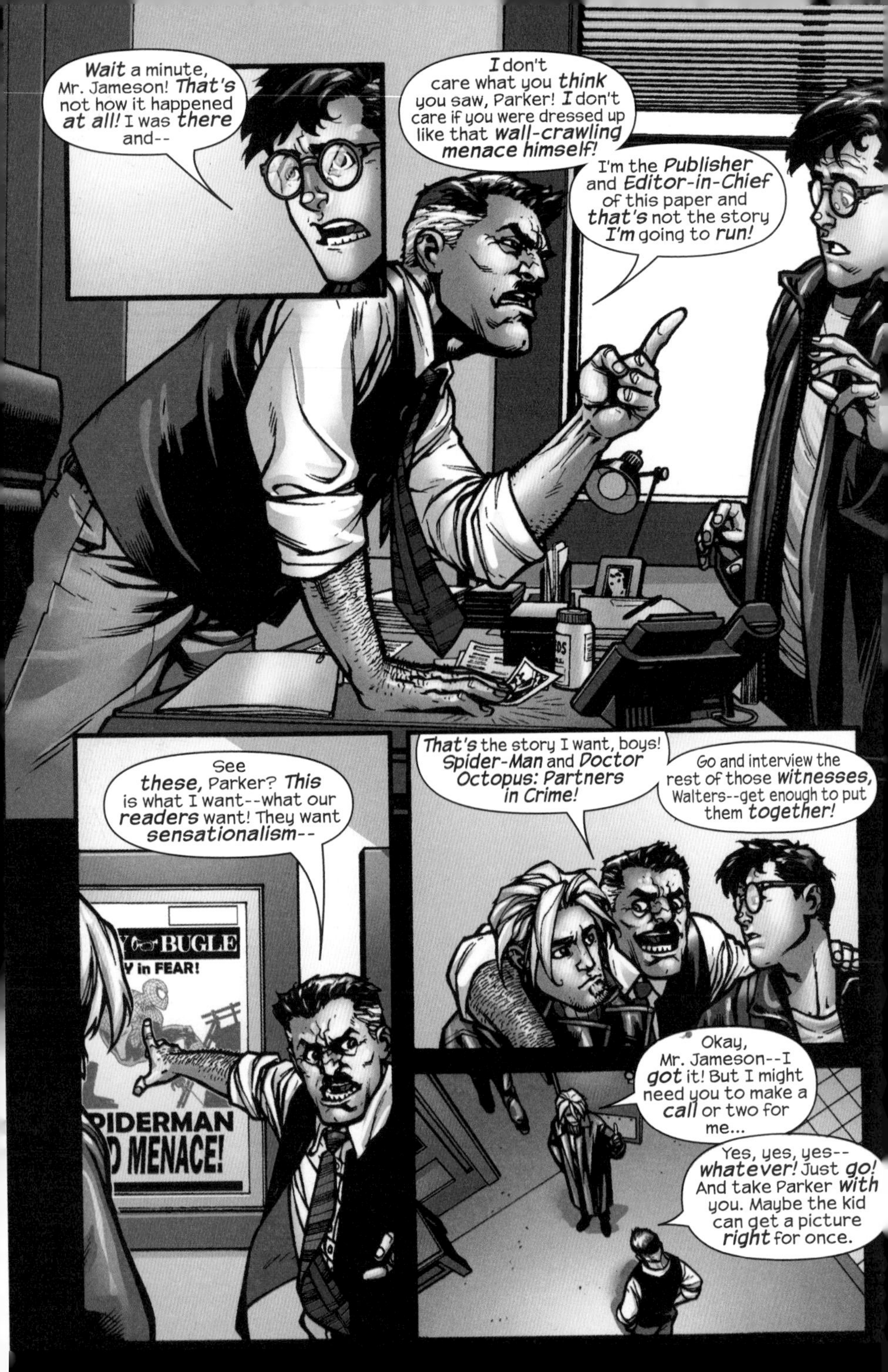

Wait a minute, Mr. Jameson! That's not how it happened at all! I was there and--
I don't care what you think you saw, Parker! I don't care if you were dressed up like that wall-crawling menace himself!
I'm the Publisher and Editor-in-Chief of this paper and that's not the story I'm going to run!
See these, Parker? This is what I want--what our readers want! They want sensationalism--
BUGLE
Y in FEAR!
PIDERMAN
D MENACE!
That's the story I want, boys! Spider-Man and Doctor Octopus: Partners in Crime!
Go and interview the rest of those witnesses, Walters--get enough to put them together!
Okay, Mr. Jameson--I got it! But I might need you to make a call or two for me...
Yes, yes, yes-- whatever! Just go! And take Parker with you. Maybe the kid can get a picture right for once.

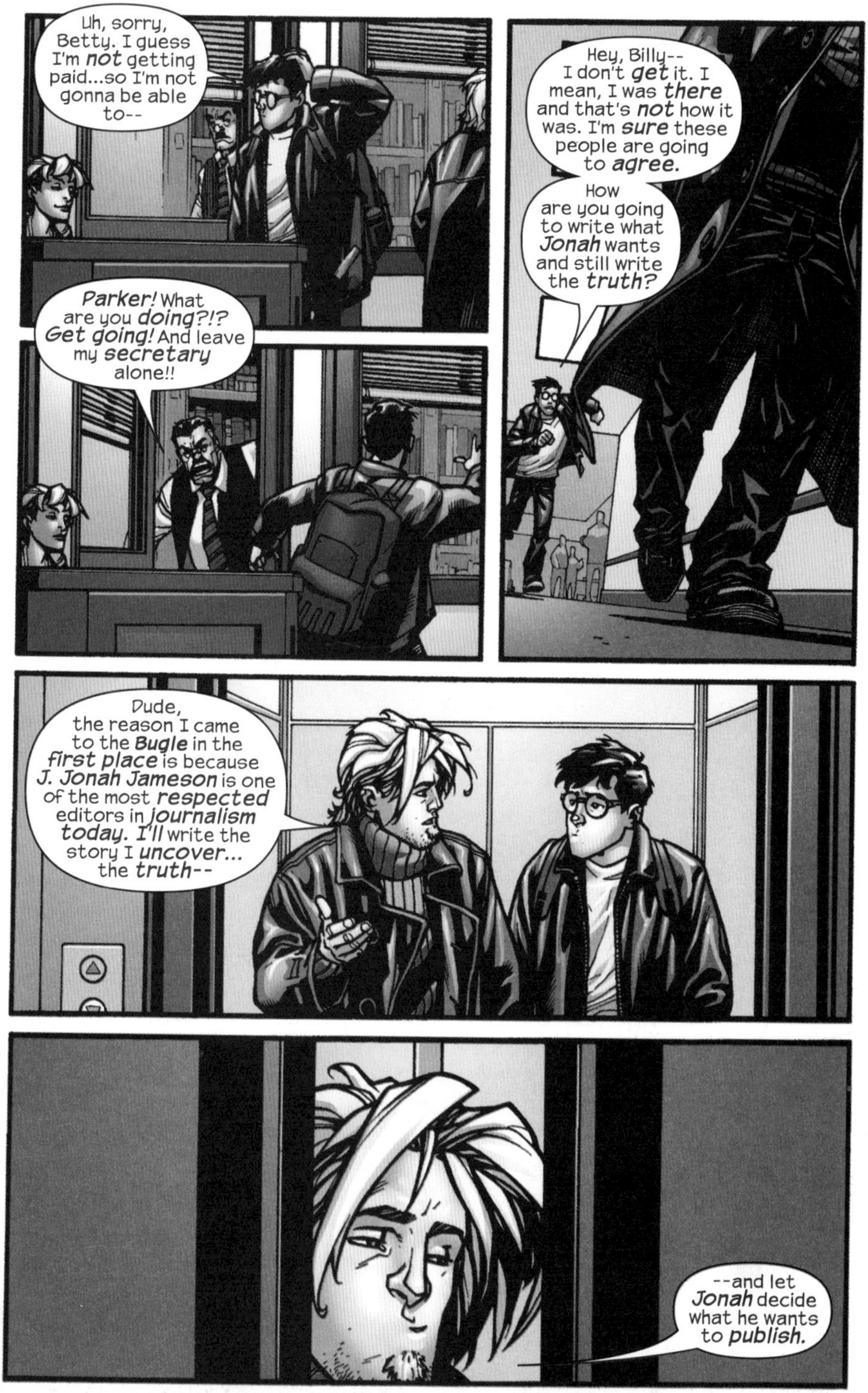
Uh, sorry, Betty. I guess I'm not getting paid...so I'm not gonna be able to--
Parker! What are you doing?!? Get going! And leave my secretary alone!!
Hey, Billy-- I don't get it. I mean, I was there and that's not how it was. I'm sure these people are going to agree.
How are you going to write what Jonah wants and still write the truth?
Dude, the reason I came to the Bugle in the first place is because J. Jonah Jameson is one of the most respected editors in journalism today. I'll write the story I uncover... the truth--
--and let Jonah decide what he wants to publish.

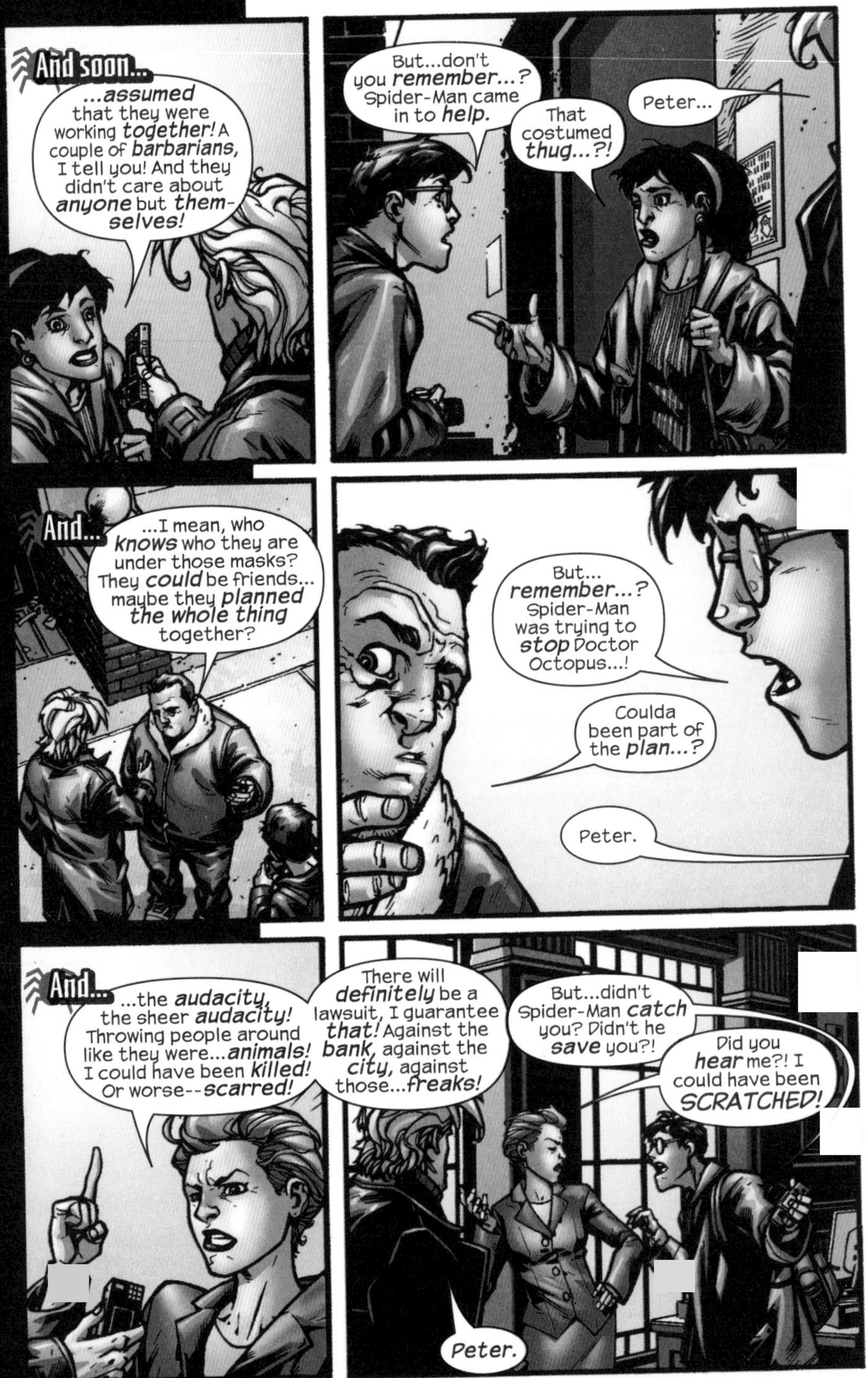
And soon...
...assumed that they were working together! A couple of barbarians, I tell you! And they didn't care about anyone but themselves!
But...don't you remember...? Spider-Man came in to help.
That costumed thug...?!
Peter...
And...
...I mean, who knows who they are under those masks? They could be friends... maybe they planned the whole thing together?
But... remember...? Spider-Man was trying to stop Doctor Octopus...!
Coulda been part of the plan...?
Peter.
And...
...the audacity, the sheer audacity! Throwing people around like they were...animals! I could have been killed! Or worse--scarred!
There will definitely be a lawsuit, I guarantee that! Against the bank, against the city, against those...freaks!
But...didn't Spider-Man catch you? Didn't he save you?!
Did you hear me?! I could have been SCRATCHED!
Peter.

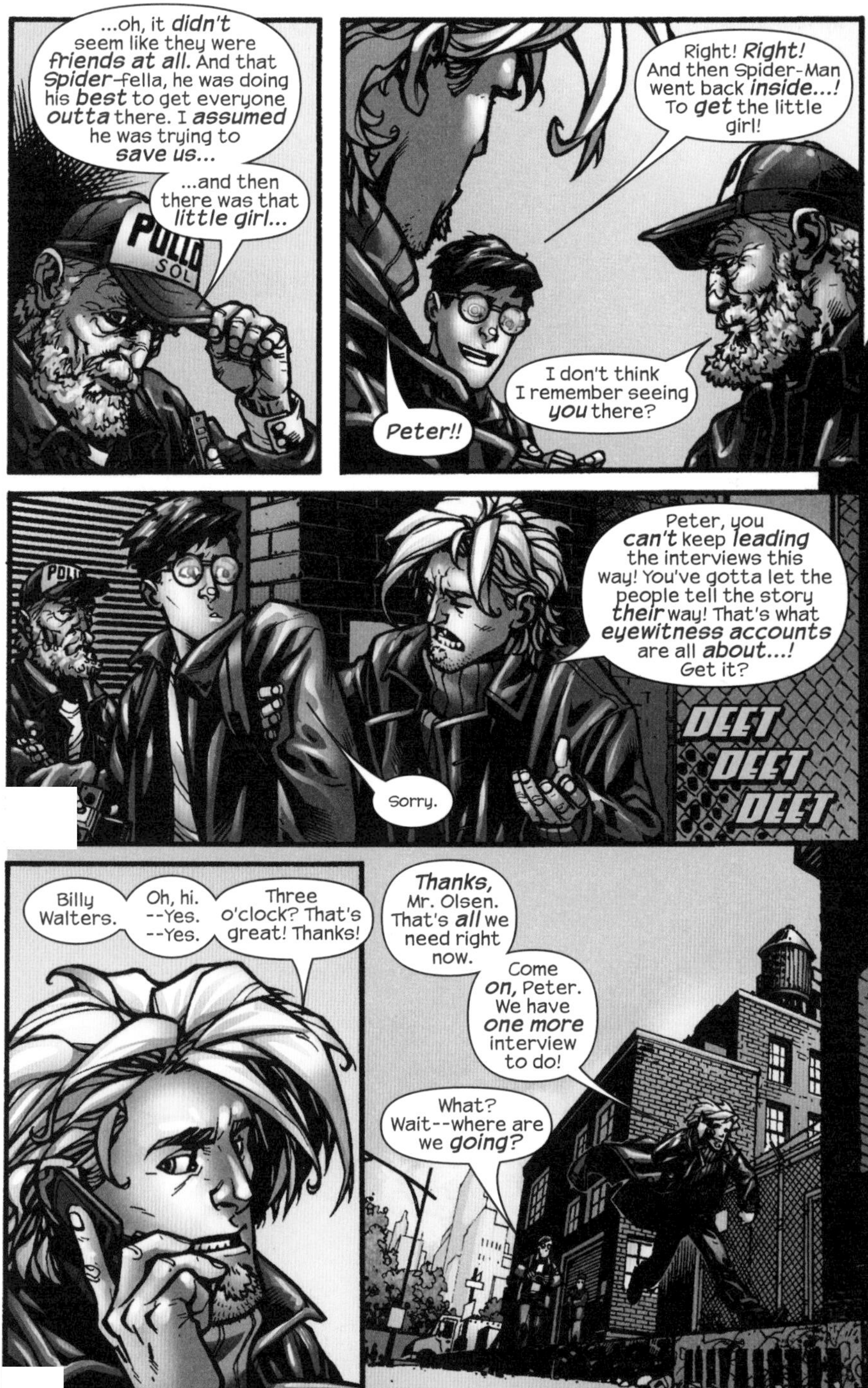
...oh, it didn't seem like they were friends at all. And that Spider-fella, he was doing his best to get everyone outta there. I assumed he was trying to save us...
...and then there was that little girl...
POLLO SOL
Right! Right! And then Spider-Man went back inside...! To get the little girl!
Peter!!
I don't think I remember seeing you there?
Peter, you can't keep leading the interviews this way! You've gotta let the people tell the story their way! That's what eyewitness accounts are all about...! Get it?
Sorry.
DEET
DEET
DEET
Billy Walters.
Oh, hi. --Yes. --Yes.
Three o'clock? That's great! Thanks!
Thanks, Mr. Olsen. That's all we need right now.
Come on, Peter. We have one more interview to do!
What? Wait--where are we going?

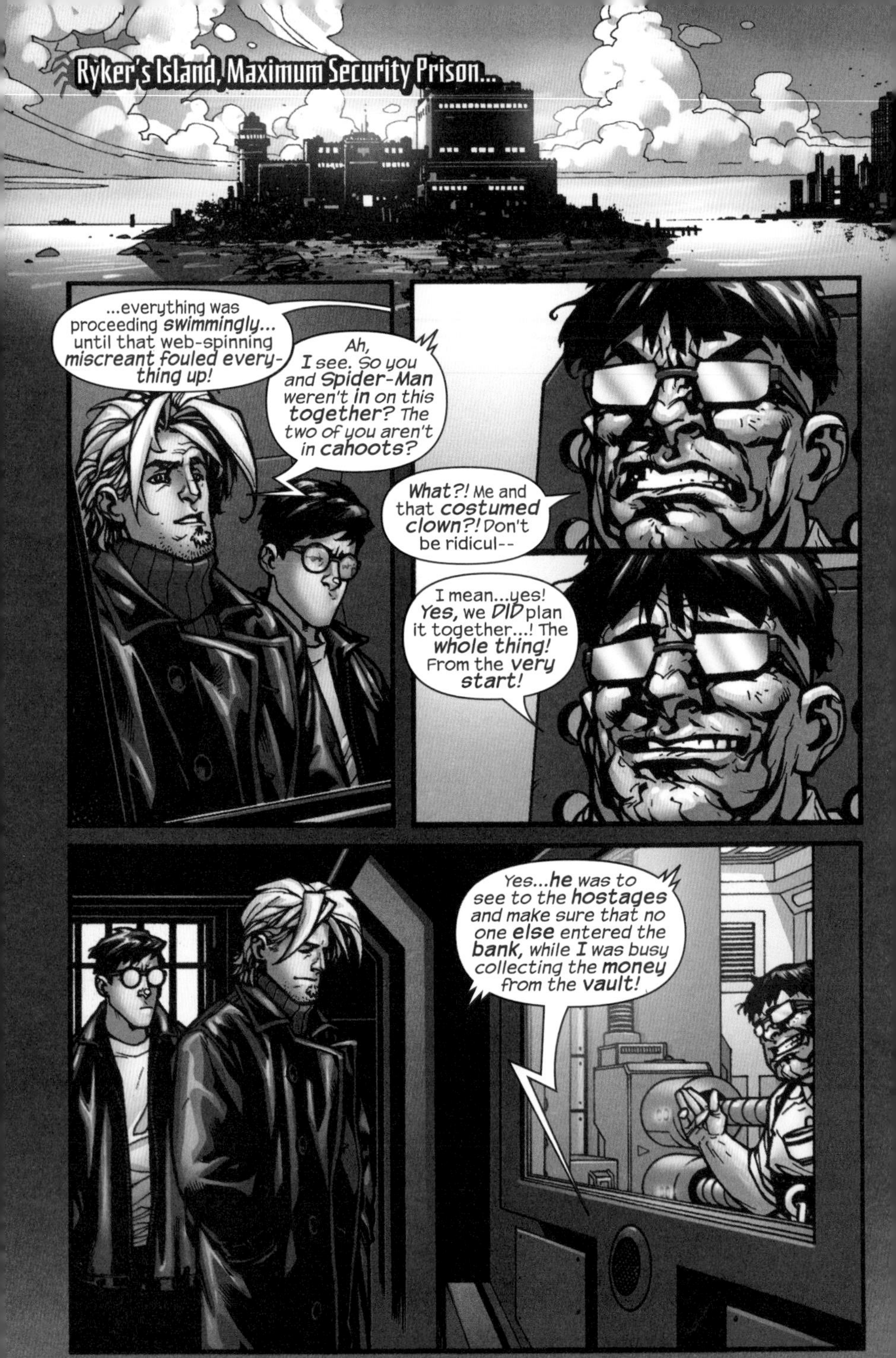
Ryker's Island, Maximum Security Prison...
...everything was proceeding swimmingly... until that web-spinning miscreant fouled every-thing up!
Ah, I see. So you and Spider-Man weren't in on this together? The two of you aren't in cahoots?
What?! Me and that costumed clown?! Don't be ridicul--
I mean...yes! Yes, we DID plan it together...! The whole thing! From the very start!
Yes...he was to see to the hostages and make sure that no one else entered the bank, while I was busy collecting the money from the vault!

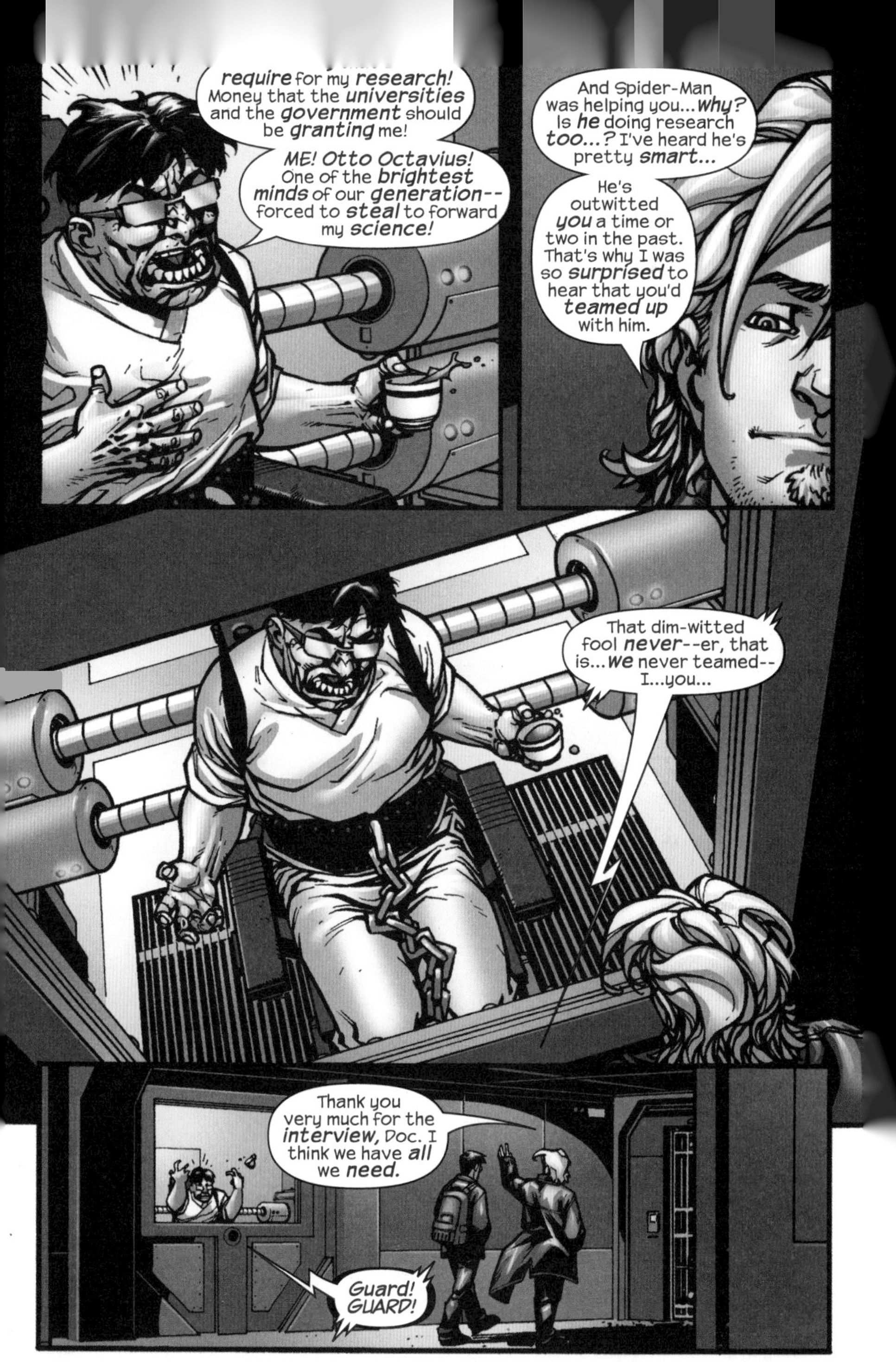
require for my research! Money that the universities and the government should be granting me!
ME! Otto Octavius! One of the brightest minds of our generation-- forced to steal to forward my science!
And Spider-Man was helping you...why? Is he doing research too...? I've heard he's pretty smart...
He's outwitted you a time or two in the past. That's why I was so surprised to hear that you'd teamed up with him.
That dim-witted fool never--er, that is...we never teamed-- I...you...
Thank you very much for the interview, Doc. I think we have all we need.
Guard! GUARD!

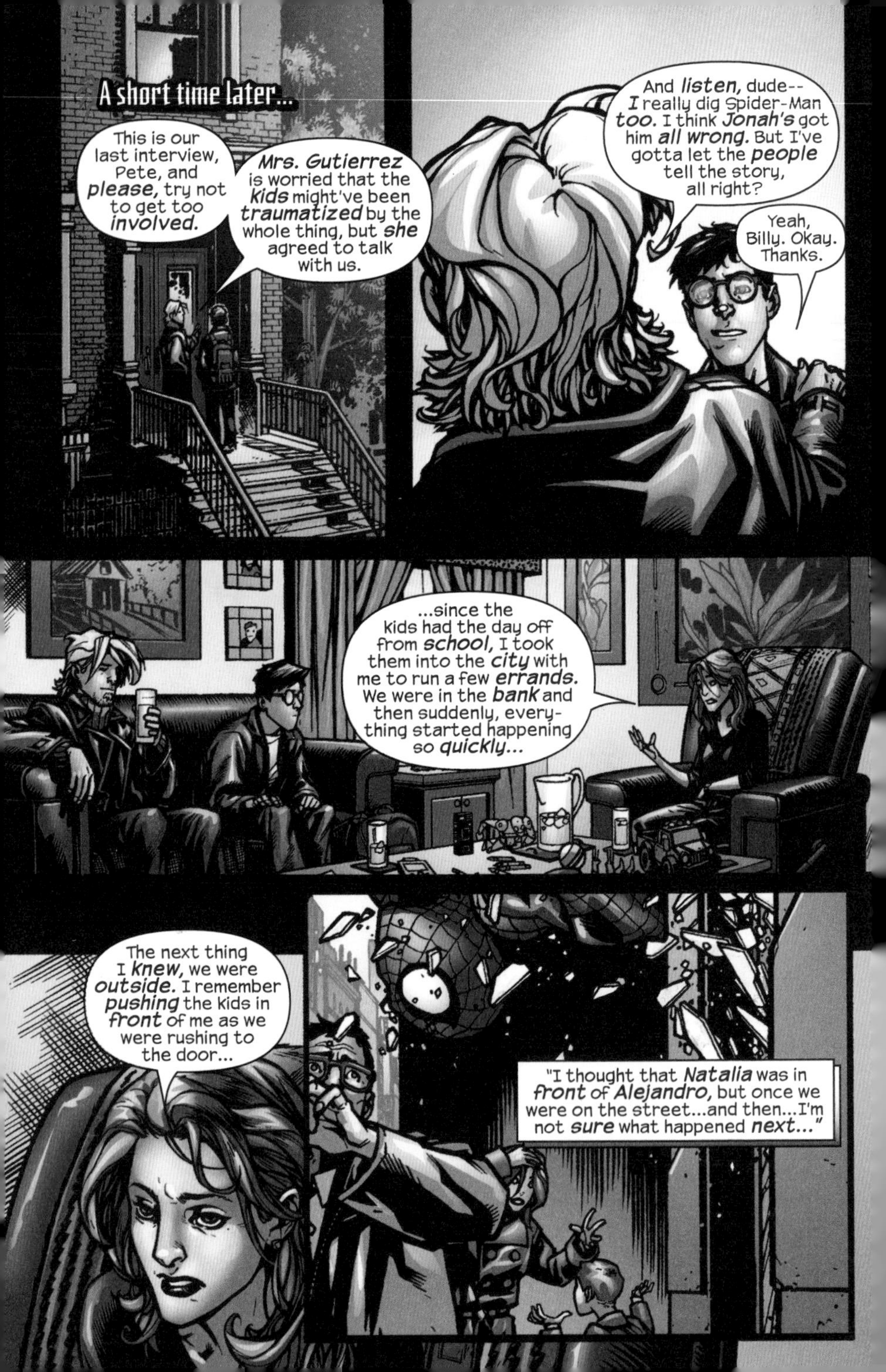
A short time later...
This is our last interview, Pete, and please, try not to get too involved.
Mrs. Gutierrez is worried that the kids might've been traumatized by the whole thing, but she agreed to talk with us.
And listen, dude-- I really dig Spider-Man too. I think Jonah's got him all wrong. But I've gotta let the people tell the story, all right?
Yeah, Billy. Okay. Thanks.
...since the kids had the day off from school, I took them into the city with me to run a few errands. We were in the bank and then suddenly, everything started happening so quickly...
The next thing I knew, we were outside. I remember pushing the kids in front of me as we were rushing to the door...
"I thought that Natalia was in front of Alejandro, but once we were on the street...and then...I'm not sure what happened next..."

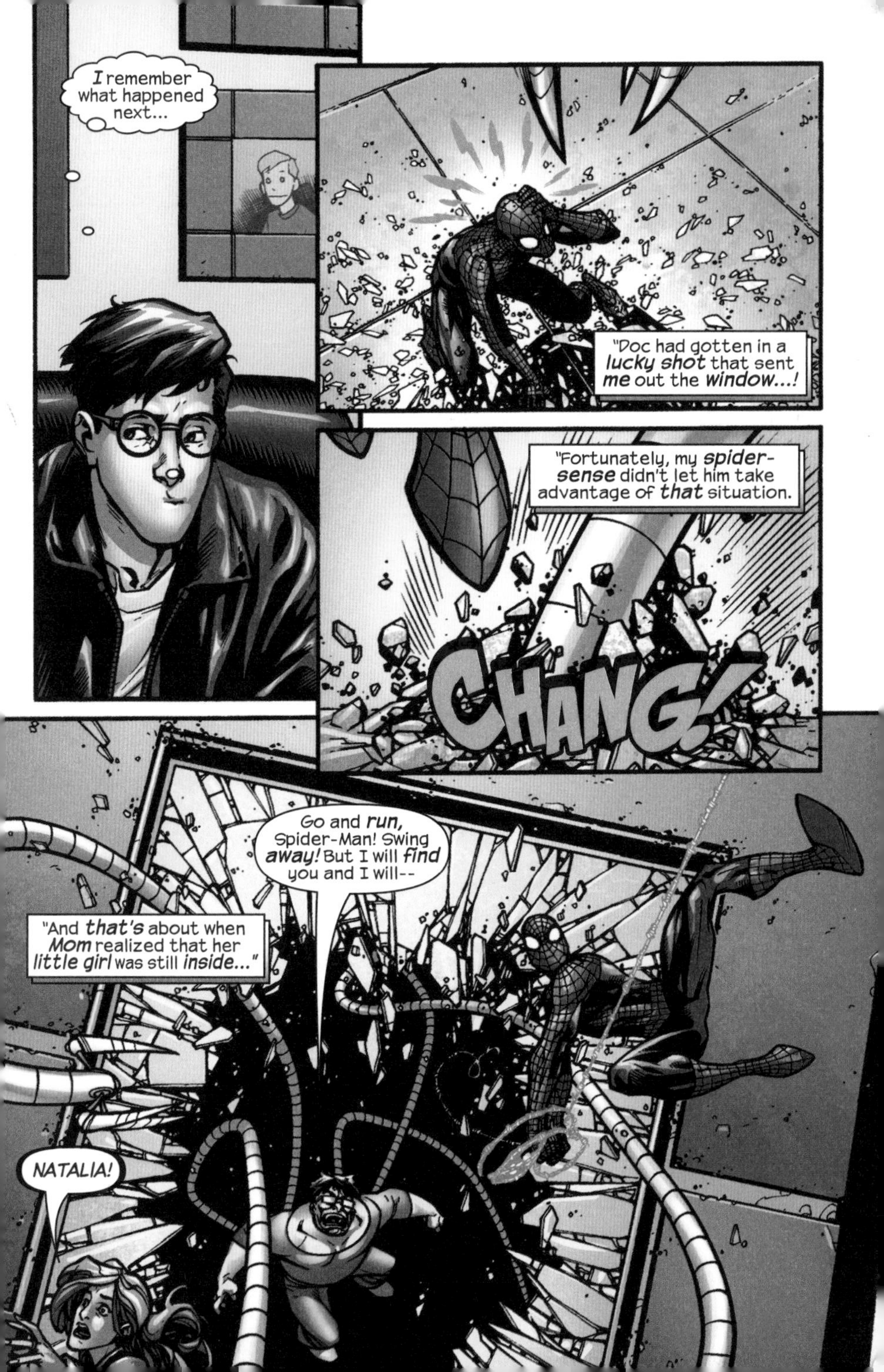
I remember what happened next...
"Doc had gotten in a lucky shot that sent me out the window...!
"Fortunately, my spider-sense didn't let him take advantage of that situation.
CHANG!
Go and run, Spider-Man! Swing away! But I will find you and I will--
"And that's about when Mom realized that her little girl was still inside..."
NATALIA!

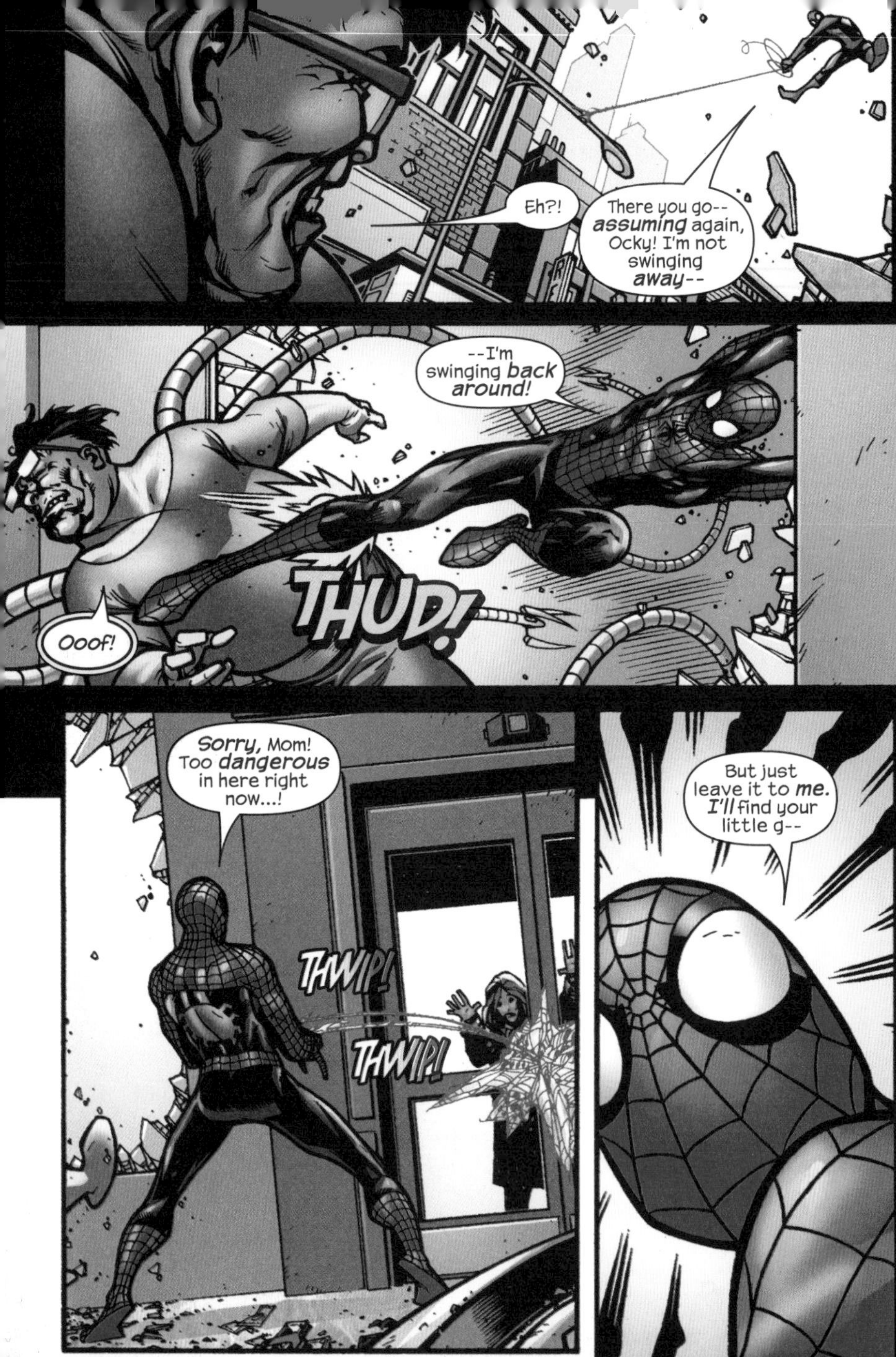

Eh?!
There you go-- assuming again, Ocky! I'm not swinging away--
--I'm swinging back around!
THUD!
Ooof!
Sorry, Mom! Too dangerous in here right now...!
THWIP!
THWIP!
But just leave it to me. I'll find your little g--

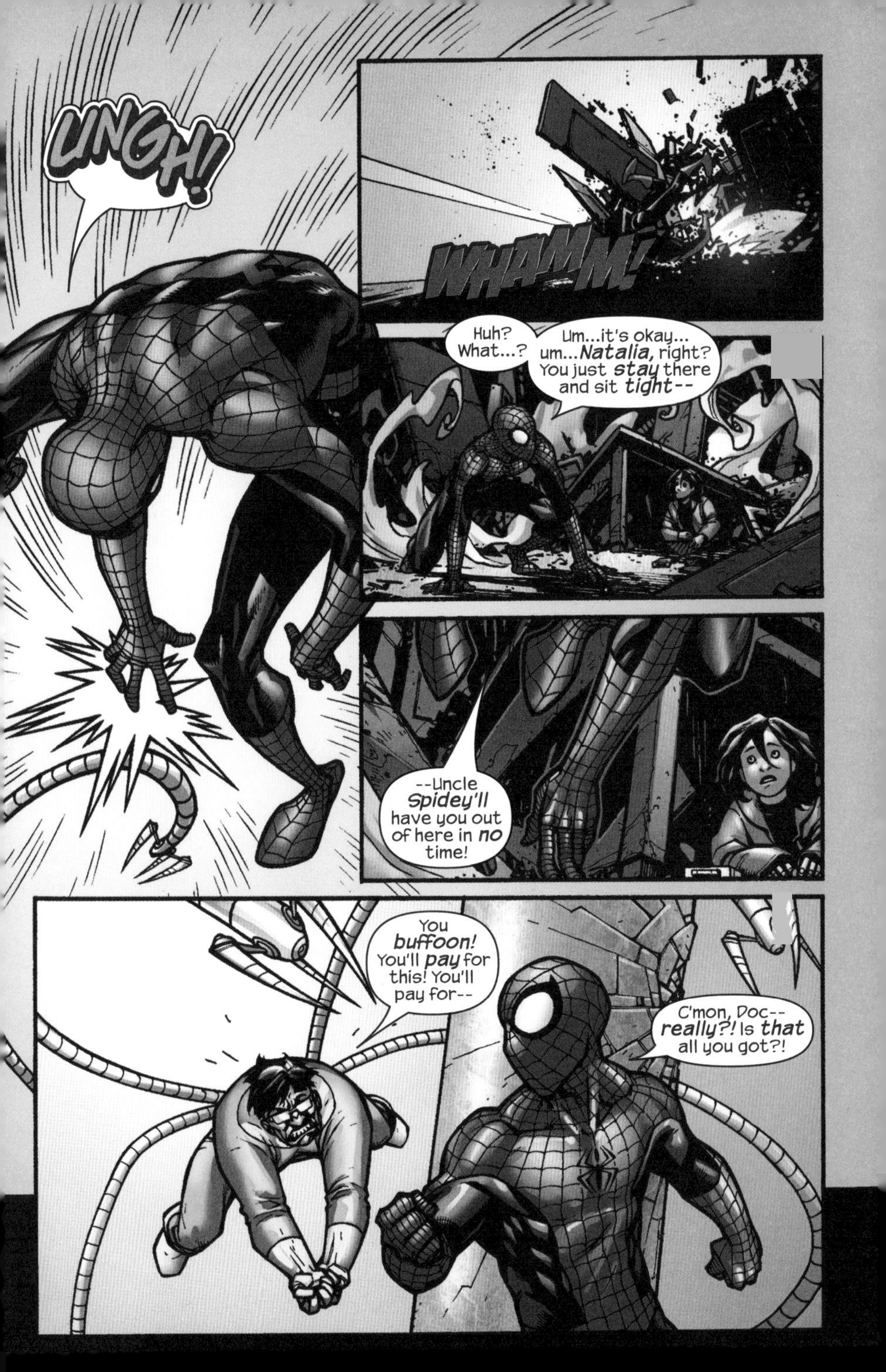
UNGH!
WHAMM!
Huh? What...?
Um...it's okay... um...Natalia, right? You just stay there and sit tight--
--Uncle Spidey'll have you out of here in no time!
You buffoon! You'll pay for this! You'll pay for--
C'mon, Doc-- really?! Is that all you got?!

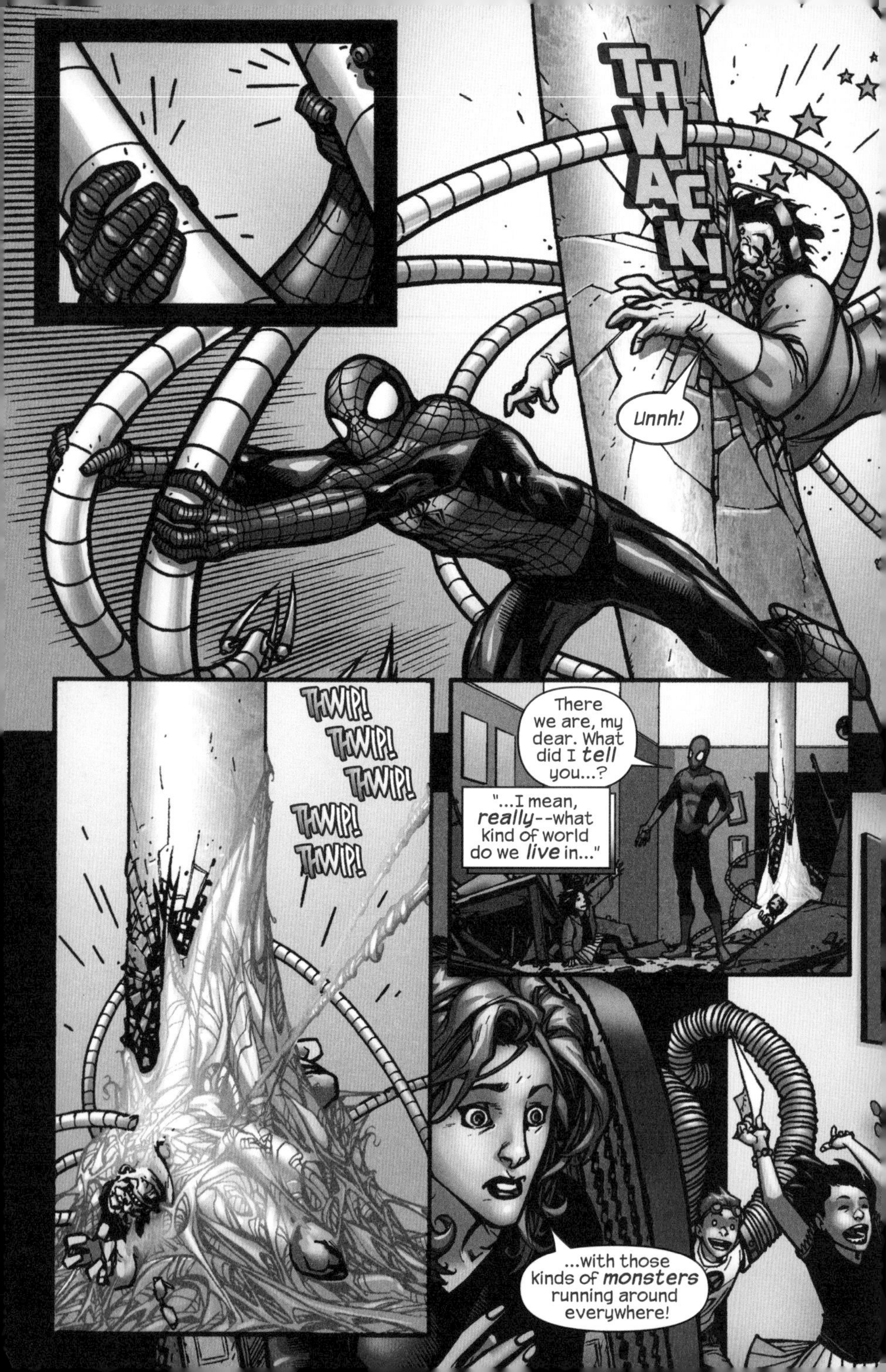

THWACK!
Unnh!
THWIP! THWIP! THWIP! THWIP! THWIP!
There we are, my dear. What did I *tell* you...?
"...I mean, *really*--what kind of world do we *live* in..."
...with those kinds of *monsters* running around everywhere!

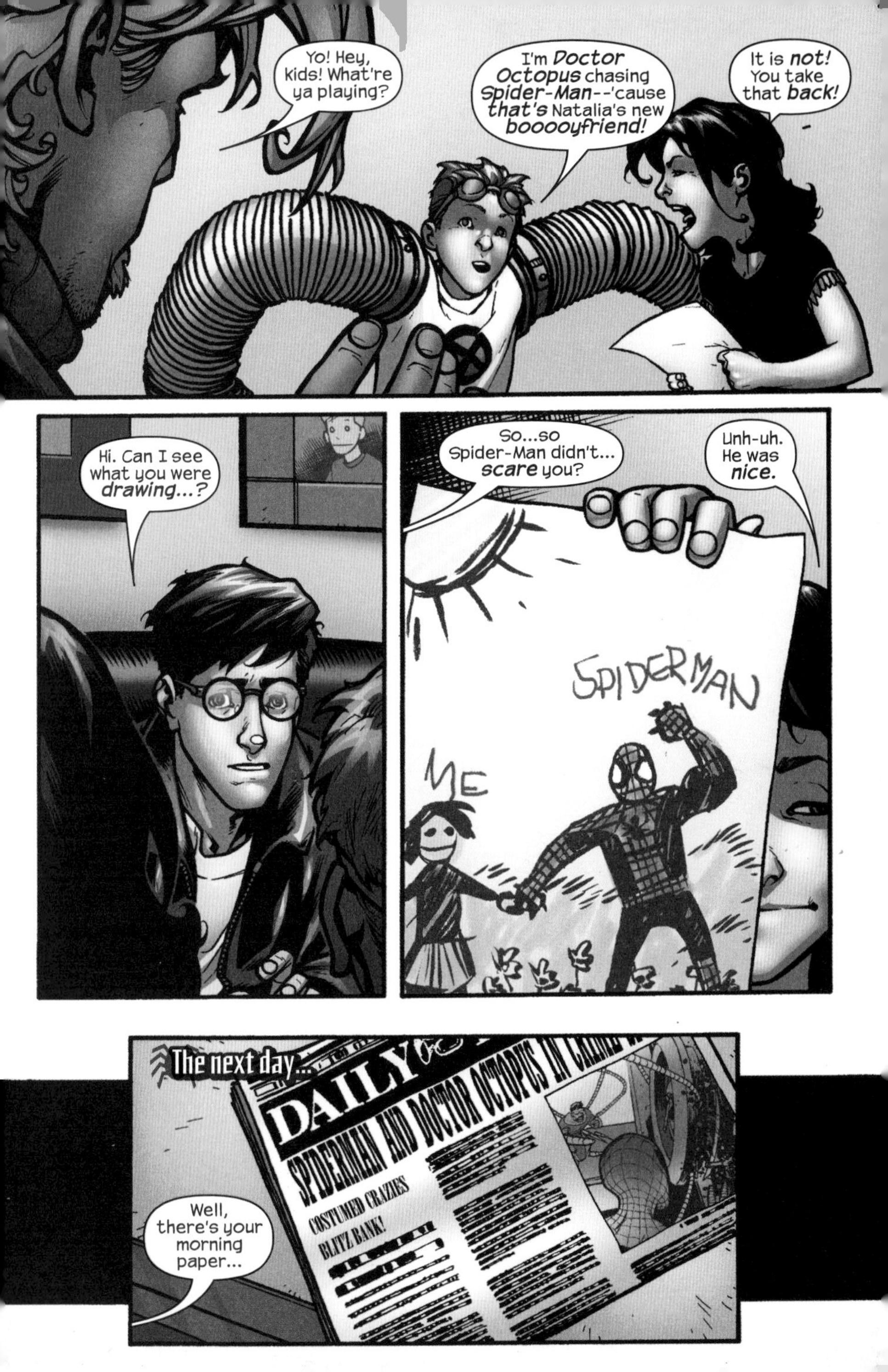

Yo! Hey, kids! What're ya playing?
I'm *Doctor Octopus* chasing *Spider-Man*--'cause *that's* Natalia's new *booooyfriend!*
It is *not!* You take that *back!*
Hi. Can I see what you were *drawing...?*
So...so Spider-Man didn't... *scare* you?
Unh-uh. He was *nice.*
SPIDERMAN
ME
The next day...
DAILY
SPIDERMAN AND DOCTOR OCTOPUS IN CRIME
COSTUMED CRAZIES BLITZ BANK!
Well, there's your morning paper...

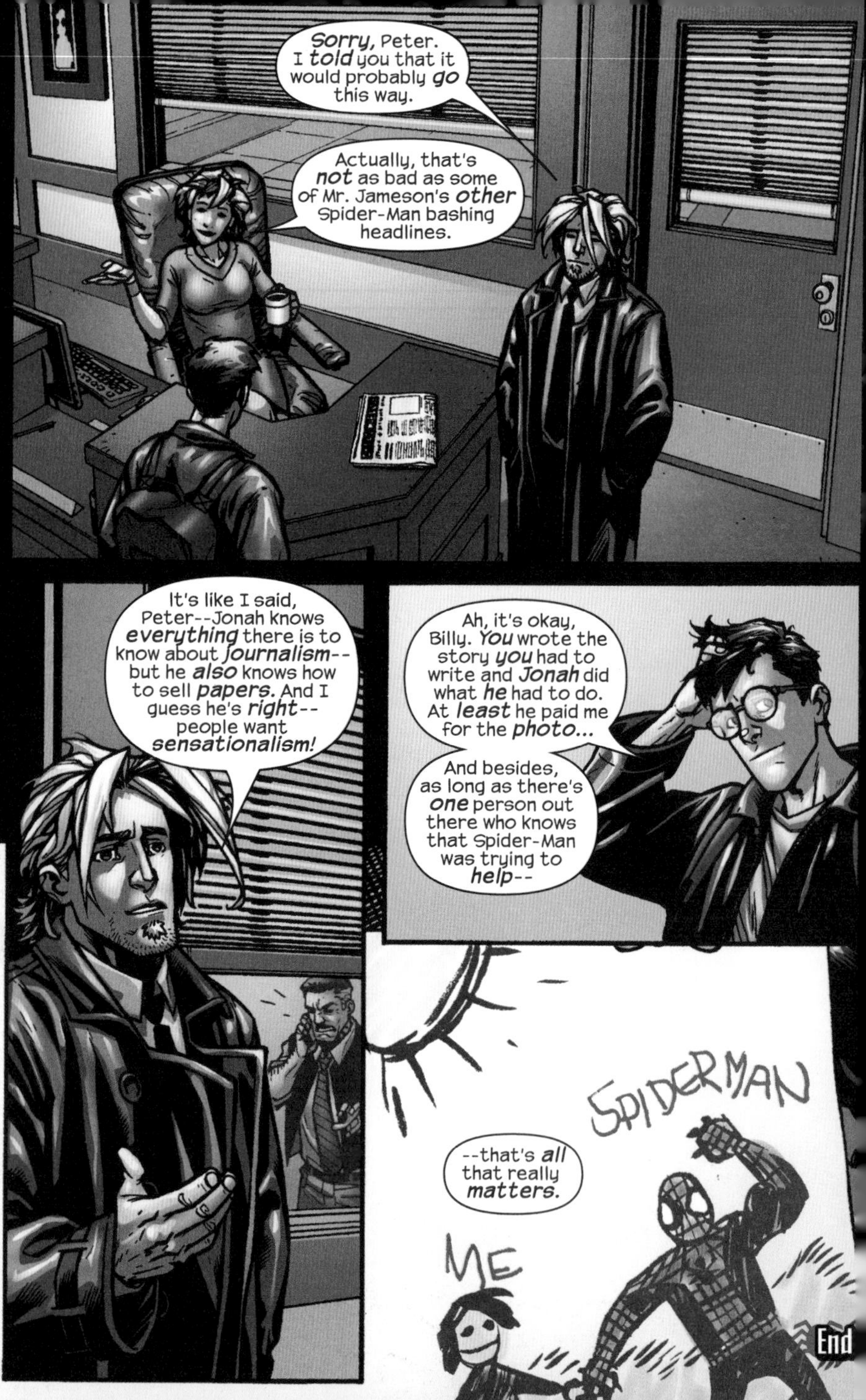
Sorry, Peter. I told you that it would probably go this way.
Actually, that's not as bad as some of Mr. Jameson's other Spider-Man bashing headlines.
It's like I said, Peter--Jonah knows everything there is to know about journalism--but he also knows how to sell papers. And I guess he's right--people want sensationalism!
Ah, it's okay, Billy. You wrote the story you had to write and Jonah did what he had to do. At least he paid me for the photo...
And besides, as long as there's one person out there who knows that Spider-Man was trying to help--
SPIDERMAN
--that's all that really matters.
ME
End

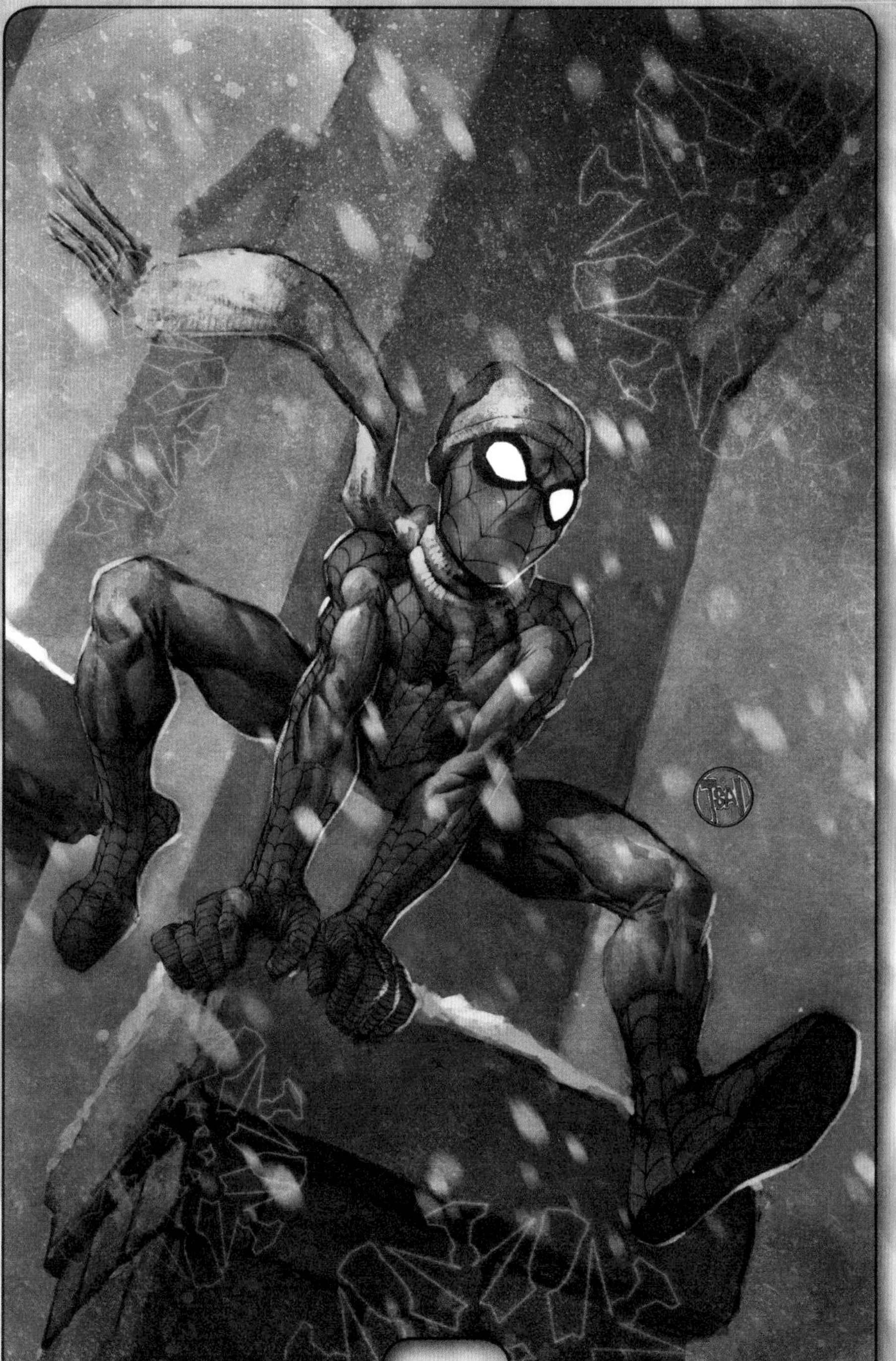

#46

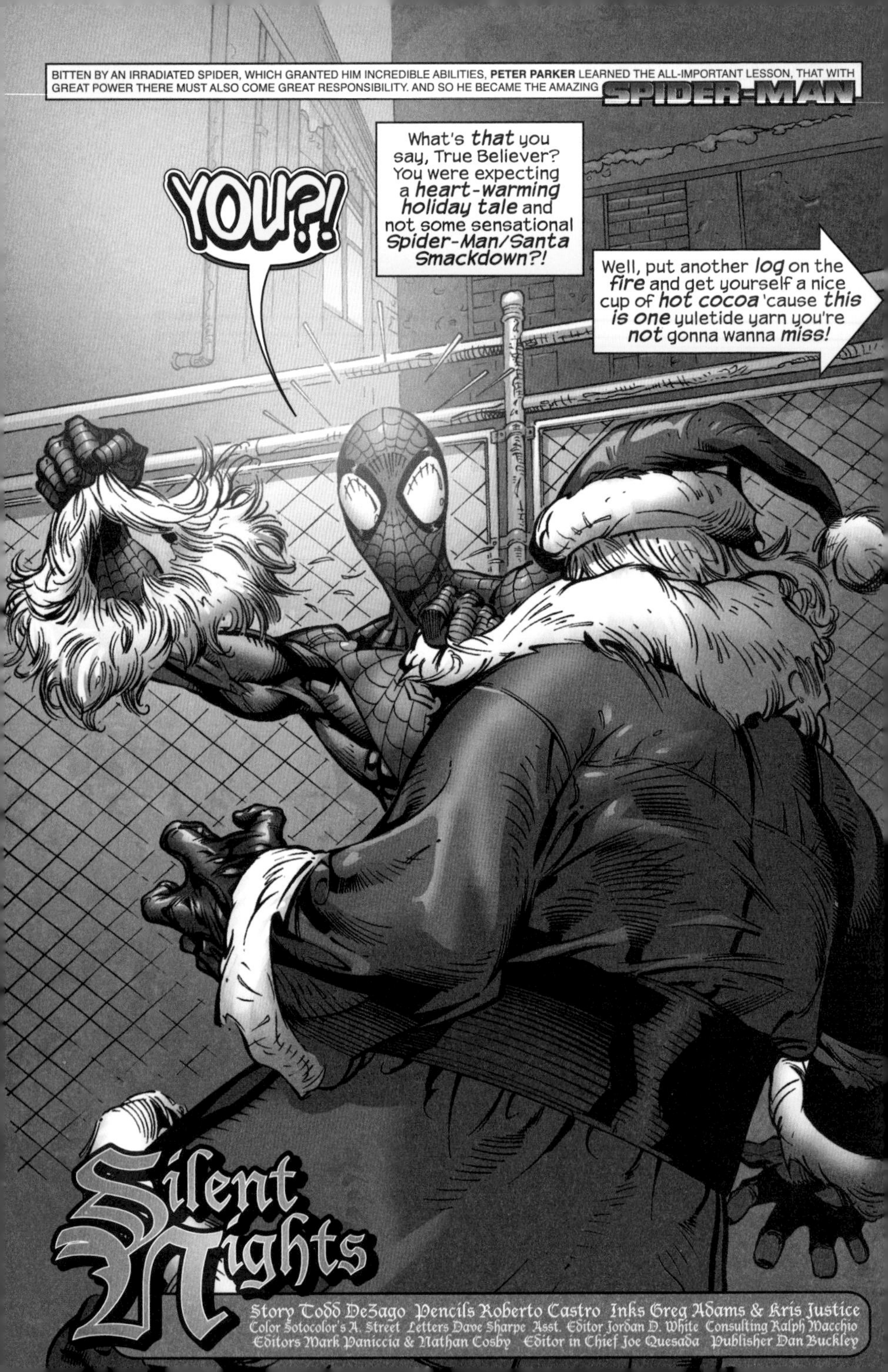
BITTEN BY AN IRRADIATED SPIDER, WHICH GRANTED HIM INCREDIBLE ABILITIES, PETER PARKER LEARNED THE ALL-IMPORTANT LESSON, THAT WITH GREAT POWER THERE MUST ALSO COME GREAT RESPONSIBILITY. AND SO HE BECAME THE AMAZING SPIDER-MAN
YOU?!
What's that you say, True Believer? You were expecting a heart-warming holiday tale and not some sensational Spider-Man/Santa Smackdown?!
Well, put another log on the fire and get yourself a nice cup of hot cocoa 'cause this is one yuletide yarn you're not gonna wanna miss!
Silent Nights
Story Todd DeZago Pencils Roberto Castro Inks Greg Adams & Kris Justice
Color Sotocolor's A. Street Letters Dave Sharpe Asst. Editor Jordan D. White Consulting Ralph Macchio
Editors Mark Paniccia & Nathan Cosby Editor in Chief Joe Quesada Publisher Dan Buckley

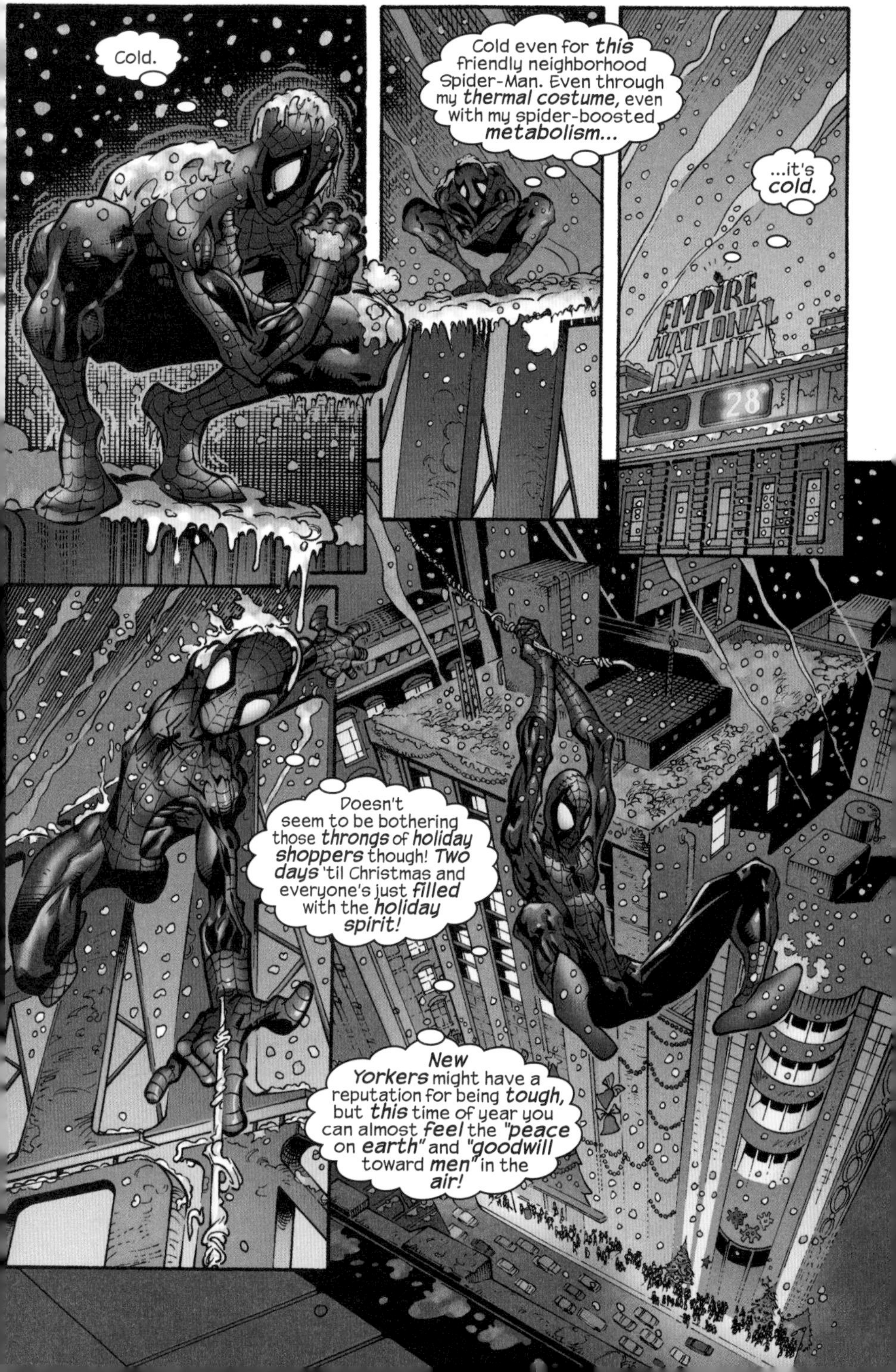
Cold.
Cold even for this friendly neighborhood Spider-Man. Even through my thermal costume, even with my spider-boosted metabolism...
...it's cold.
EMPIRE NATIONAL BANK
28
Doesn't seem to be bothering those throngs of holiday shoppers though! Two days 'til Christmas and everyone's just filled with the holiday spirit!
New Yorkers might have a reputation for being tough, but this time of year you can almost feel the "peace on earth" and "goodwill toward men" in the air!

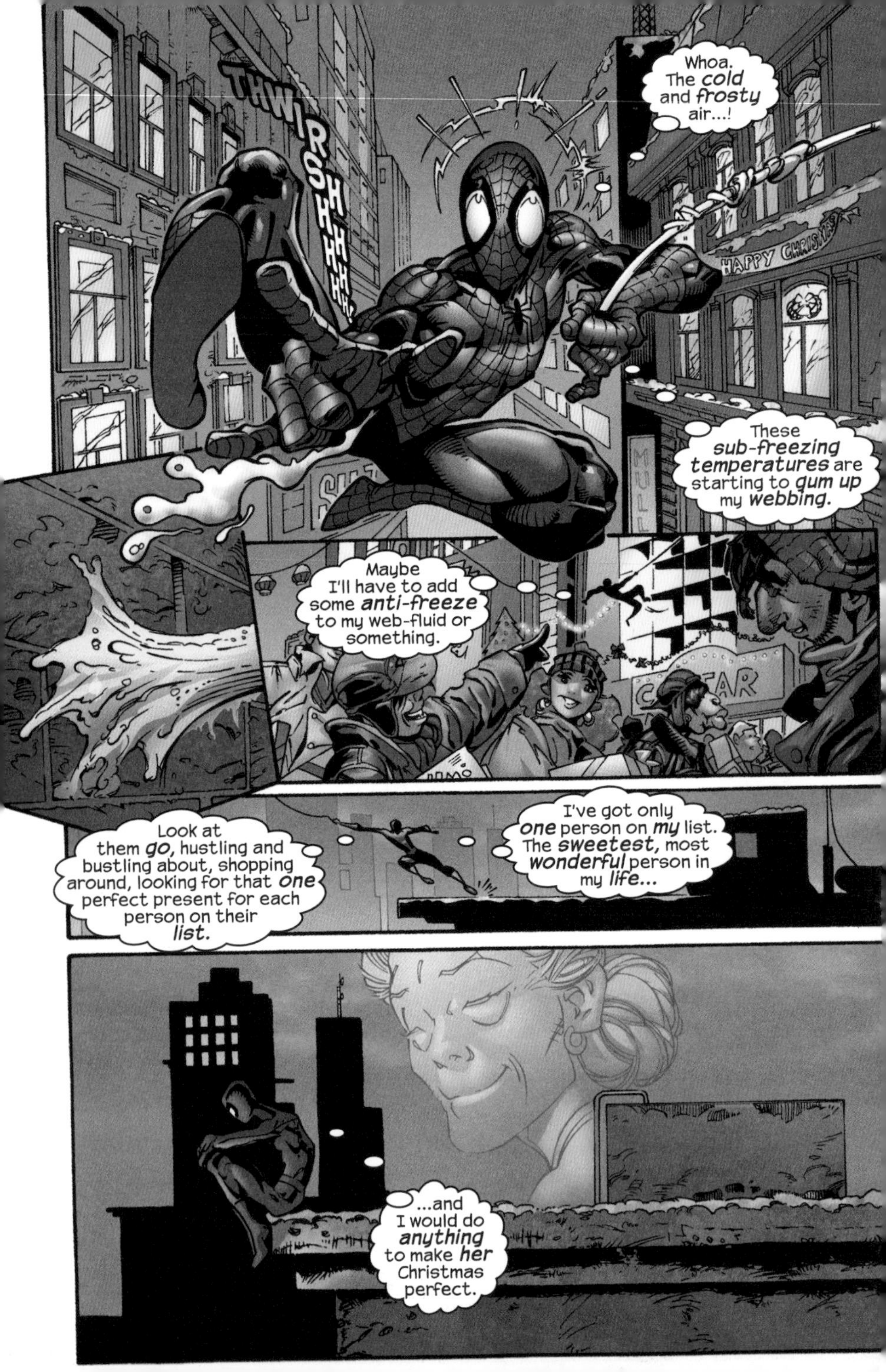
THWIRSHHHHHH
Whoa. The cold and frosty air...!
HAPPY CHRISTMAS
These sub-freezing temperatures are starting to gum up my webbing.
Maybe I'll have to add some anti-freeze to my web-fluid or something.
Look at them go, hustling and bustling about, shopping around, looking for that one perfect present for each person on their list.
I've got only one person on my list. The sweetest, most wonderful person in my life...
...and I would do anything to make her Christmas perfect.

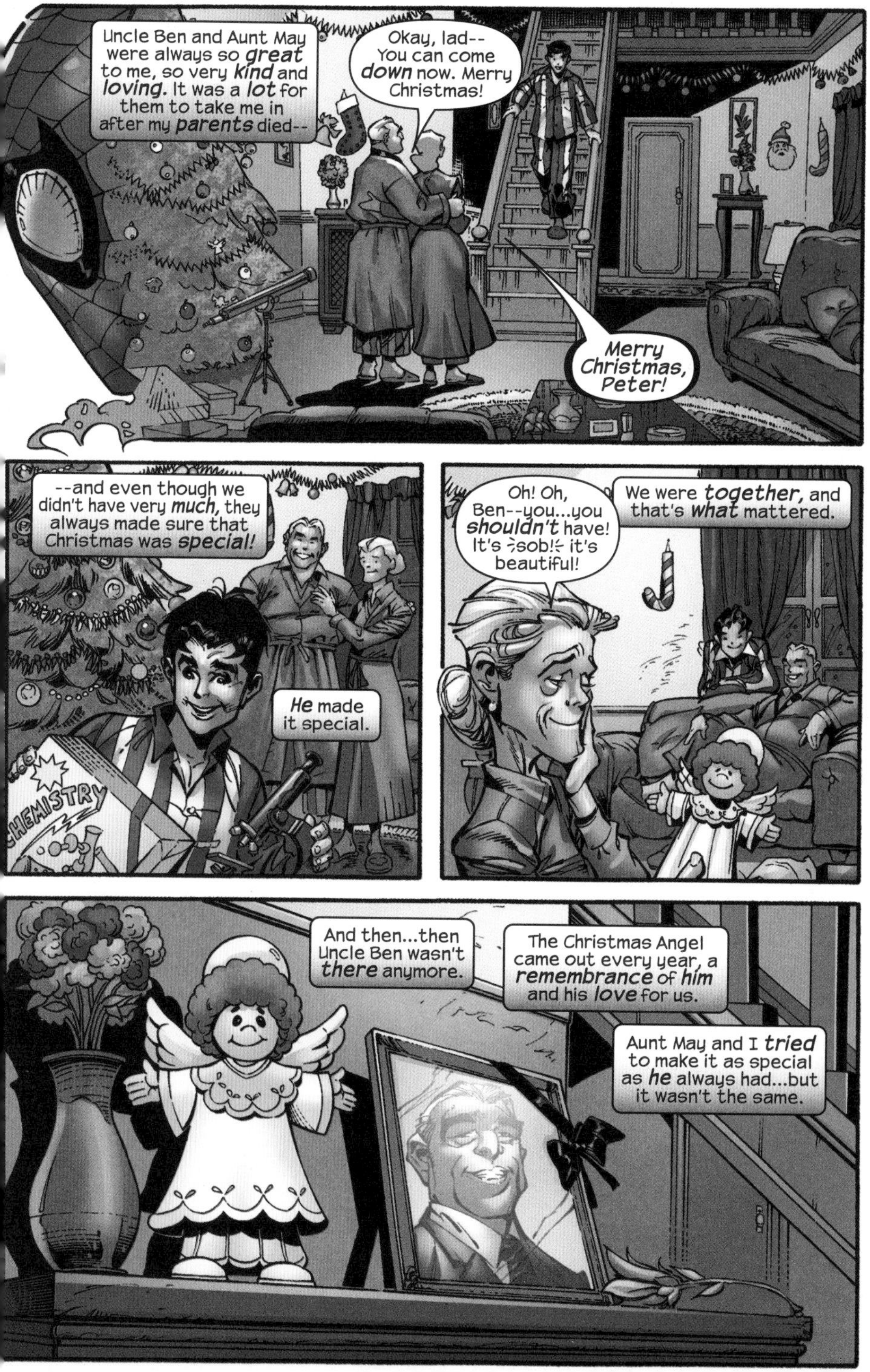
Uncle Ben and Aunt May were always so great to me, so very kind and loving. It was a lot for them to take me in after my parents died--
Okay, lad-- You can come down now. Merry Christmas!
Merry Christmas, Peter!
--and even though we didn't have very much, they always made sure that Christmas was special!
He made it special.
CHEMISTRY
Oh! Oh, Ben--you...you shouldn't have! It's *sob!* it's beautiful!
We were together, and that's what mattered.
And then...then Uncle Ben wasn't there anymore.
The Christmas Angel came out every year, a remembrance of him and his love for us.
Aunt May and I tried to make it as special as he always had...but it wasn't the same.

And then, last year...

I'm *fine*, Peter! You take care of *those* boxes. I may be *old* but I can still handle *one* box of Christmas deco--

WHUNK!

--oh!

She cried so *much*. It was as if she'd *shattered* all her *memories* of *Uncle Ben*. She was so sad...

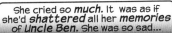

Spider-sense says that there's nobody *looking*, so...

...*presto!* From the *sensational*, *spectacular* Spider-Man... to plain old *Peter Parker*... who *still* doesn't have a gift for his aunt for Christmas.

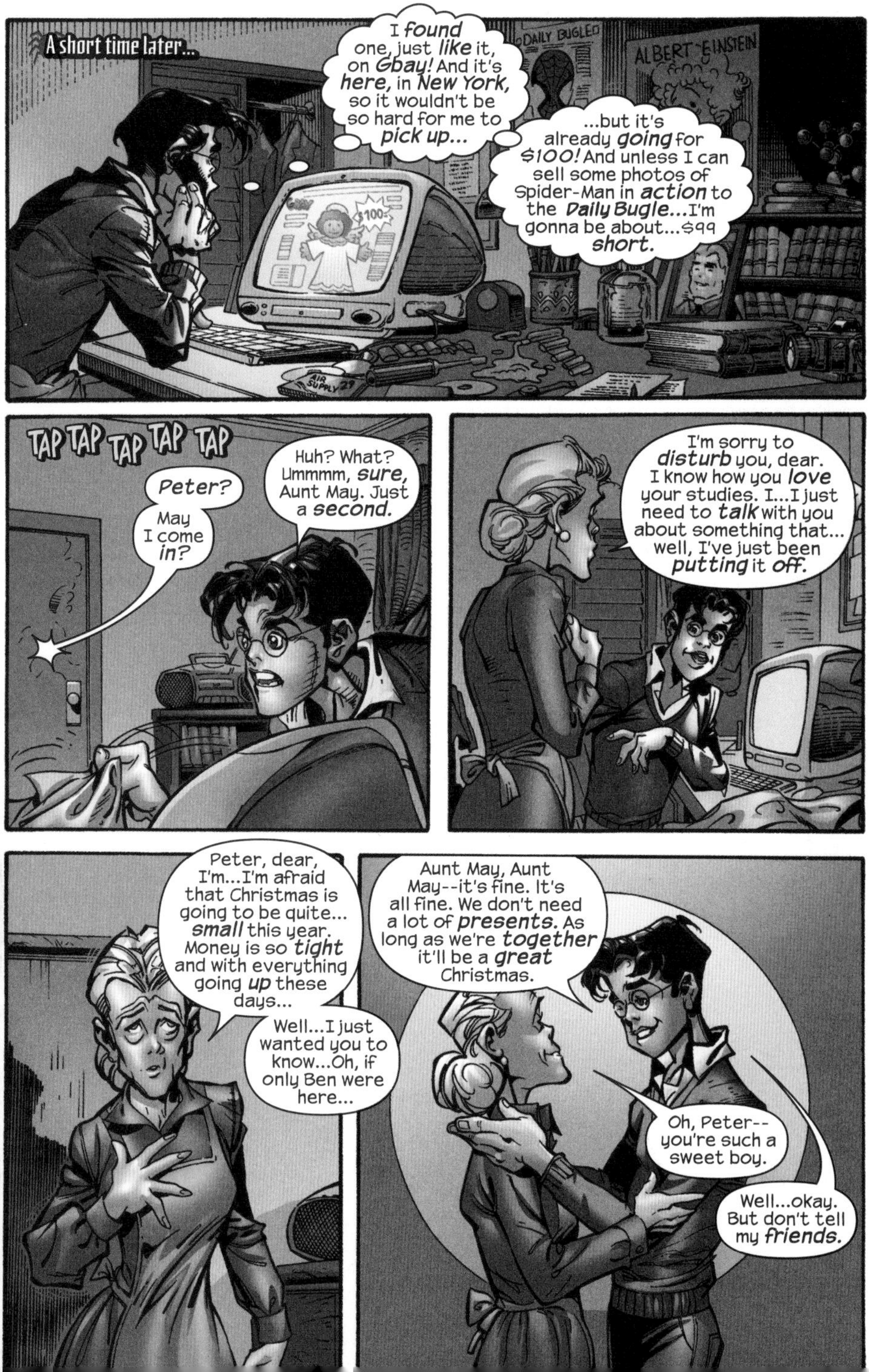
A short time later...
I found one, just like it, on Gbay! And it's here, in New York, so it wouldn't be so hard for me to pick up...
...but it's already going for $100! And unless I can sell some photos of Spider-Man in action to the Daily Bugle...I'm gonna be about...$99 short.
DAILY BUGLE
ALBERT EINSTEIN
$100
AIR SUPPLY
TAP TAP TAP TAP TAP
Peter?
May I come in?
Huh? What? Ummmm, sure, Aunt May. Just a second.
I'm sorry to disturb you, dear. I know how you love your studies. I...I just need to talk with you about something that... well, I've just been putting it off.
Peter, dear, I'm...I'm afraid that Christmas is going to be quite... small this year. Money is so tight and with everything going up these days...
Well...I just wanted you to know...Oh, if only Ben were here...
Aunt May, Aunt May--it's fine. It's all fine. We don't need a lot of presents. As long as we're together it'll be a great Christmas.
Oh, Peter--you're such a sweet boy.
Well...okay. But don't tell my friends.

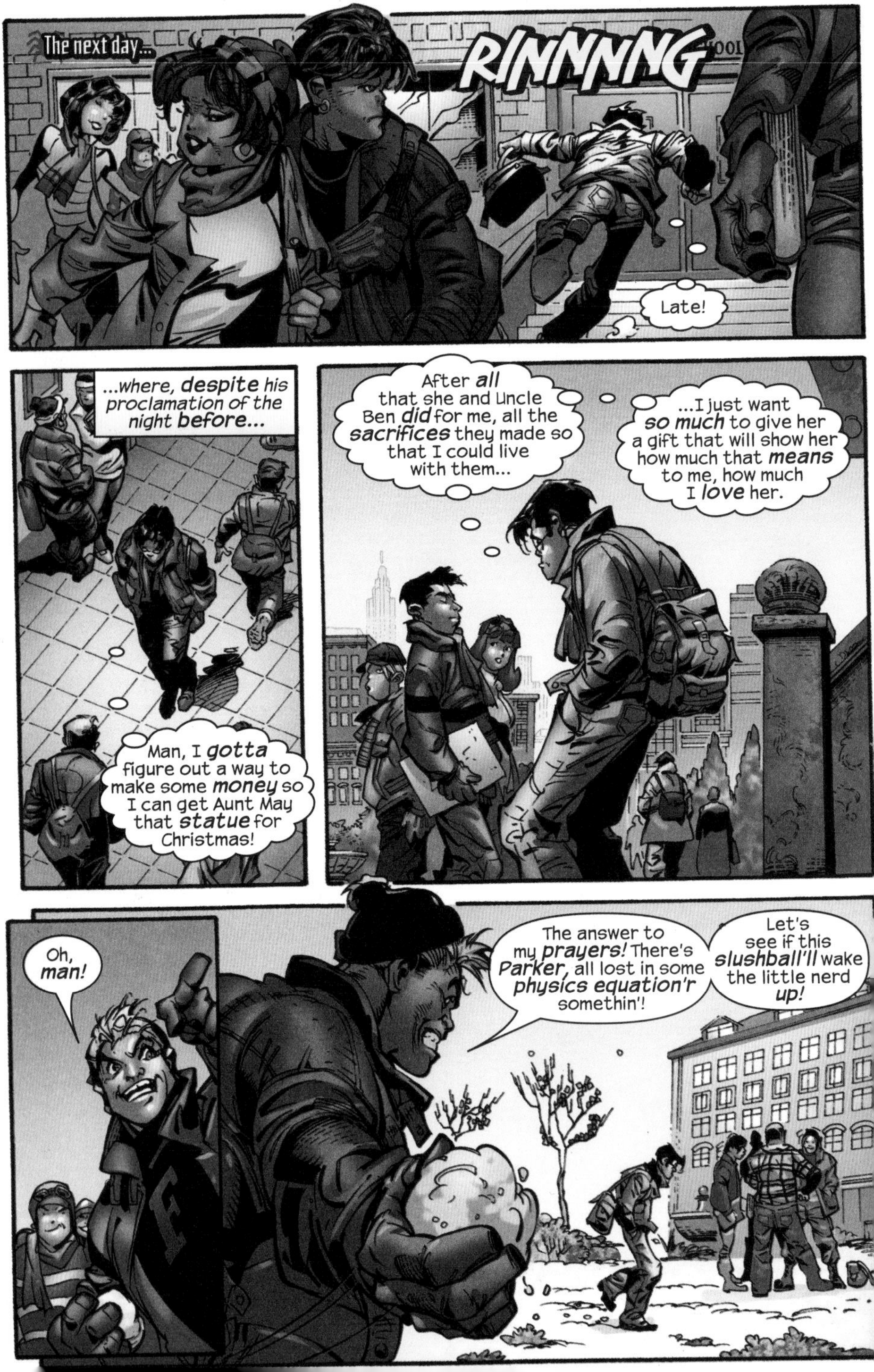
The next day...
RINNNNG
Late!
...where, despite his proclamation of the night before...
Man, I gotta figure out a way to make some money so I can get Aunt May that statue for Christmas!
After all that she and Uncle Ben did for me, all the sacrifices they made so that I could live with them...
...I just want so much to give her a gift that will show her how much that means to me, how much I love her.
Oh, man!
The answer to my prayers! There's Parker, all lost in some physics equation'r somethin'!
Let's see if this slushball'll wake the little nerd up!

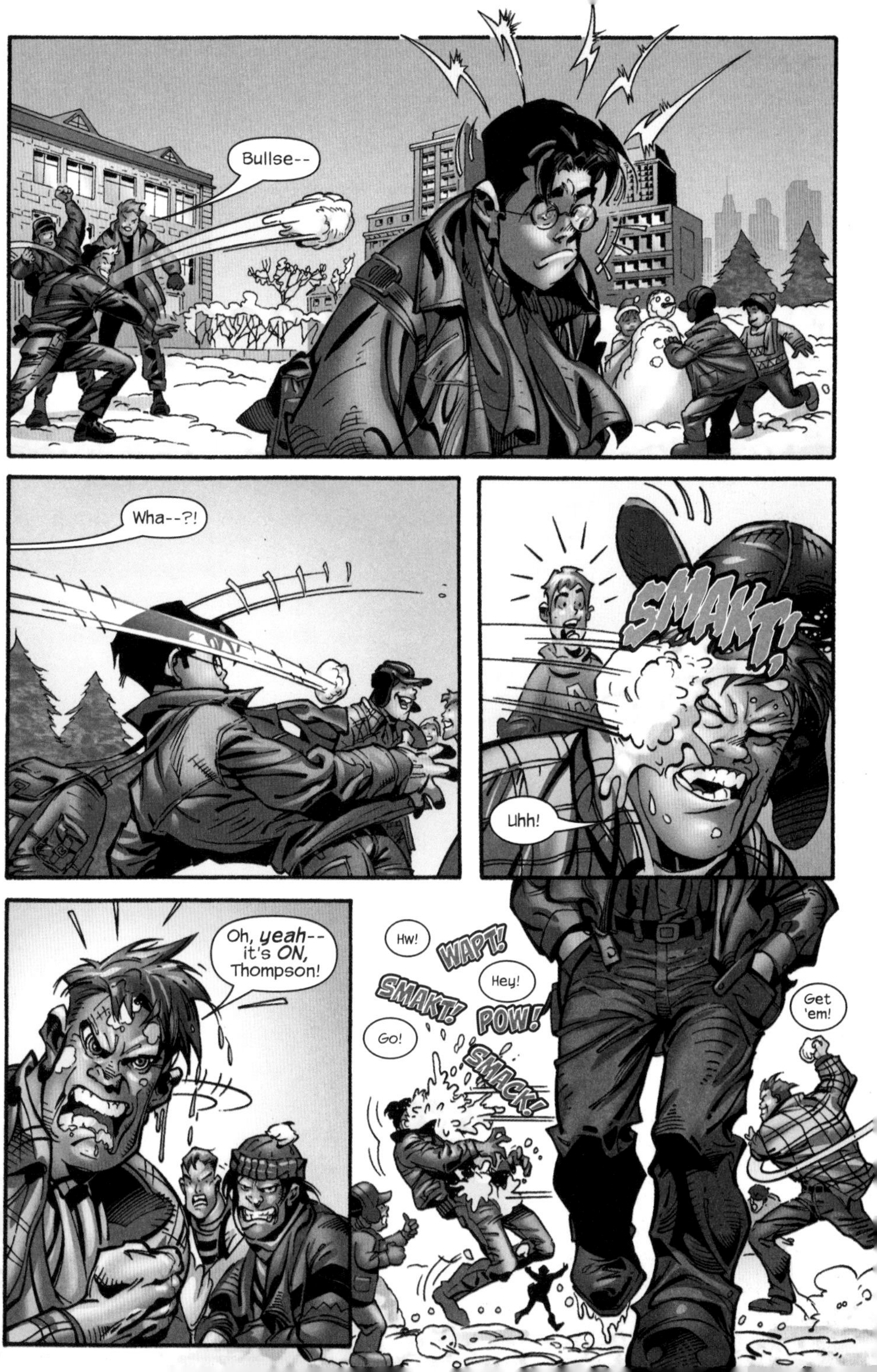
Bullse--
Wha--?!
SMAKT!
Uhh!
Oh, *yeah*--
it's *ON*,
Thompson!
Hw!
WAPT!
Hey!
SMAKT!
POW!
Go!
SMACK!
Get
'em!

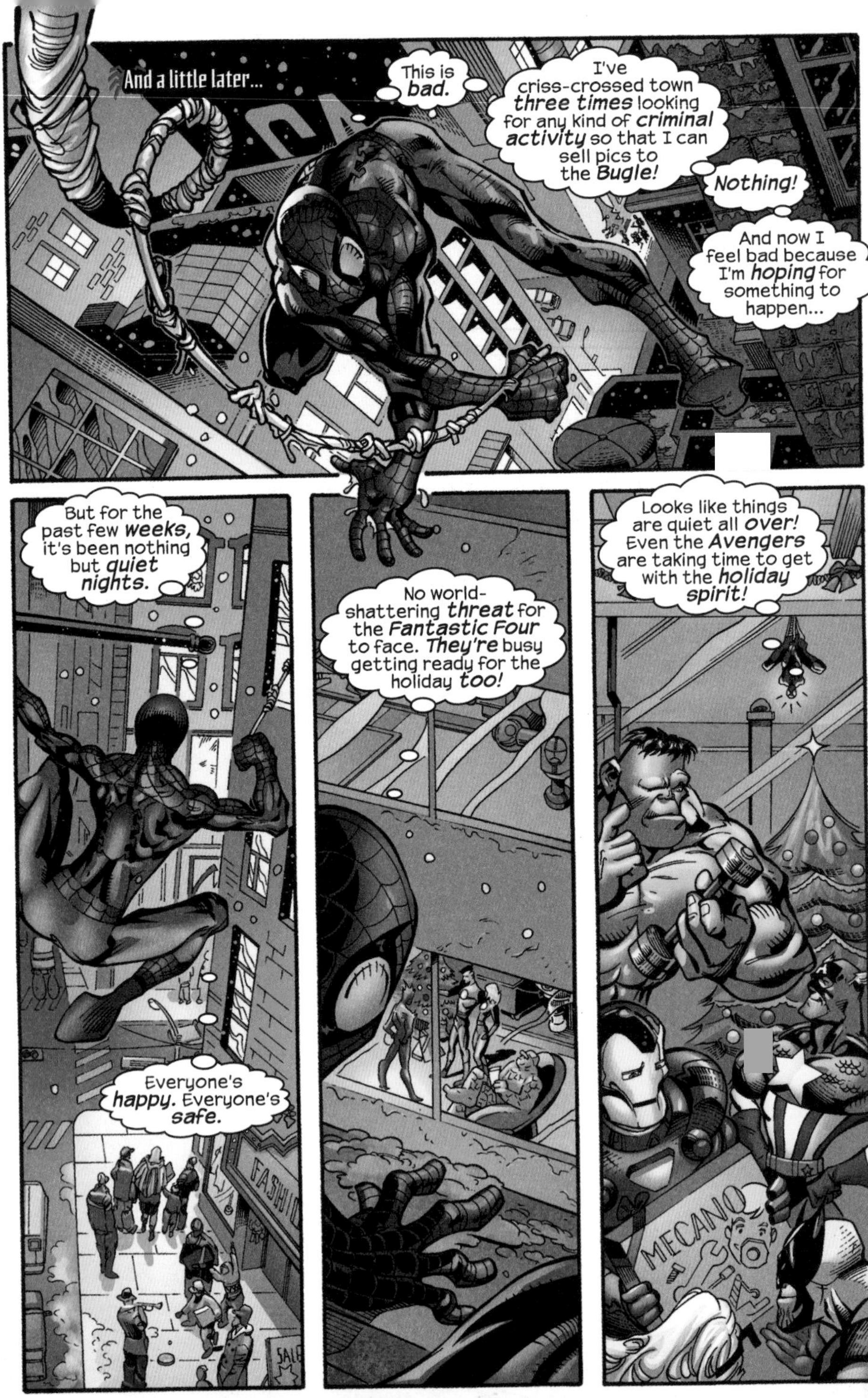

And a little later...
This is bad.
I've criss-crossed town three times looking for any kind of criminal activity so that I can sell pics to the Bugle!
Nothing!
And now I feel bad because I'm hoping for something to happen...
But for the past few weeks, it's been nothing but quiet nights.
Everyone's happy. Everyone's safe.
No world-shattering threat for the Fantastic Four to face. They're busy getting ready for the holiday too!
Looks like things are quiet all over! Even the Avengers are taking time to get with the holiday spirit!
FASHIO
SALE
MECANO

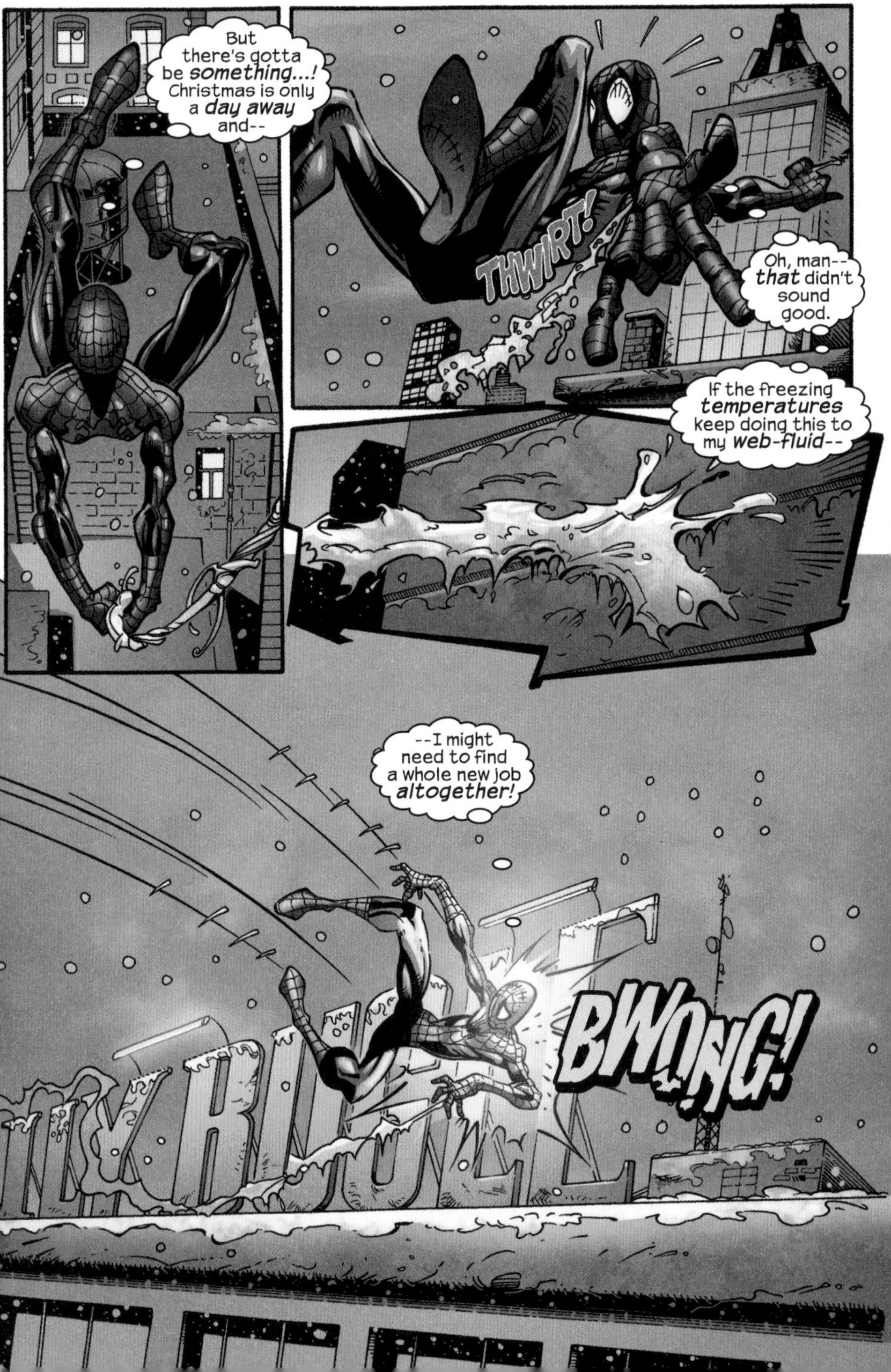
But there's gotta be something...! Christmas is only a day away and--
THWIRT!
Oh, man--that didn't sound good.
If the freezing temperatures keep doing this to my web-fluid--
--I might need to find a whole new job altogether!
BWONG!

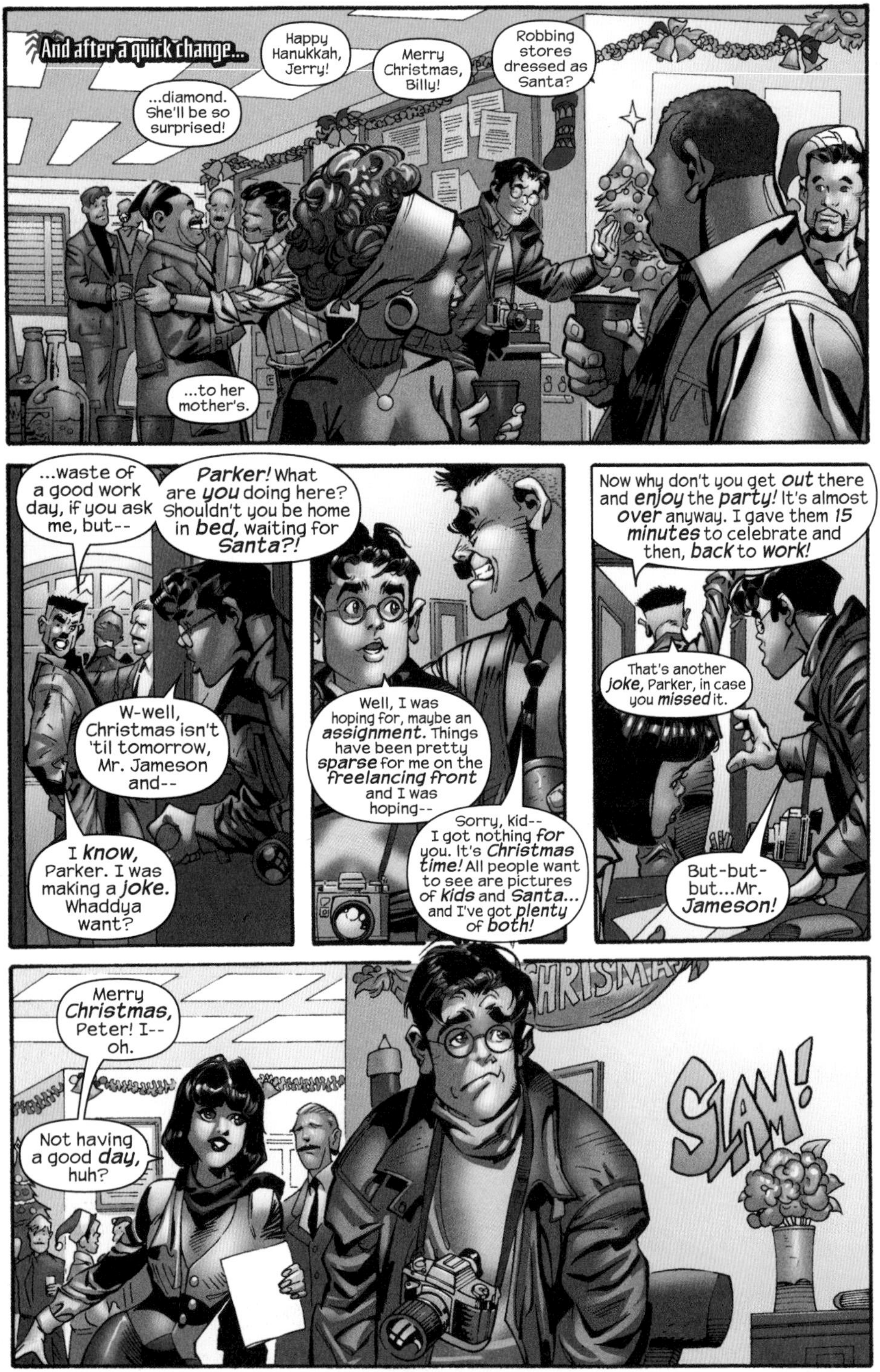

And after a quick change...
...diamond. She'll be so surprised!
...to her mother's.
Happy Hanukkah, Jerry!
Merry Christmas, Billy!
Robbing stores dressed as Santa?
...waste of a good work day, if you ask me, but--
Parker! What are you doing here? Shouldn't you be home in bed, waiting for Santa?!
W-well, Christmas isn't 'til tomorrow, Mr. Jameson and--
I know, Parker. I was making a joke. Whaddya want?
Well, I was hoping for, maybe an assignment. Things have been pretty sparse for me on the freelancing front and I was hoping--
Sorry, kid-- I got nothing for you. It's Christmas time! All people want to see are pictures of kids and Santa... and I've got plenty of both!
Now why don't you get out there and enjoy the party! It's almost over anyway. I gave them 15 minutes to celebrate and then, back to work!
That's another joke, Parker, in case you missed it.
But-but-but...Mr. Jameson!
Merry Christmas, Peter! I-- oh.
Not having a good day, huh?
SLAM!

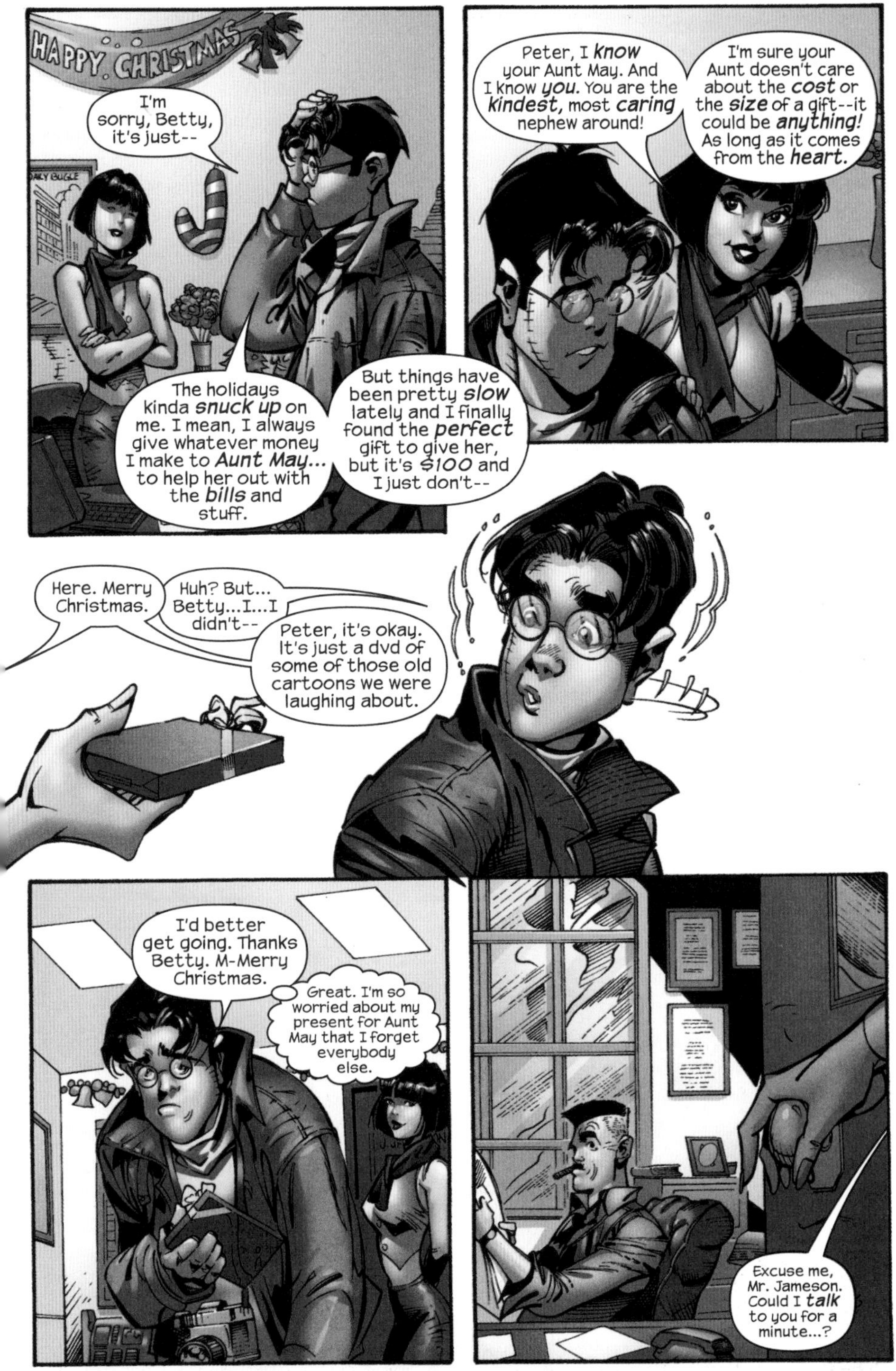
HAPPY CHRISTMAS
I'm sorry, Betty, it's just--
The holidays kinda snuck up on me. I mean, I always give whatever money I make to Aunt May... to help her out with the bills and stuff.
But things have been pretty slow lately and I finally found the perfect gift to give her, but it's $100 and I just don't--
Peter, I know your Aunt May. And I know you. You are the kindest, most caring nephew around!
I'm sure your Aunt doesn't care about the cost or the size of a gift--it could be anything! As long as it comes from the heart.
Here. Merry Christmas.
Huh? But... Betty...I...I didn't--
Peter, it's okay. It's just a dvd of some of those old cartoons we were laughing about.
I'd better get going. Thanks Betty. M-Merry Christmas.
Great. I'm so worried about my present for Aunt May that I forget everybody else.
Excuse me, Mr. Jameson. Could I talk to you for a minute...?

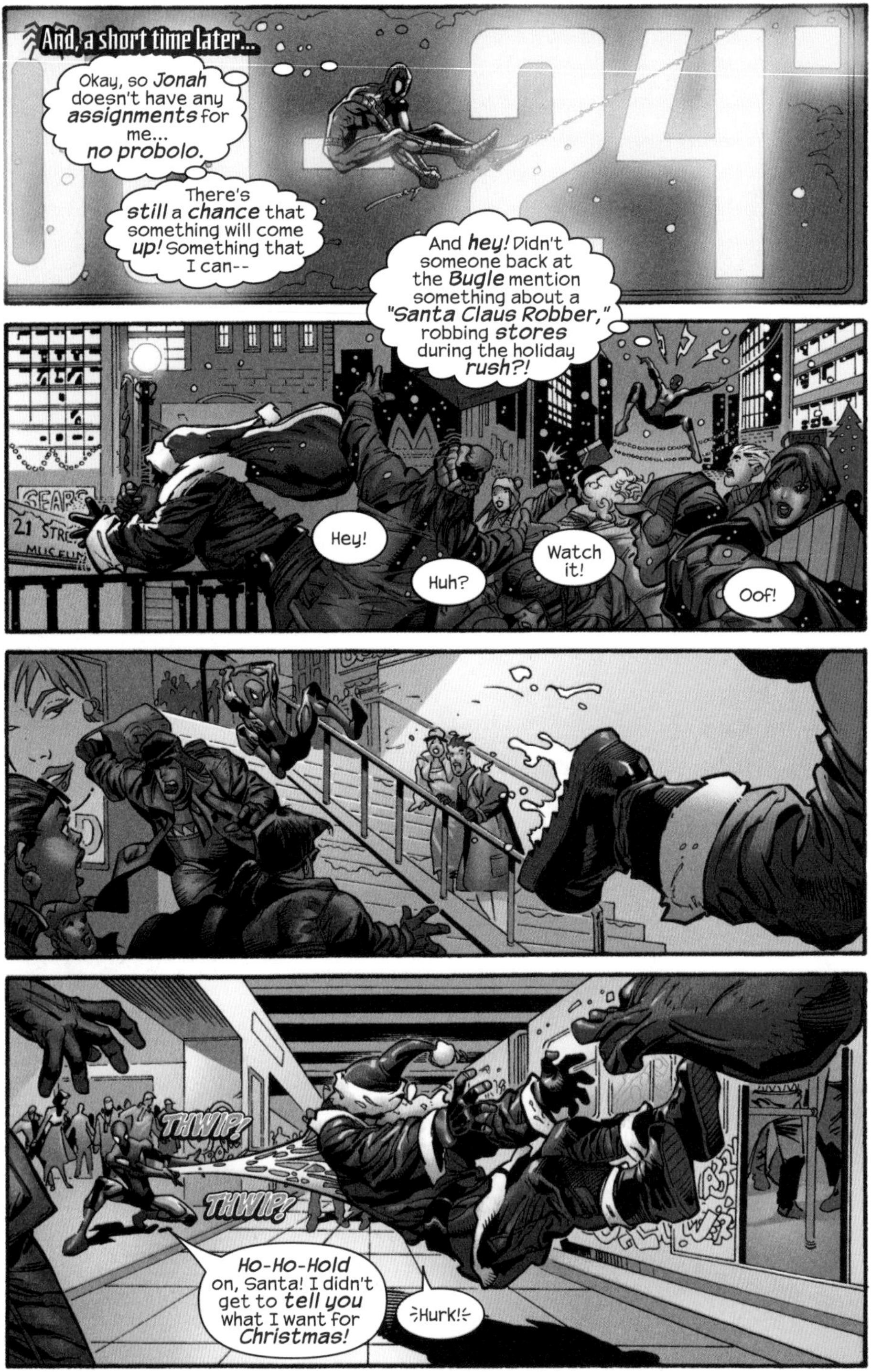

And, a short time later...
Okay, so Jonah doesn't have any assignments for me... no probolo.
There's still a chance that something will come up! Something that I can--
And hey! Didn't someone back at the Bugle mention something about a "Santa Claus Robber," robbing stores during the holiday rush?!
Hey!
Huh?
Watch it!
Oof!
THWIP!
THWIP!
Ho-Ho-Hold on, Santa! I didn't get to tell you what I want for Christmas!
Hurk!

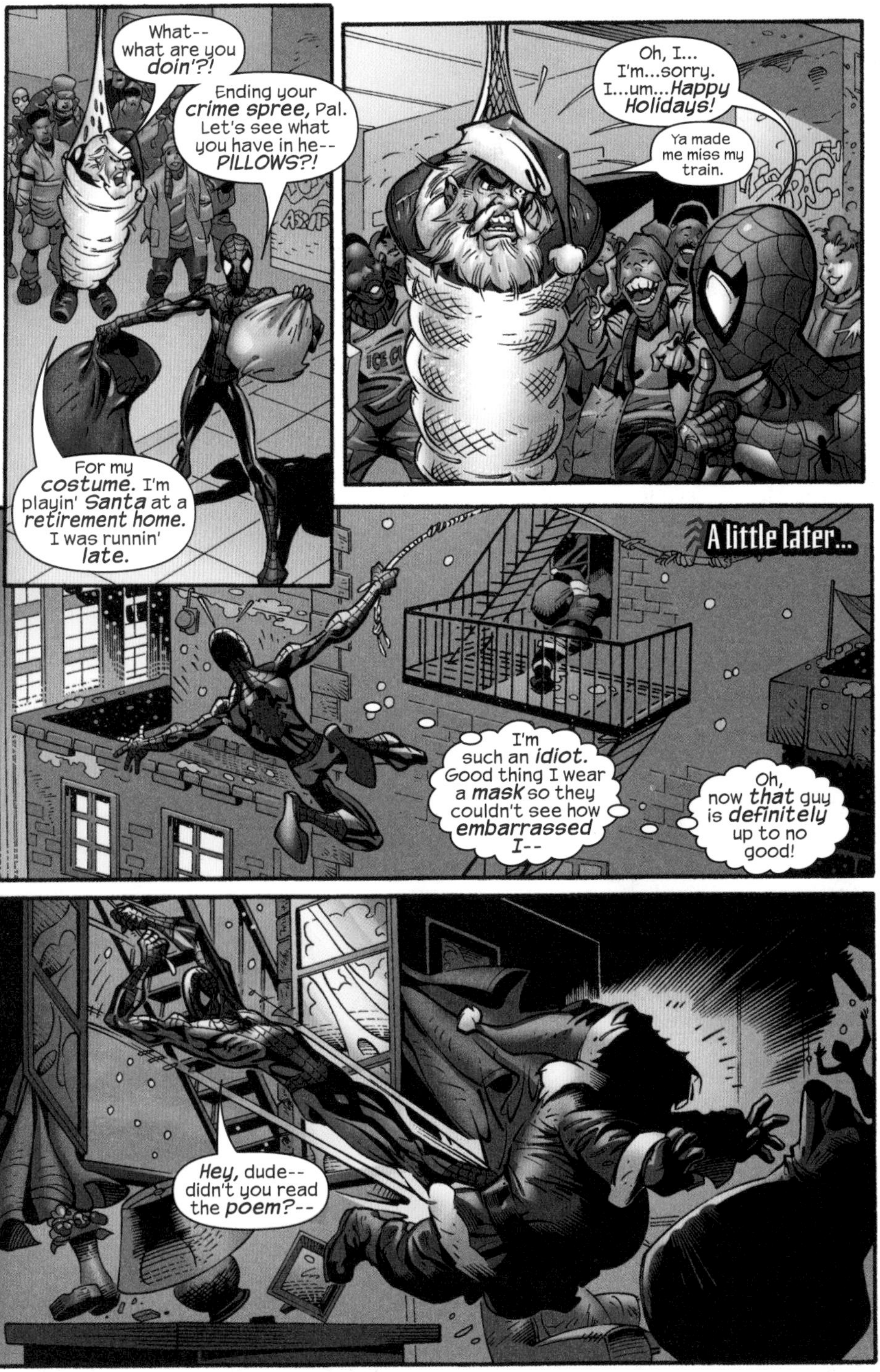
What--
what are you
doin'?!
Ending your
crime spree, Pal.
Let's see what
you have in he--
PILLOWS?!
For my
costume. I'm
playin' Santa at a
retirement home.
I was runnin'
late.
Oh, I...
I'm...sorry.
I...um...Happy
Holidays!
Ya made
me miss my
train.
A little later...
I'm
such an idiot.
Good thing I wear
a mask so they
couldn't see how
embarrassed
I--
Oh,
now that guy
is definitely
up to no
good!
Hey, dude--
didn't you read
the poem?--

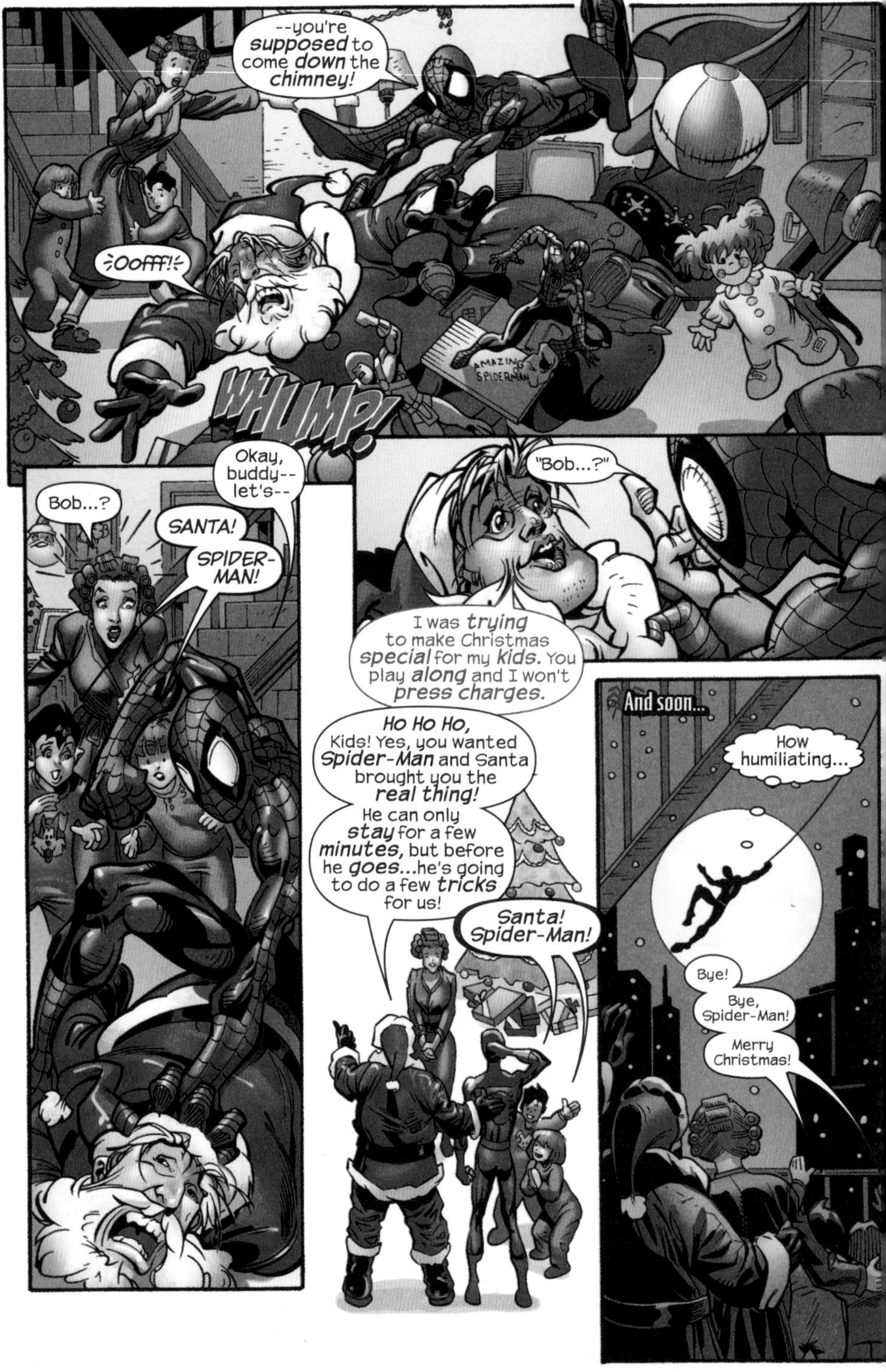
--you're supposed to come down the chimney!
Oofff!
WHUMP!
AMAZING SPIDERMAN
Bob...?
Okay, buddy--let's--
SANTA!
SPIDER-MAN!
"Bob...?"
I was trying to make Christmas special for my kids. You play along and I won't press charges.
Ho Ho Ho, Kids! Yes, you wanted Spider-Man and Santa brought you the real thing!
He can only stay for a few minutes, but before he goes...he's going to do a few tricks for us!
Santa! Spider-Man!
And soon...
How humiliating...
Bye!
Bye, Spider-Man!
Merry Christmas!

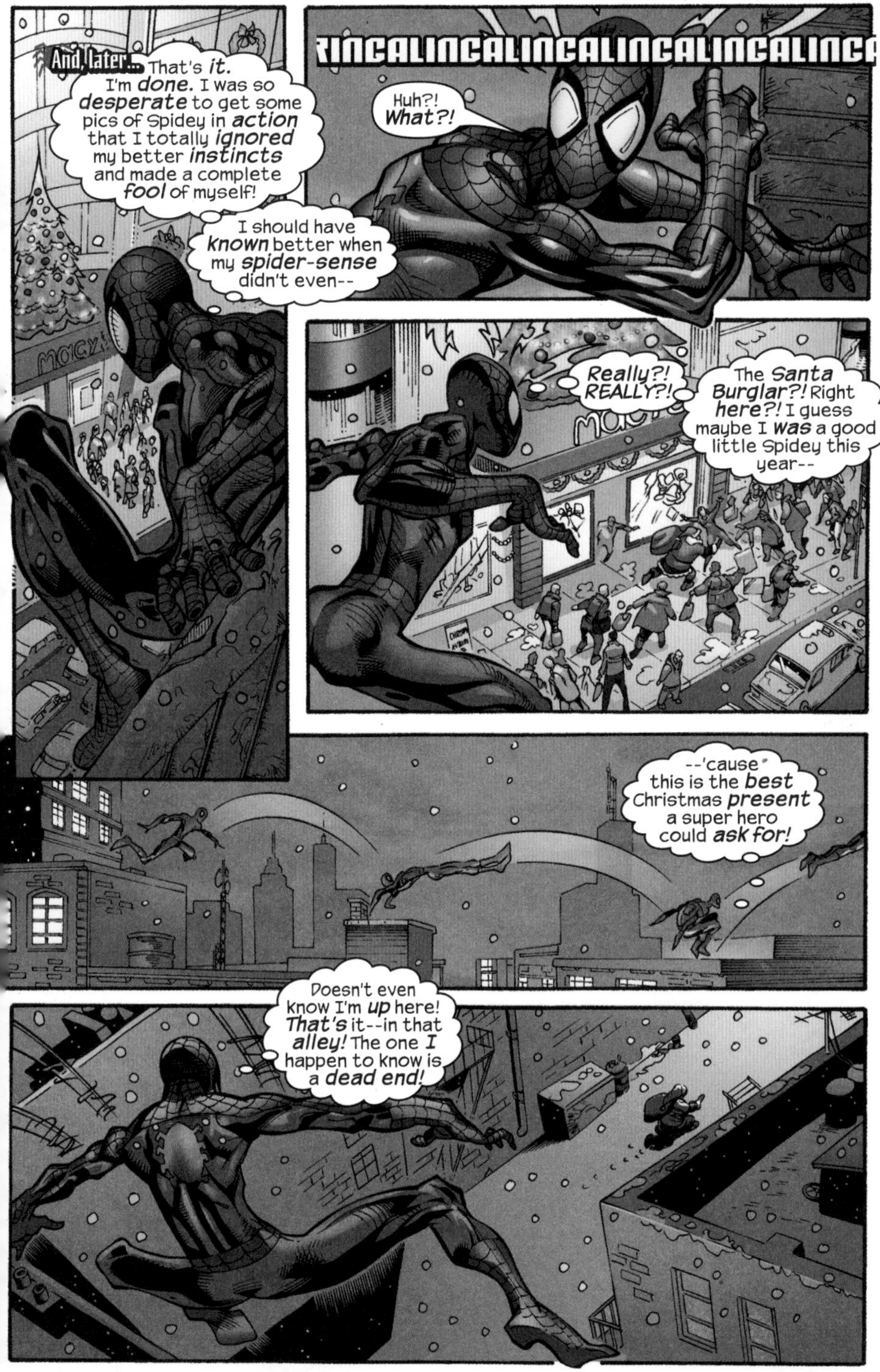
And, later...
That's it. I'm done. I was so desperate to get some pics of Spidey in action that I totally ignored my better instincts and made a complete fool of myself!
I should have known better when my spider-sense didn't even--
RINGALINGALINGALINGALINGALINGALINGA
Huh?! What?!
Really?! REALLY?!
The Santa Burglar?! Right here?! I guess maybe I was a good little Spidey this year--
--'cause this is the best Christmas present a super hero could ask for!
Doesn't even know I'm up here! That's it--in that alley! The one I happen to know is a dead end!

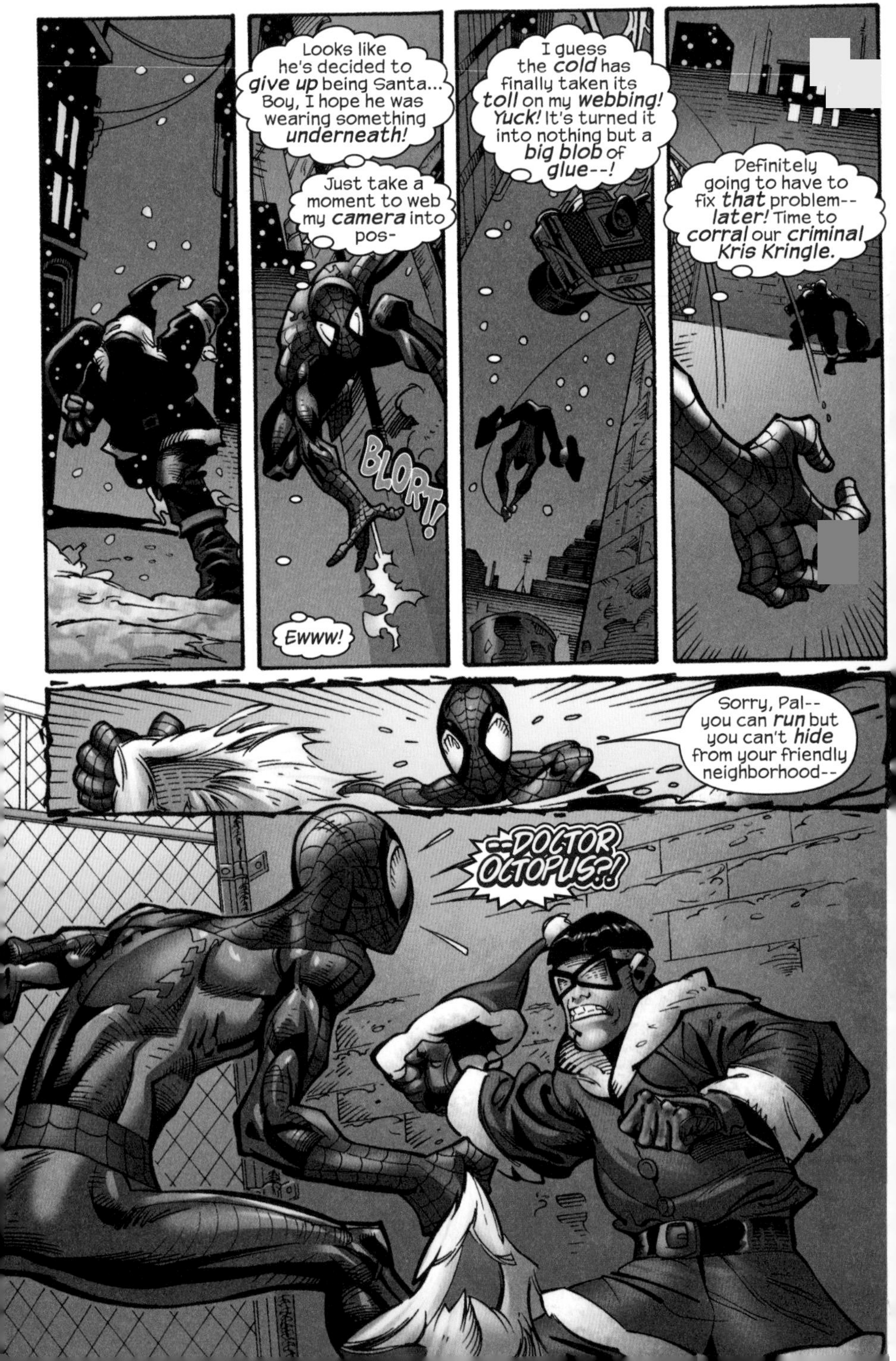

Looks like he's decided to give up being Santa... Boy, I hope he was wearing something underneath!
Just take a moment to web my camera into pos-
BLORT!
Ewww!
I guess the cold has finally taken its toll on my webbing! Yuck! It's turned it into nothing but a big blob of glue--!
Definitely going to have to fix that problem--later! Time to corral our criminal Kris Kringle.
Sorry, Pal--you can run but you can't hide from your friendly neighborhood--
--DOCTOR OCTOPUS?!

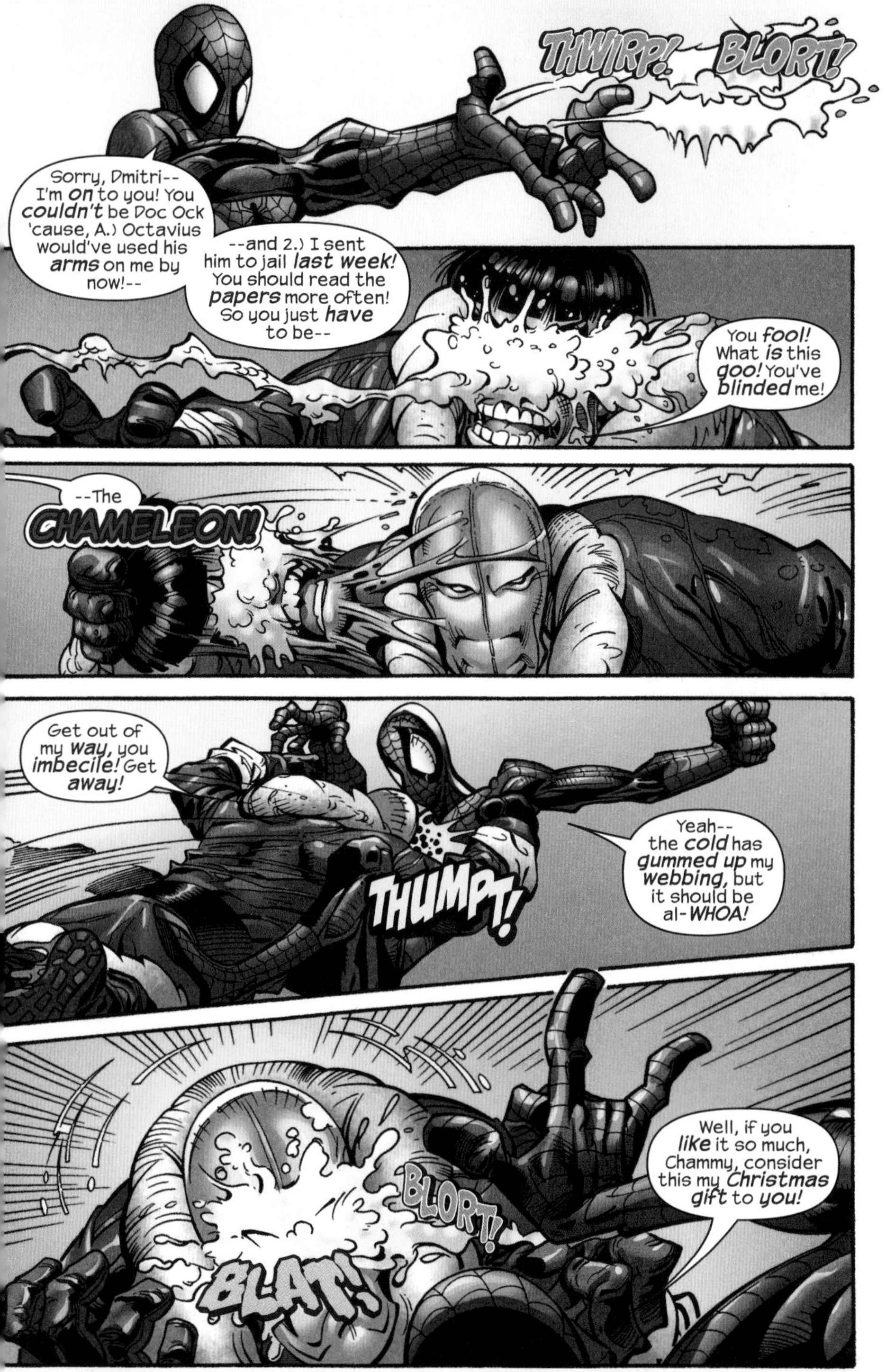
THWIRP!
BLORT!
Sorry, Dmitri-- I'm on to you! You couldn't be Doc Ock 'cause, A.) Octavius would've used his arms on me by now!--
--and 2.) I sent him to jail last week! You should read the papers more often! So you just have to be--
You fool! What is this goo! You've blinded me!
--The CHAMELEON!
Get out of my way, you imbecile! Get away!
Yeah-- the cold has gummed up my webbing, but it should be al-WHOA!
THUMPT!
Well, if you like it so much, Chammy, consider this my Christmas gift to you!
BLORT!
BLAT!

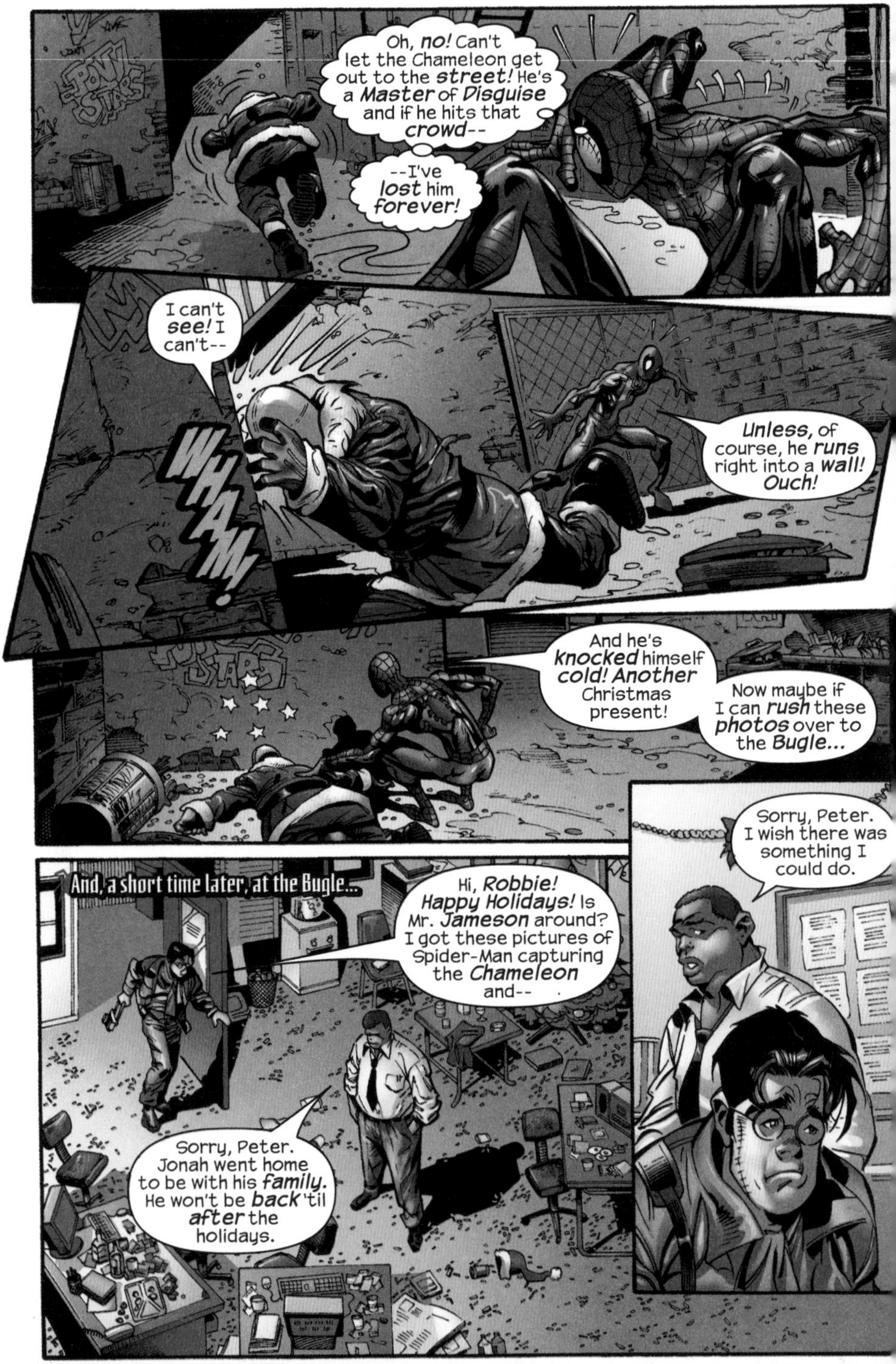
Oh, no! Can't let the Chameleon get out to the street! He's a Master of Disguise and if he hits that crowd--
--I've lost him forever!
I can't see! I can't--
WHAM!
Unless, of course, he runs right into a wall! Ouch!
And he's knocked himself cold! Another Christmas present!
Now maybe if I can rush these photos over to the Bugle...
And, a short time later, at the Bugle...
Hi, Robbie! Happy Holidays! Is Mr. Jameson around? I got these pictures of Spider-Man capturing the Chameleon and--
Sorry, Peter. Jonah went home to be with his family. He won't be back 'til after the holidays.
Sorry, Peter. I wish there was something I could do.

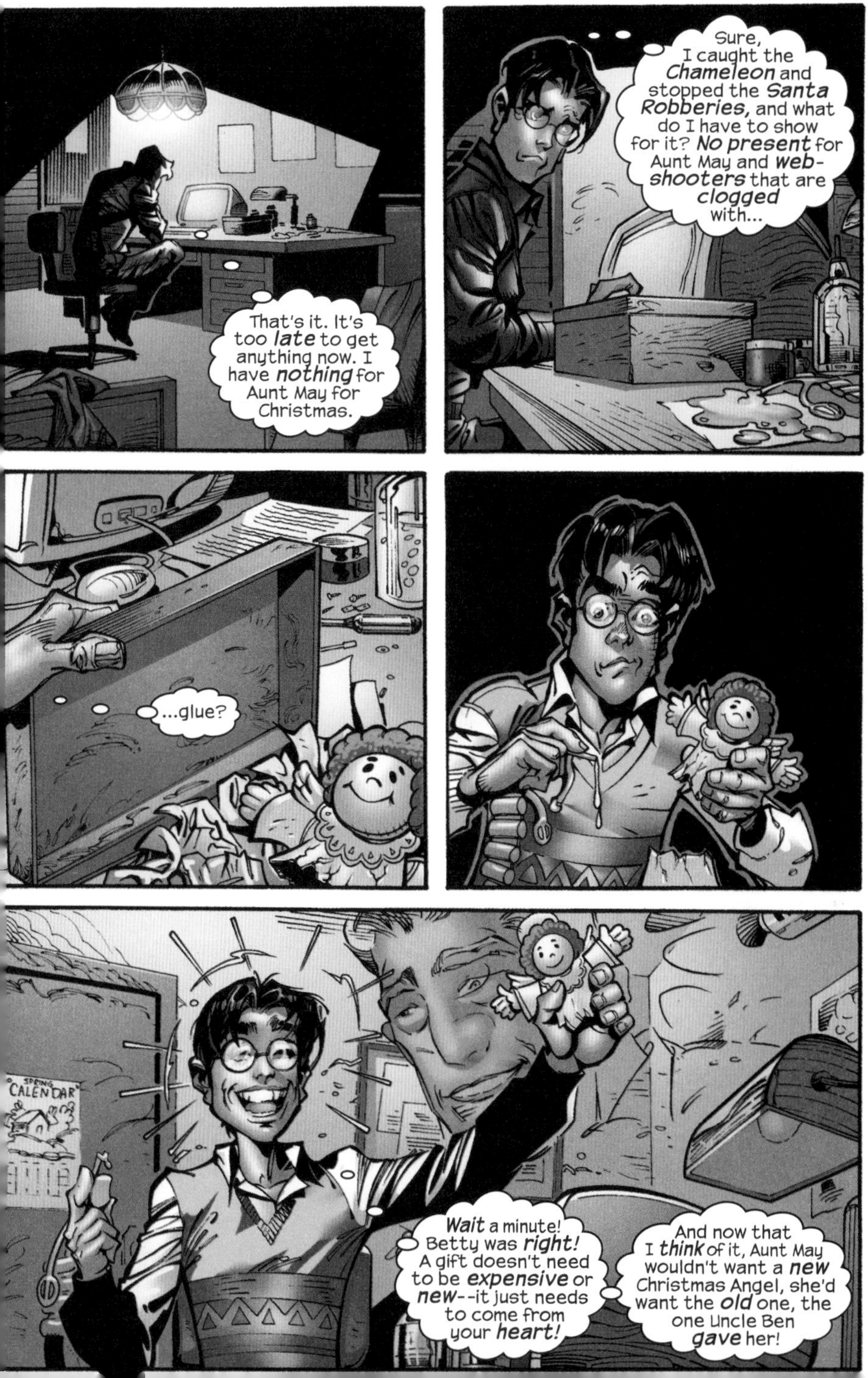
That's it. It's too *late* to get anything now. I have *nothing* for Aunt May for Christmas.
Sure, I caught the *Chameleon* and stopped the *Santa Robberies,* and what do I have to show for it? *No present* for Aunt May and *web-shooters* that are *clogged* with...
...glue?
Wait a minute! Betty was *right!* A gift doesn't need to be *expensive* or *new*--it just needs to come from your *heart!*
And now that I *think* of it, Aunt May wouldn't want a *new* Christmas Angel, she'd want the *old* one, the one Uncle Ben *gave* her!
SPRING CALENDAR

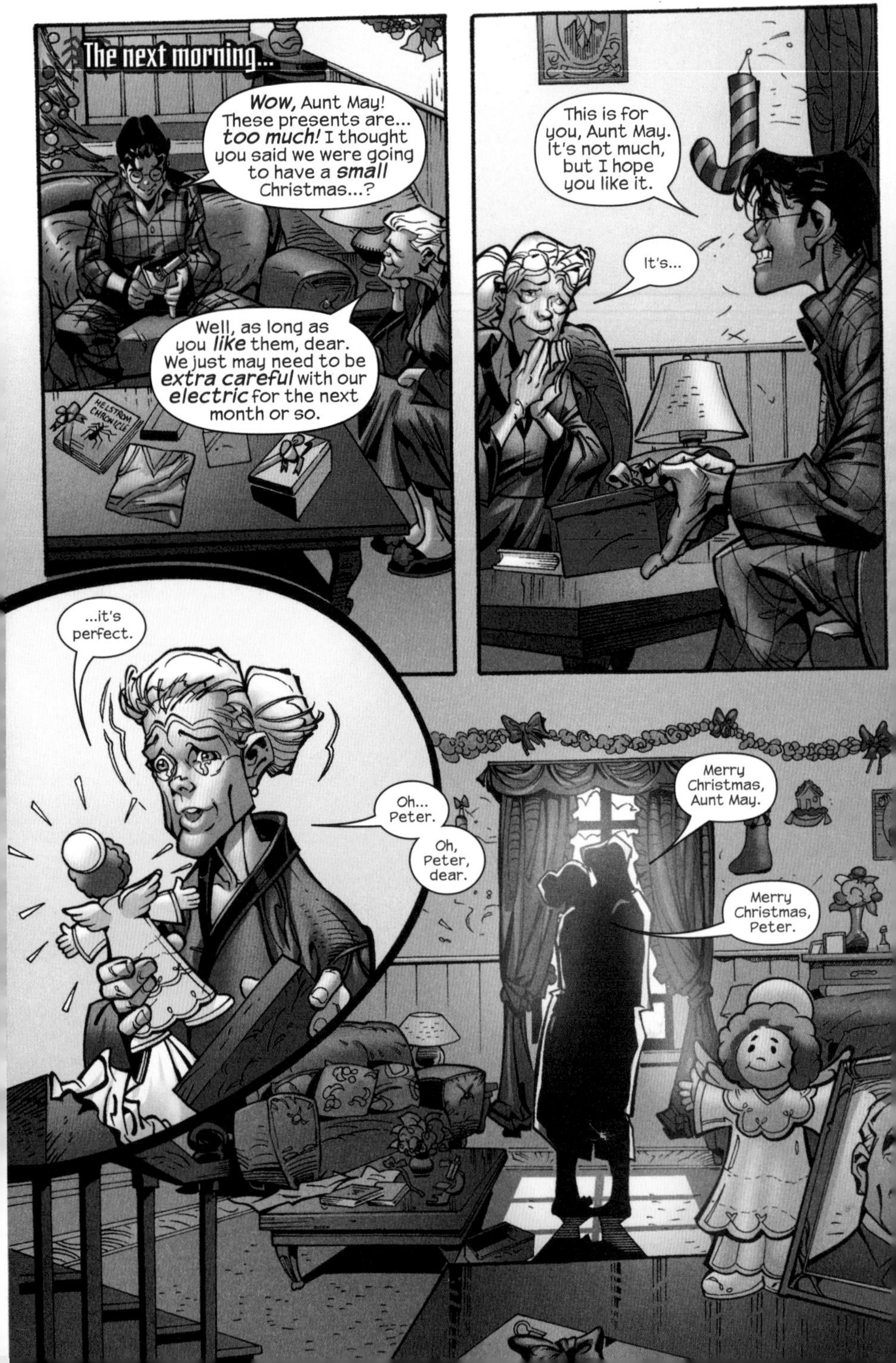
The next morning...
Wow, Aunt May! These presents are... too much! I thought you said we were going to have a small Christmas...?
Well, as long as you like them, dear. We just may need to be extra careful with our electric for the next month or so.
HELSTROM CHRONICLE
This is for you, Aunt May. It's not much, but I hope you like it.
It's...
...it's perfect.
Oh... Peter.
Oh, Peter, dear.
Merry Christmas, Aunt May.
Merry Christmas, Peter.

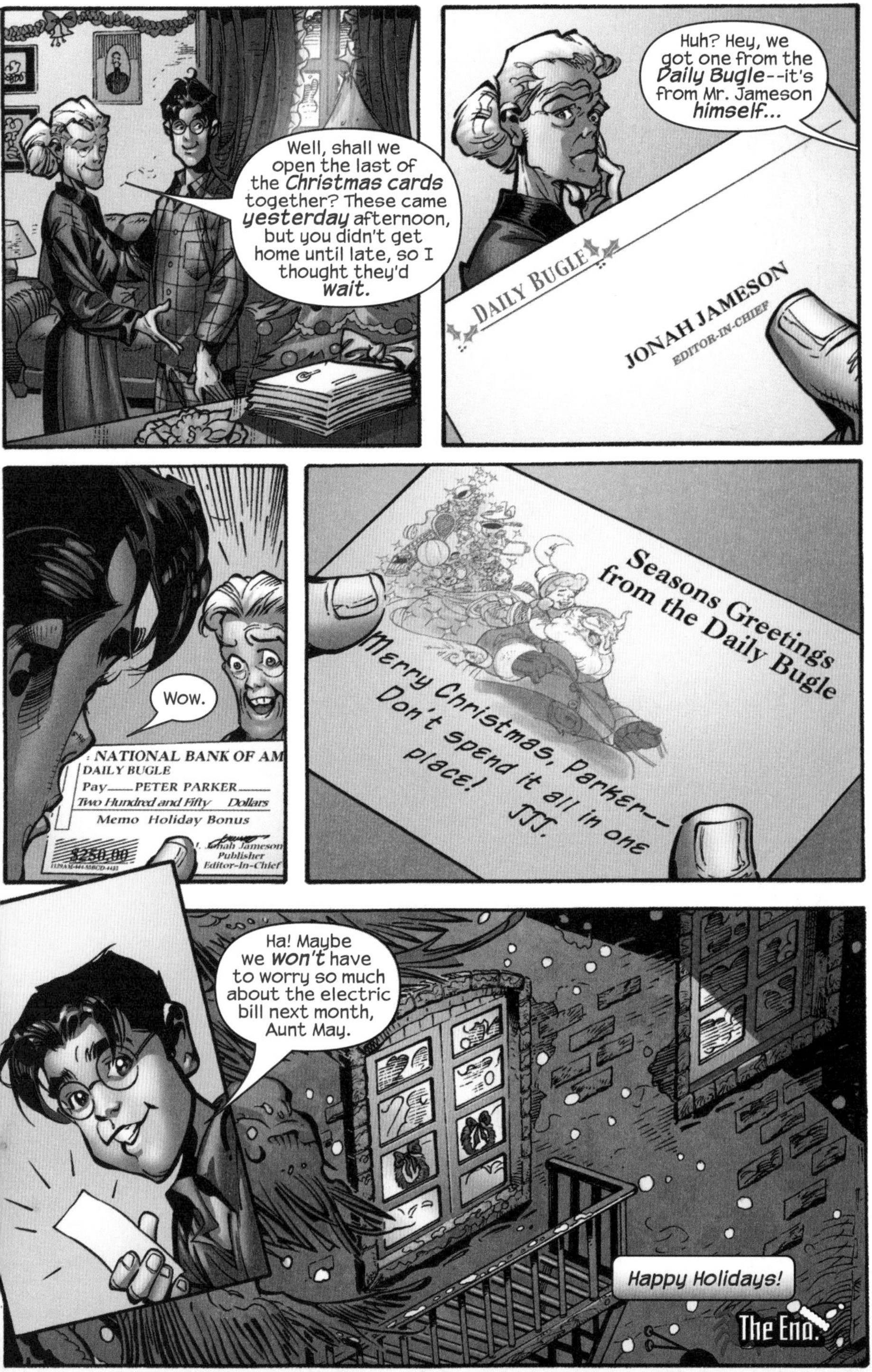
Well, shall we open the last of the Christmas cards together? These came yesterday afternoon, but you didn't get home until late, so I thought they'd wait.
Huh? Hey, we got one from the Daily Bugle--it's from Mr. Jameson himself...
DAILY BUGLE
JONAH JAMESON
EDITOR-IN-CHIEF
Wow.
NATIONAL BANK OF AM
DAILY BUGLE
Pay PETER PARKER
Two Hundred and Fifty Dollars
Memo Holiday Bonus
$250.00
J. Jonah Jameson
Publisher
Editor-In-Chief
Seasons Greetings from the Daily Bugle
Merry Christmas, Parker-- Don't spend it all in one place! JJJ.
Ha! Maybe we won't have to worry so much about the electric bill next month, Aunt May.
Happy Holidays!
The End.

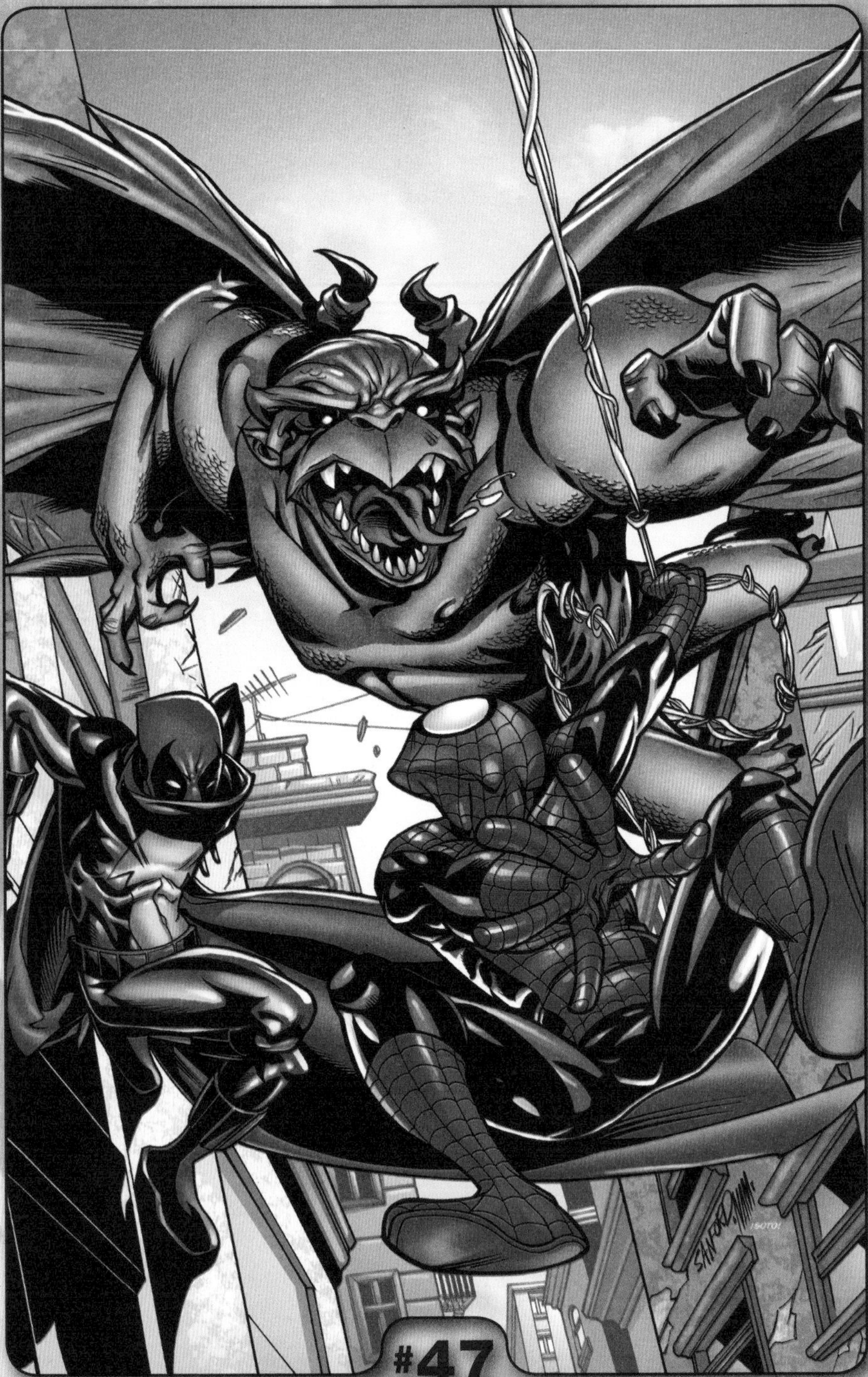

#47

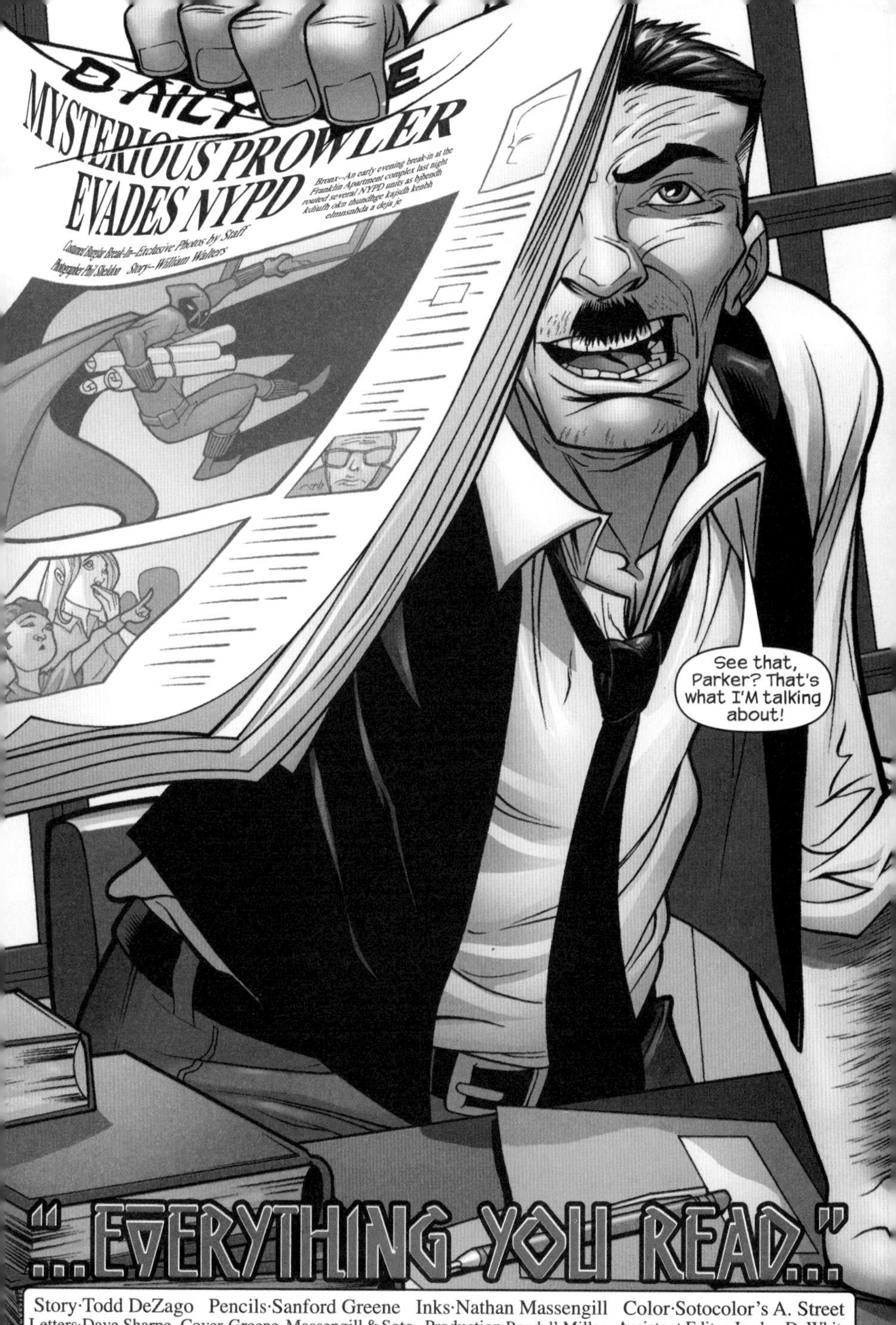
MYSTERIOUS PROWLER EVADES NYPD
Bronx--An early evening break-in at the Franklin Apartment complex last night routed several NYPD units as bjhendh kdiufh okn thundhge kajsdh kenbh elmnsnbda a deja je
Costumed Burglar Break-In--Exclusive Photos by Staff Photographer Phil Sheldon Story--William Walters
See that, Parker? That's what I'M talking about!
"...EVERYTHING YOU READ..."

Story·Todd DeZago Pencils·Sanford Greene Inks·Nathan Massengill Color·Sotocolor's A. Street
Letters·Dave Sharpe Cover·Greene, Massengill & Soto Production·Randall Miller Assistant Editor·Jordan D. White
Consulting·Mark Paniccia & Ralph Macchio Editor·Nathan Cosby Editor in Chief·Joe Quesada Publisher·Dan Buckley

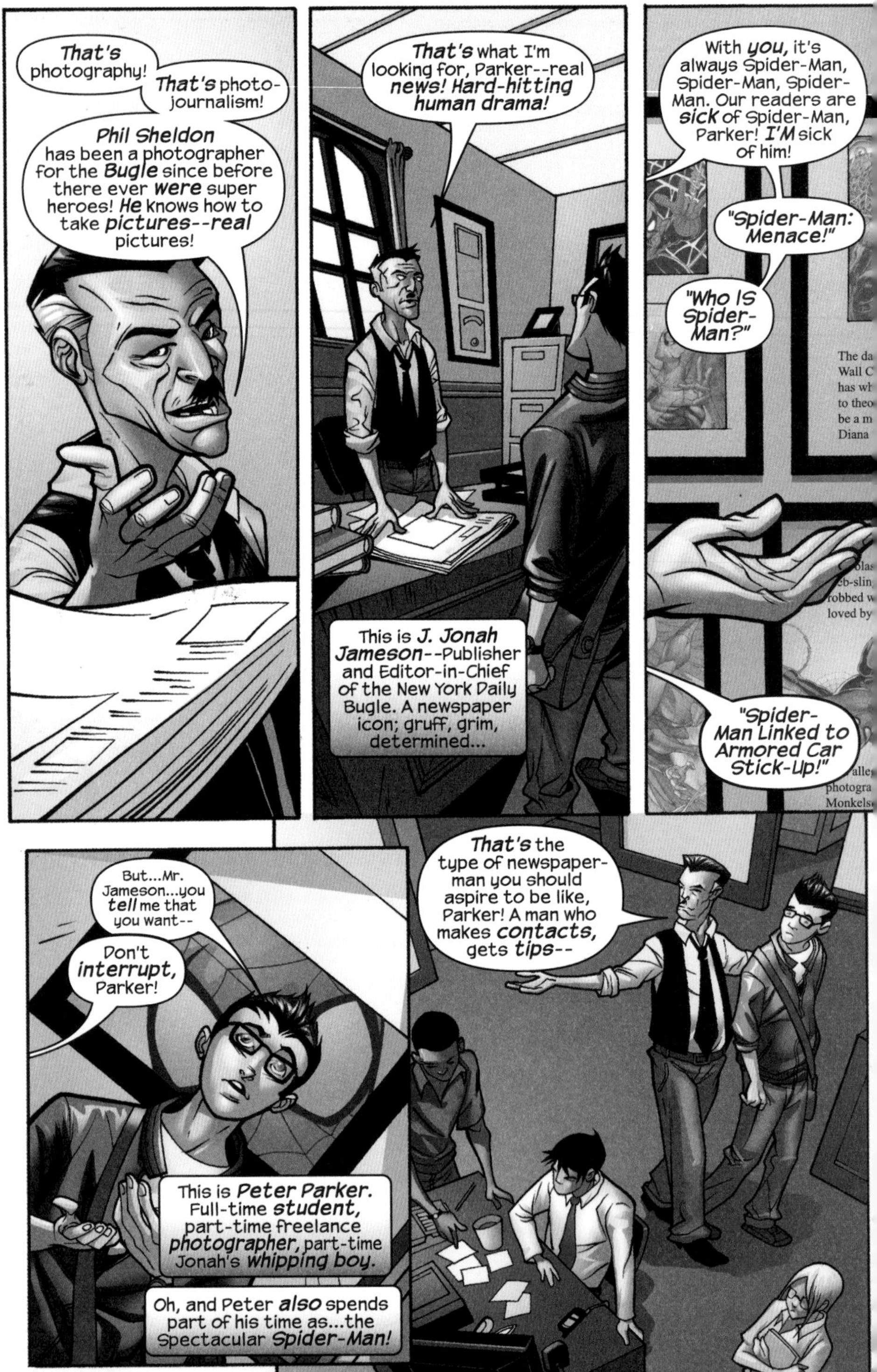
That's photography!
That's photo-journalism!
Phil Sheldon has been a photographer for the Bugle since before there ever were super heroes! He knows how to take pictures--real pictures!
That's what I'm looking for, Parker--real news! Hard-hitting human drama!
This is J. Jonah Jameson--Publisher and Editor-in-Chief of the New York Daily Bugle. A newspaper icon; gruff, grim, determined...
With you, it's always Spider-Man, Spider-Man, Spider-Man. Our readers are sick of Spider-Man, Parker! I'M sick of him!
"Spider-Man: Menace!"
"Who IS Spider-Man?"
"Spider-Man Linked to Armored Car Stick-Up!"
That's the type of newspaper-man you should aspire to be like, Parker! A man who makes contacts, gets tips--
But...Mr. Jameson...you tell me that you want--
Don't interrupt, Parker!
This is Peter Parker. Full-time student, part-time freelance photographer, part-time Jonah's whipping boy.
Oh, and Peter also spends part of his time as...the Spectacular Spider-Man!

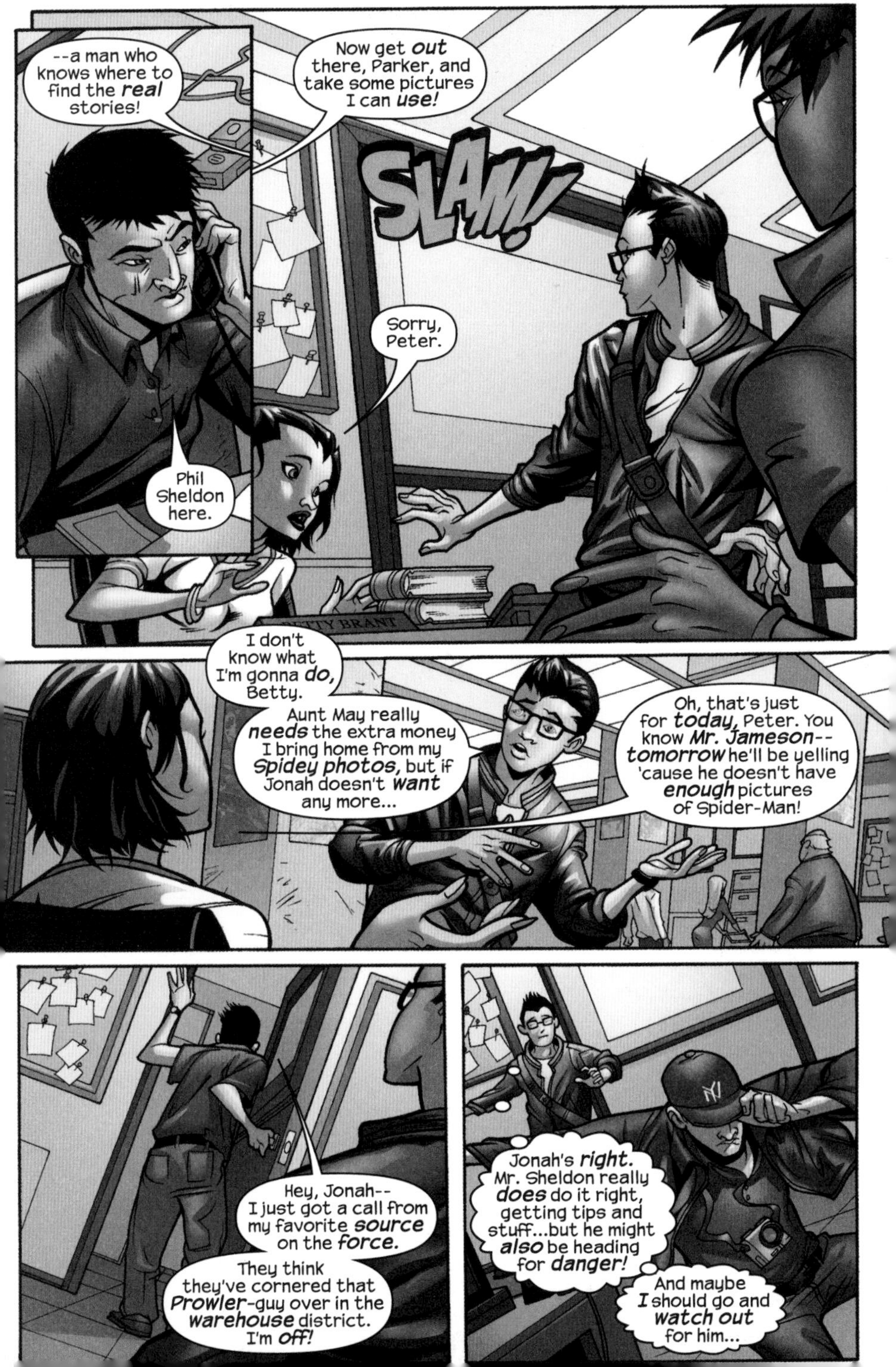
--a man who knows where to find the *real* stories!
Now get *out* there, Parker, and take some pictures I can *use!*
SLAM!
Sorry, Peter.
Phil Sheldon here.
BETTY BRANT
I don't know what I'm gonna *do,* Betty.
Aunt May really *needs* the extra money I bring home from my *Spidey photos,* but if Jonah doesn't *want* any more...
Oh, that's just for *today,* Peter. You know *Mr. Jameson*--*tomorrow* he'll be yelling 'cause he doesn't have *enough* pictures of Spider-Man!
Hey, Jonah-- I just got a call from my favorite *source* on the *force.*
They think they've cornered that *Prowler*-guy over in the *warehouse* district. I'm *off!*
Jonah's *right.* Mr. Sheldon really *does* do it right, getting tips and stuff...but he might *also* be heading for *danger!*
And maybe *I* should go and *watch out* for him...

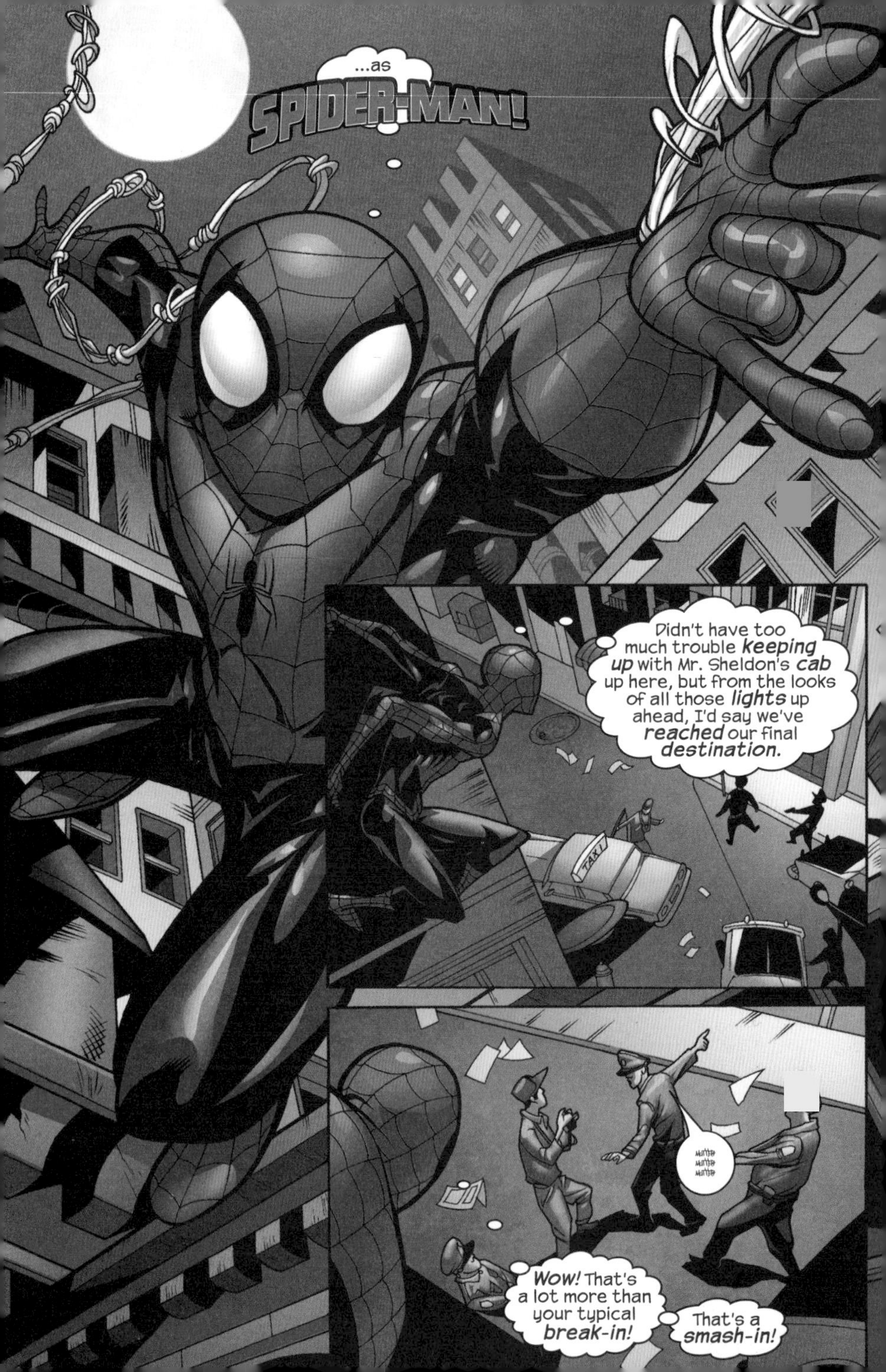
...as
SPIDER-MAN!
Didn't have too much trouble keeping up with Mr. Sheldon's cab up here, but from the looks of all those lights up ahead, I'd say we've reached our final destination.
TAXI
Wow! That's a lot more than your typical break-in!
That's a smash-in!

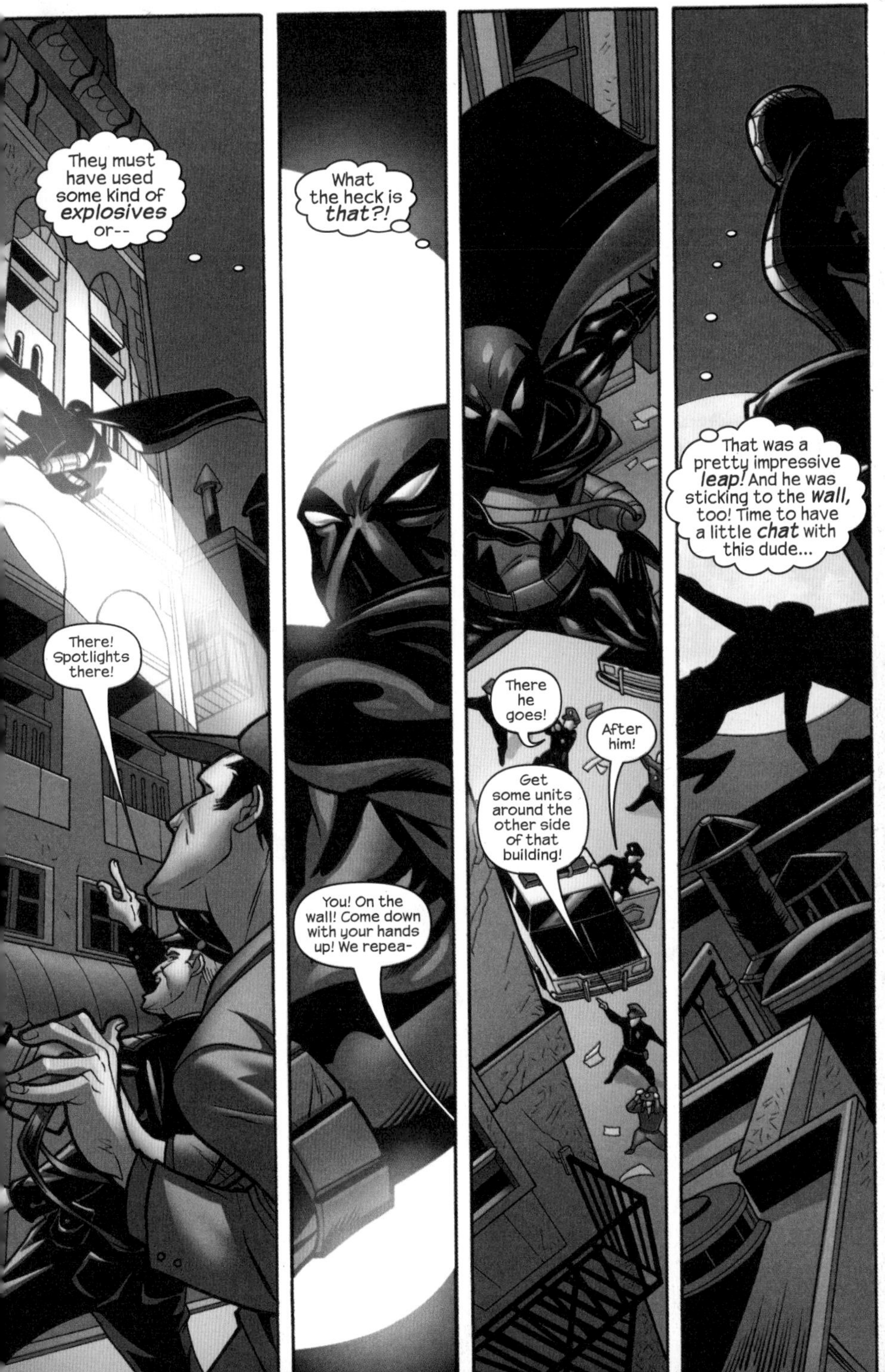
They must have used some kind of explosives or--
There! Spotlights there!
What the heck is that?!
You! On the wall! Come down with your hands up! We repea-
There he goes!
After him!
Get some units around the other side of that building!
That was a pretty impressive leap! And he was sticking to the wall, too! Time to have a little chat with this dude...

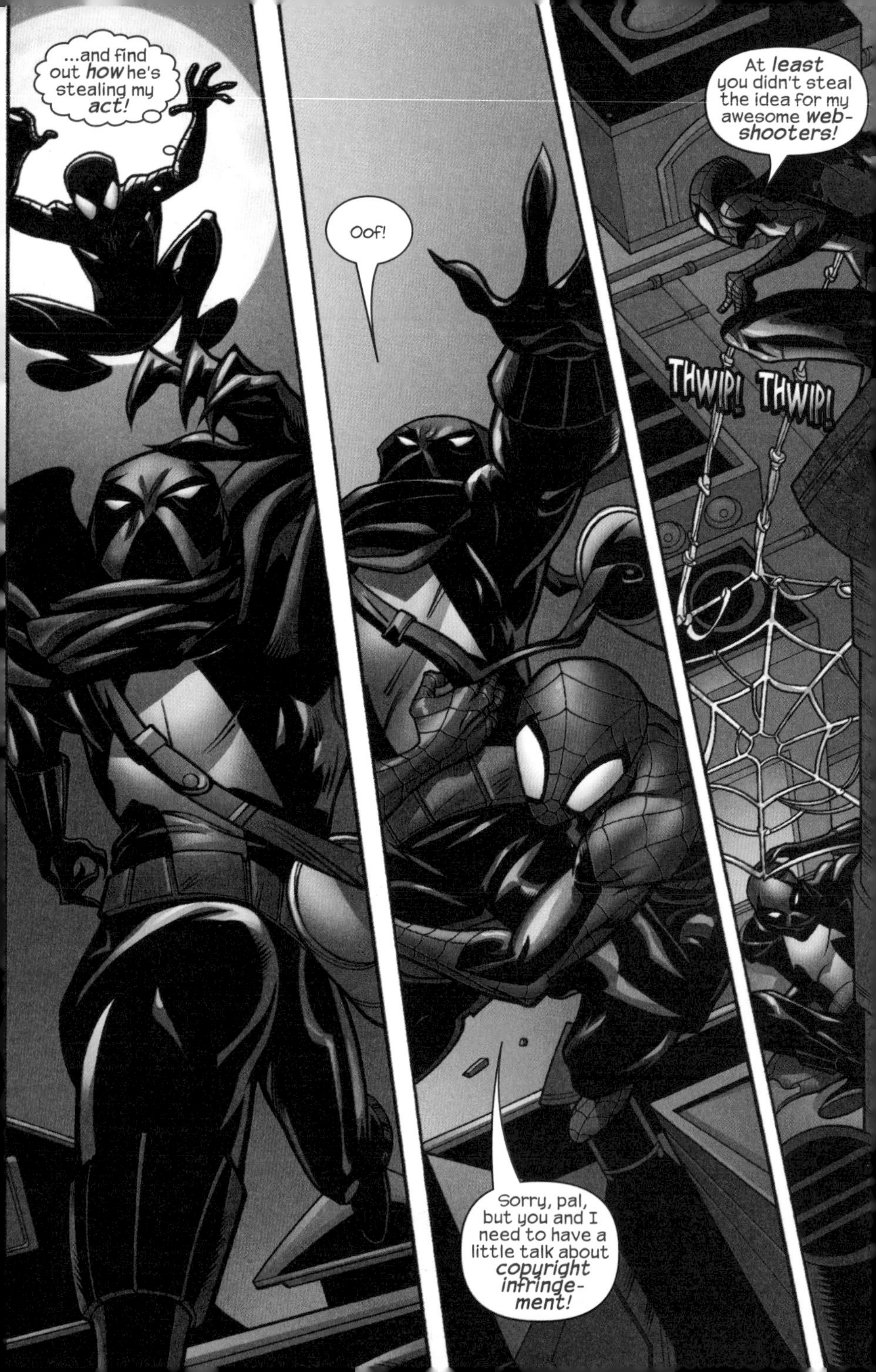
...and find out how he's stealing my act!
Oof!
Sorry, pal, but you and I need to have a little talk about copyright infringe-ment!
At least you didn't steal the idea for my awesome web-shooters!
THWIP! THWIP!

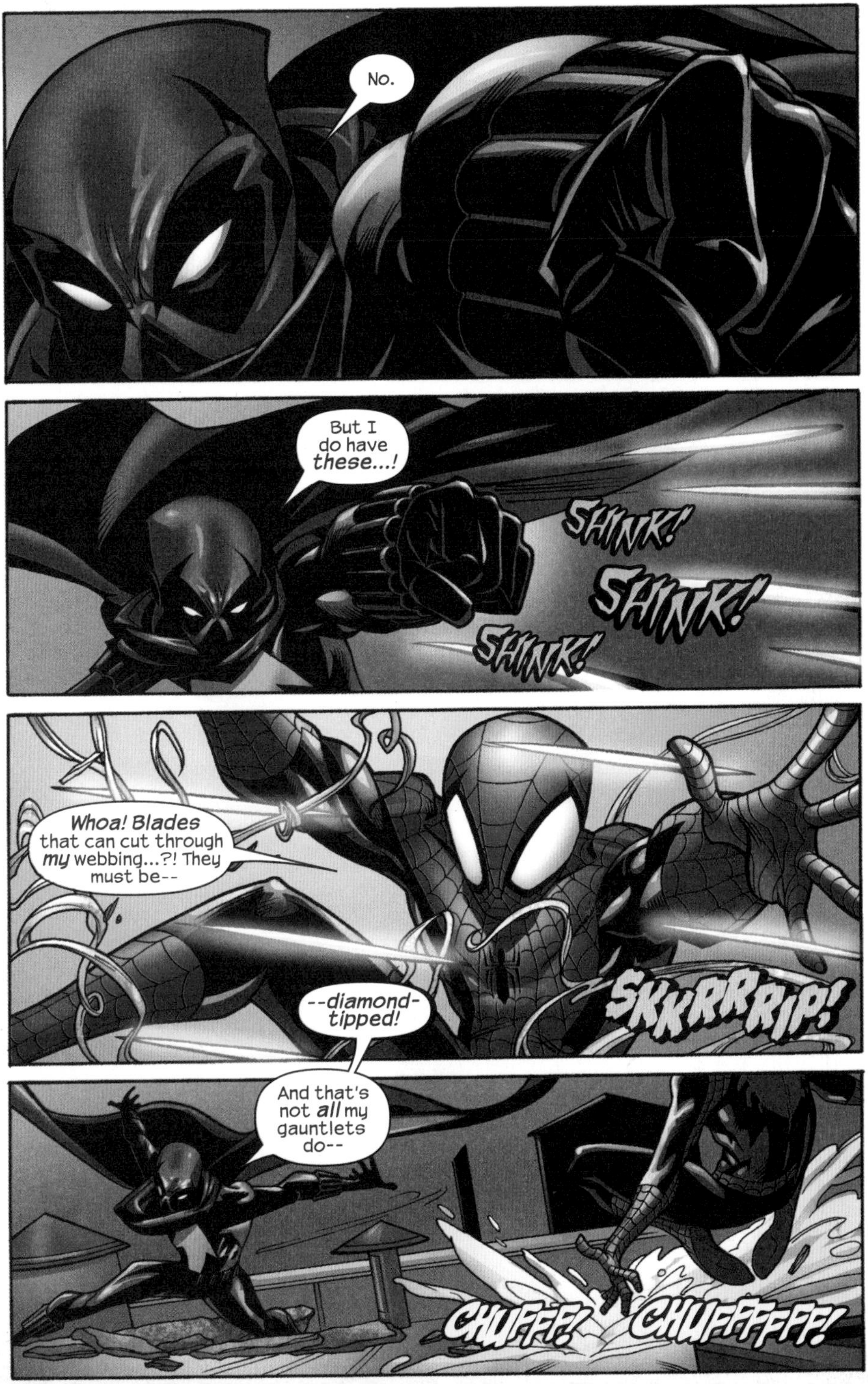
No.
But I do have *these...!*
SHINK!
SHINK!
SHINK!
Whoa! Blades that can cut through *my* webbing...?! They must be--
--diamond-tipped!
SKKRRRRIP!
And that's not *all* my gauntlets do--
CHUFFF!
CHUFFFFFFF!

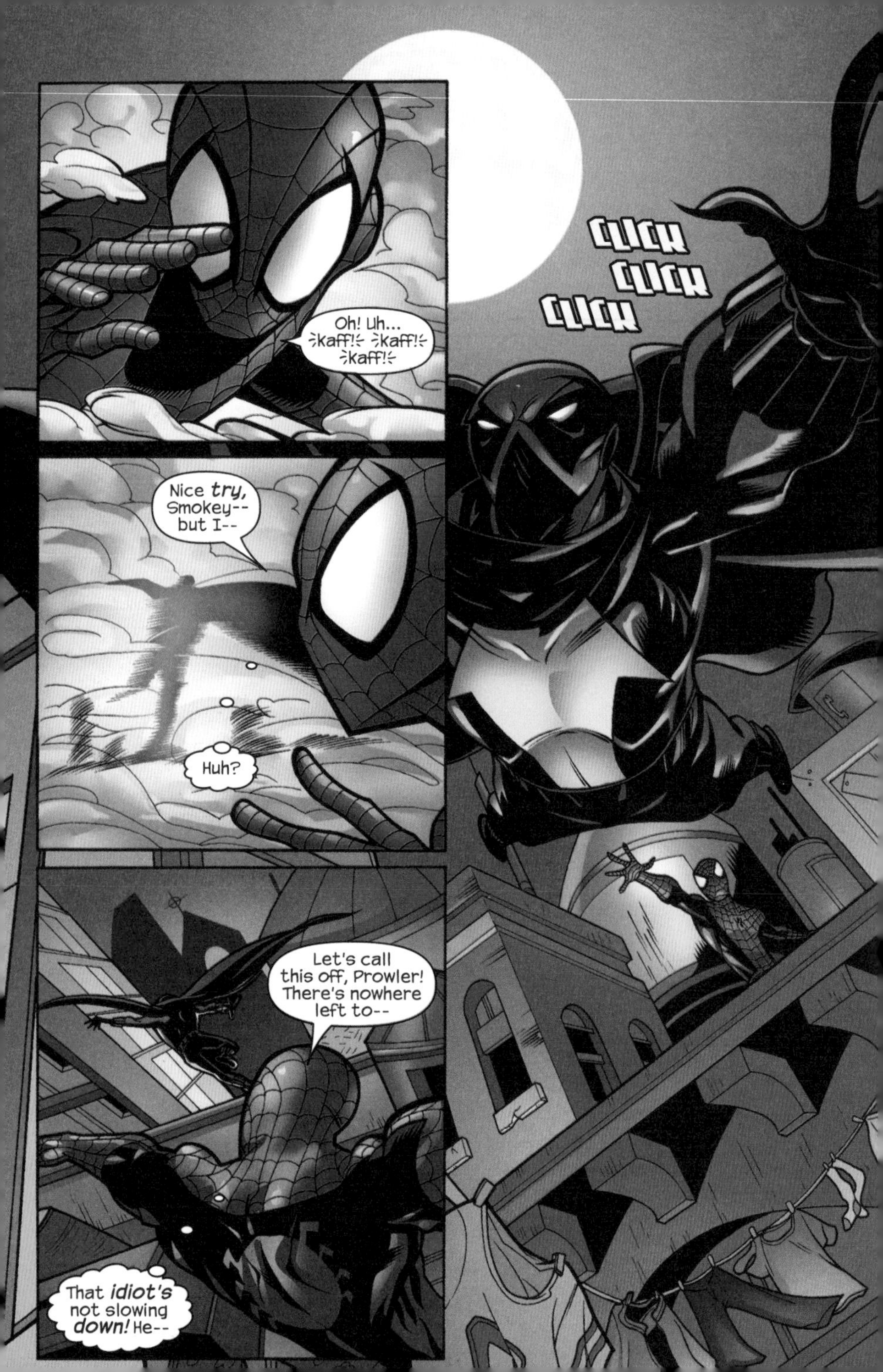
Oh! Uh...
kaff! kaff!
kaff!
Nice try,
Smokey--
but I--
Huh?
Let's call
this off, Prowler!
There's nowhere
left to--
That idiot's
not slowing
down! He--
CLICK
CLICK
CLICK

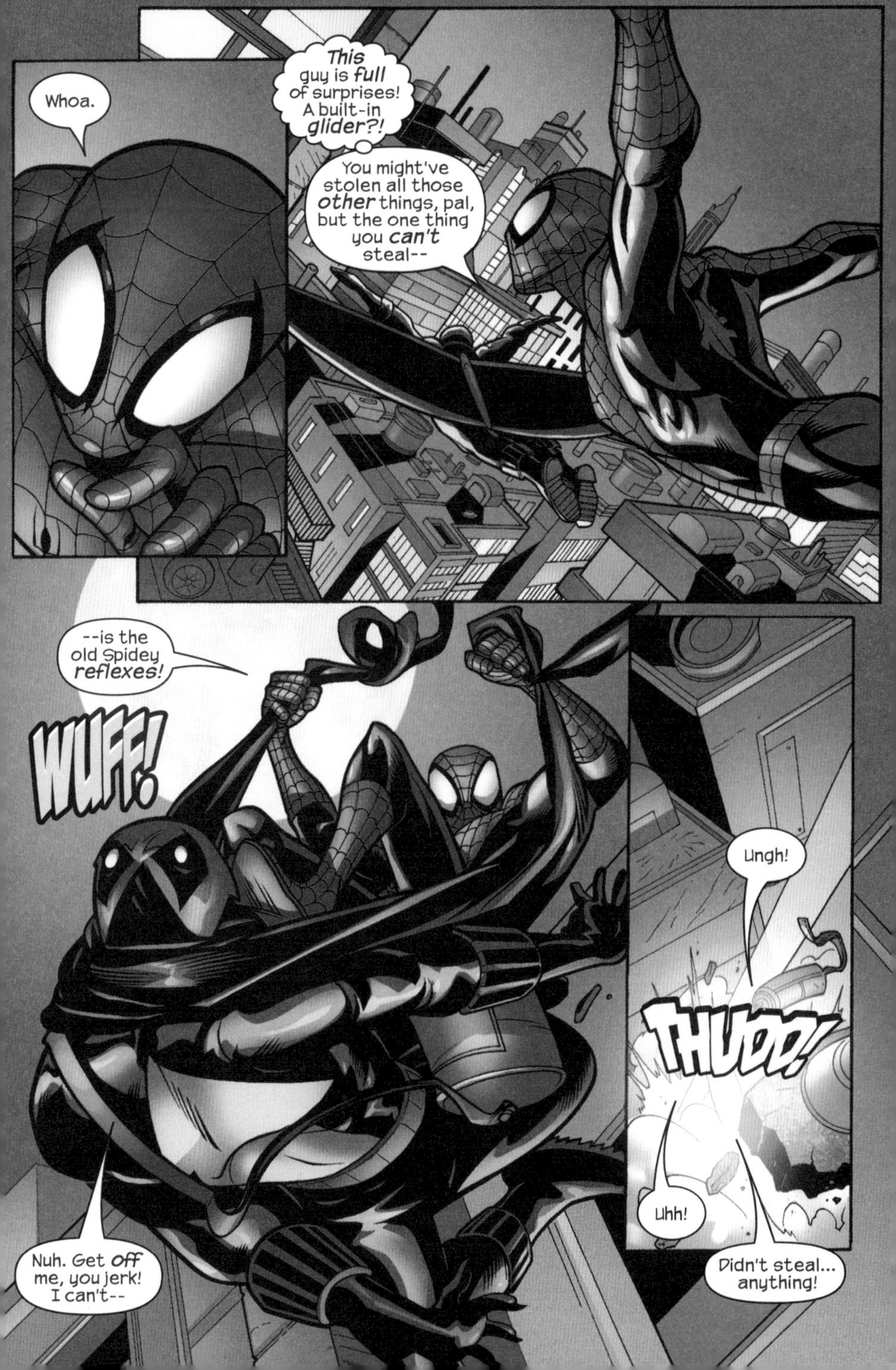
Whoa.
This guy is full of surprises! A built-in glider?!
You might've stolen all those other things, pal, but the one thing you can't steal--
--is the old Spidey reflexes!
WUFF!
Nuh. Get off me, you jerk! I can't--
Ungh!
THUDD!
Uhh!
Didn't steal... anything!

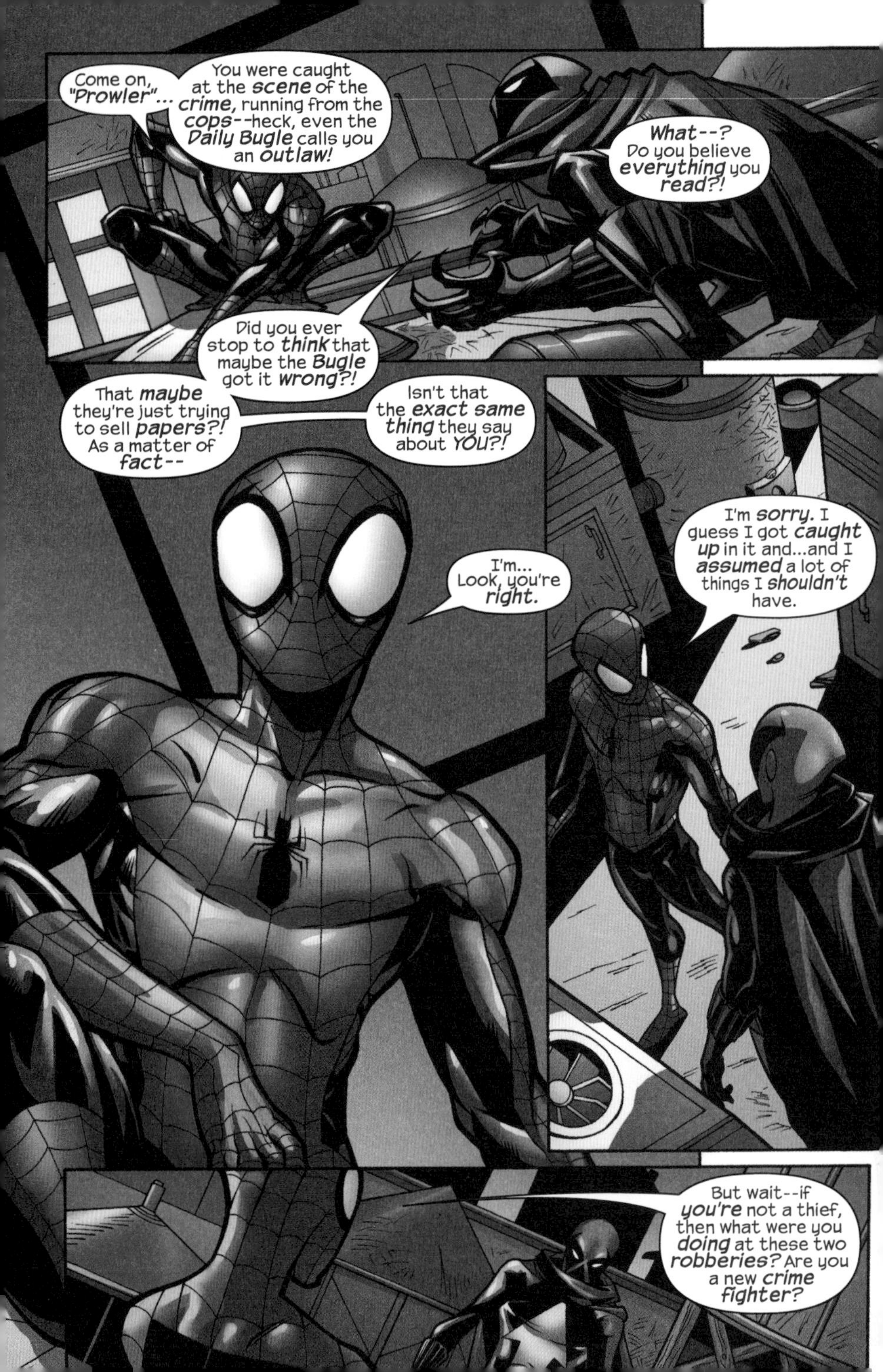
Come on, "Prowler"...
You were caught at the scene of the crime, running from the cops--heck, even the Daily Bugle calls you an outlaw!
What--? Do you believe everything you read?!
Did you ever stop to think that maybe the Bugle got it wrong?!
That maybe they're just trying to sell papers?! As a matter of fact--
Isn't that the exact same thing they say about YOU?!
I'm... Look, you're right.
I'm sorry. I guess I got caught up in it and...and I assumed a lot of things I shouldn't have.
But wait--if you're not a thief, then what were you doing at these two robberies? Are you a new crime fighter?

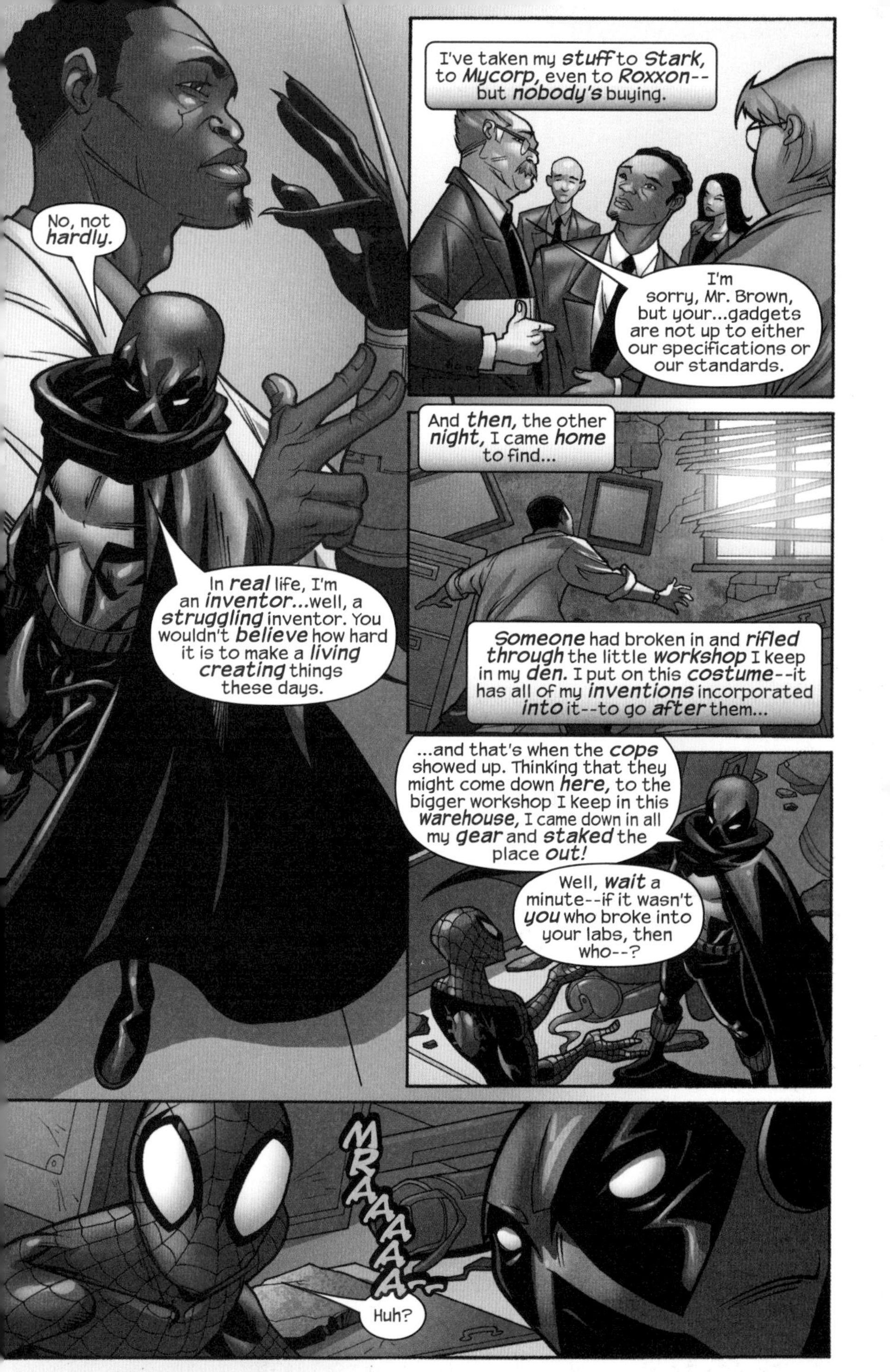
No, not hardly.
In real life, I'm an inventor...well, a struggling inventor. You wouldn't believe how hard it is to make a living creating things these days.
I've taken my stuff to Stark, to Mycorp, even to Roxxon--but nobody's buying.
I'm sorry, Mr. Brown, but your...gadgets are not up to either our specifications or our standards.
And then, the other night, I came home to find...
Someone had broken in and rifled through the little workshop I keep in my den. I put on this costume--it has all of my inventions incorporated into it--to go after them...
...and that's when the cops showed up. Thinking that they might come down here, to the bigger workshop I keep in this warehouse, I came down in all my gear and staked the place out!
Well, wait a minute--if it wasn't you who broke into your labs, then who--?
MRAAAAA--
Huh?

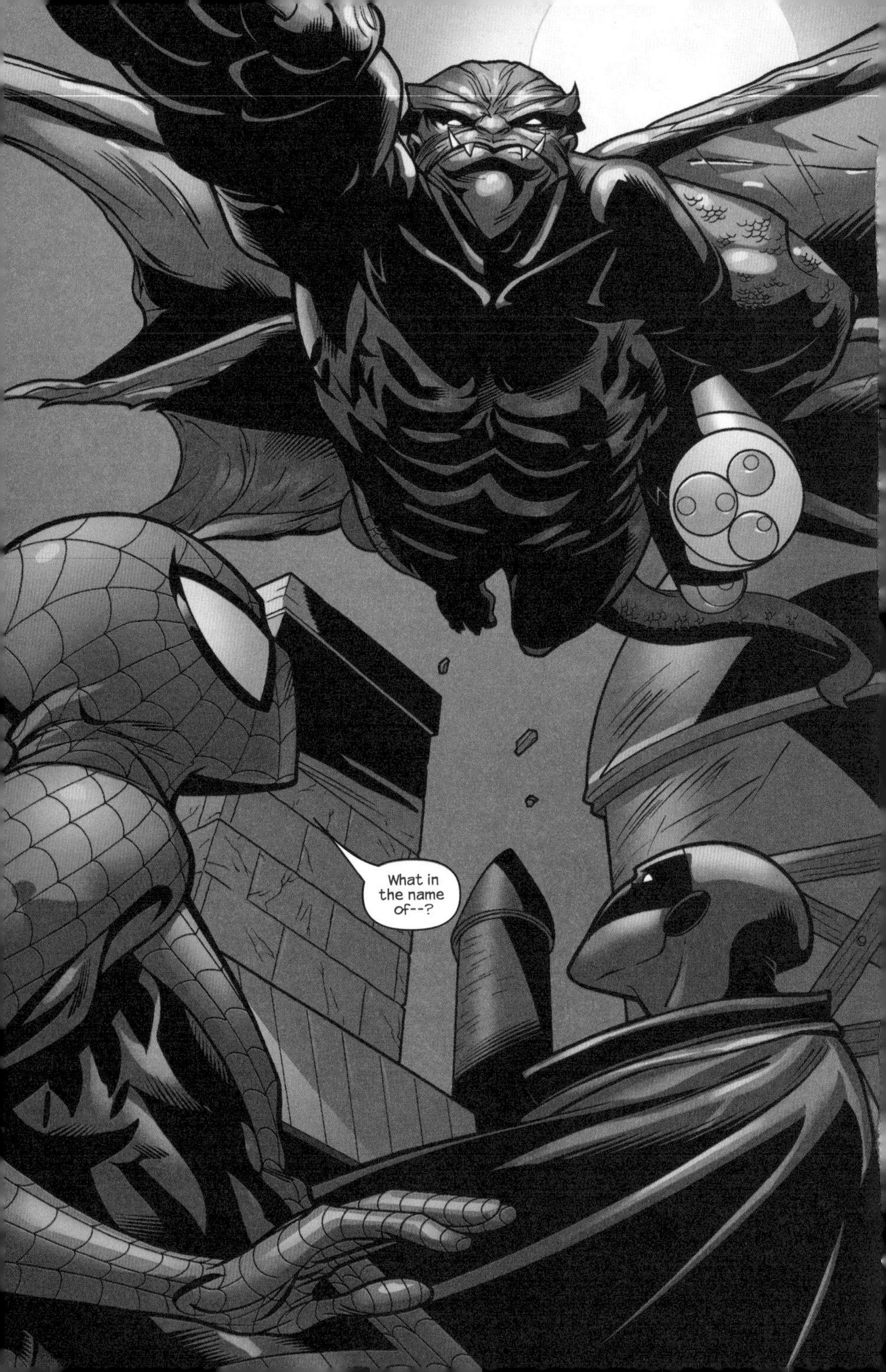
What in the name of--?

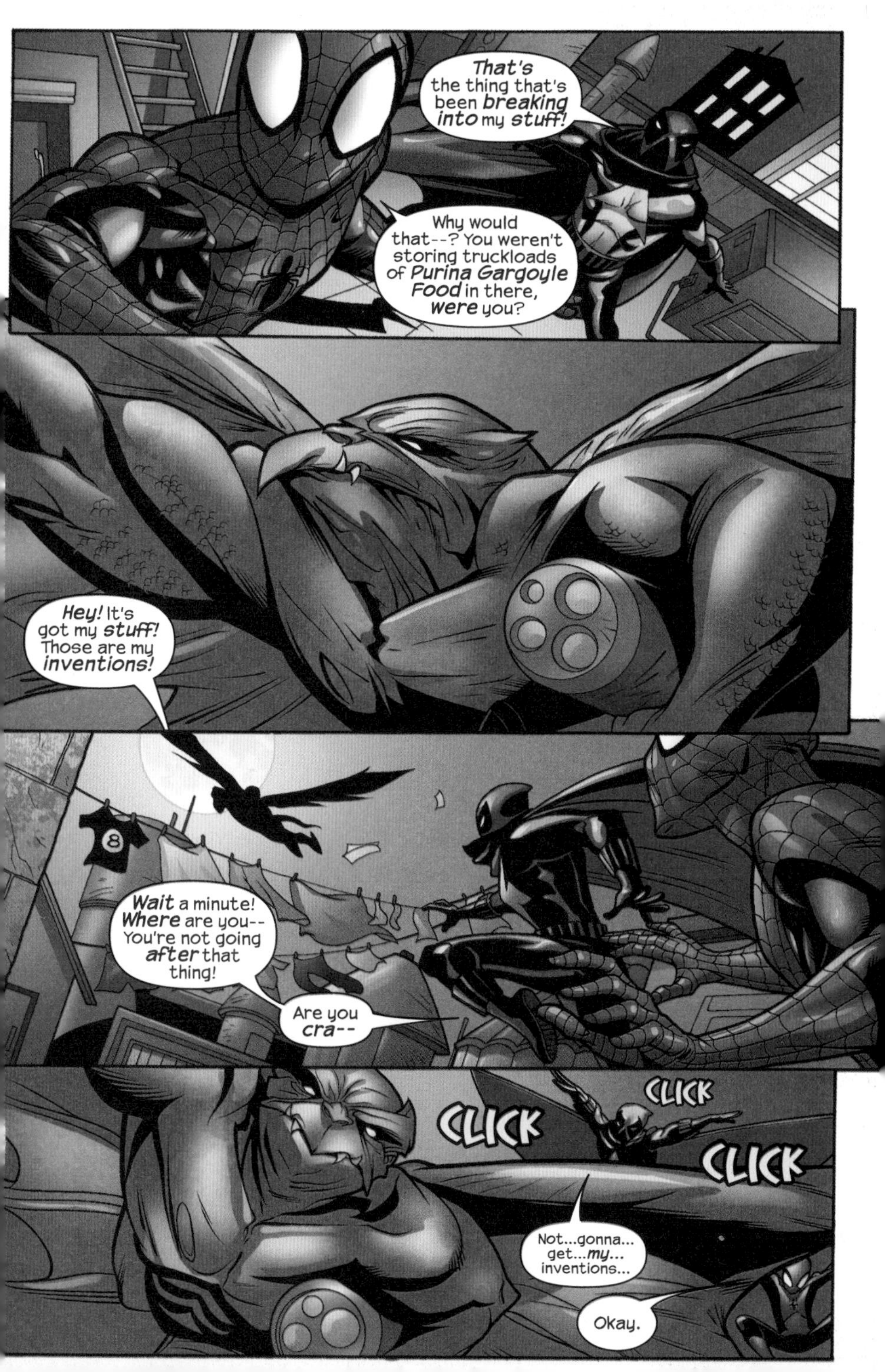
That's the thing that's been breaking into my stuff!
Why would that--? You weren't storing truckloads of Purina Gargoyle Food in there, were you?
Hey! It's got my stuff! Those are my inventions!
Wait a minute! Where are you-- You're not going after that thing!
Are you cra--
CLICK
CLICK
CLICK
Not...gonna... get...my... inventions...
Okay.

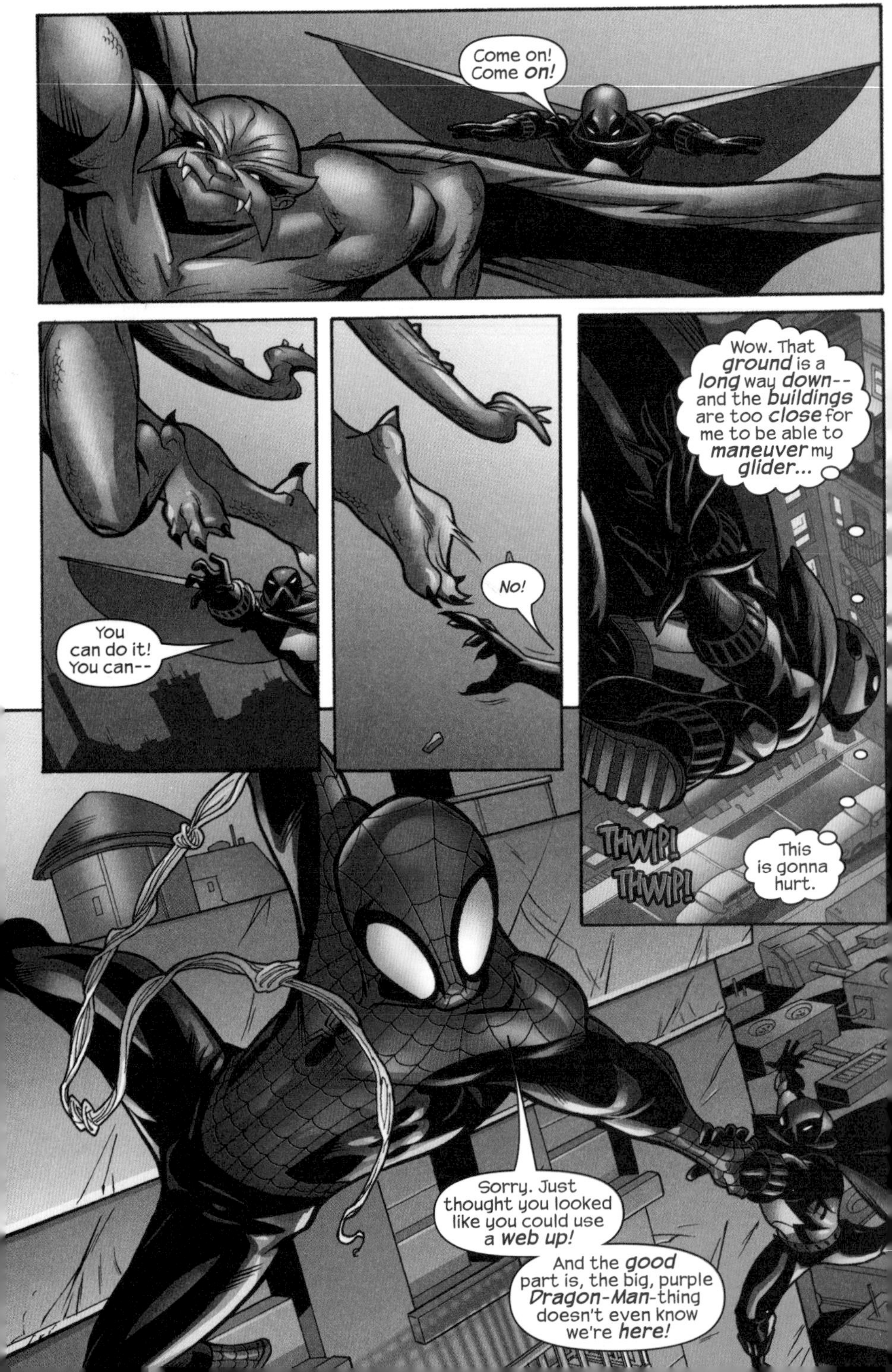
Come on! Come on!
You can do it! You can--
No!
Wow. That ground is a long way down-- and the buildings are too close for me to be able to maneuver my glider...
THWIP! THWIP!
This is gonna hurt.
Sorry. Just thought you looked like you could use a web up!
And the good part is, the big, purple Dragon-Man-thing doesn't even know we're here!

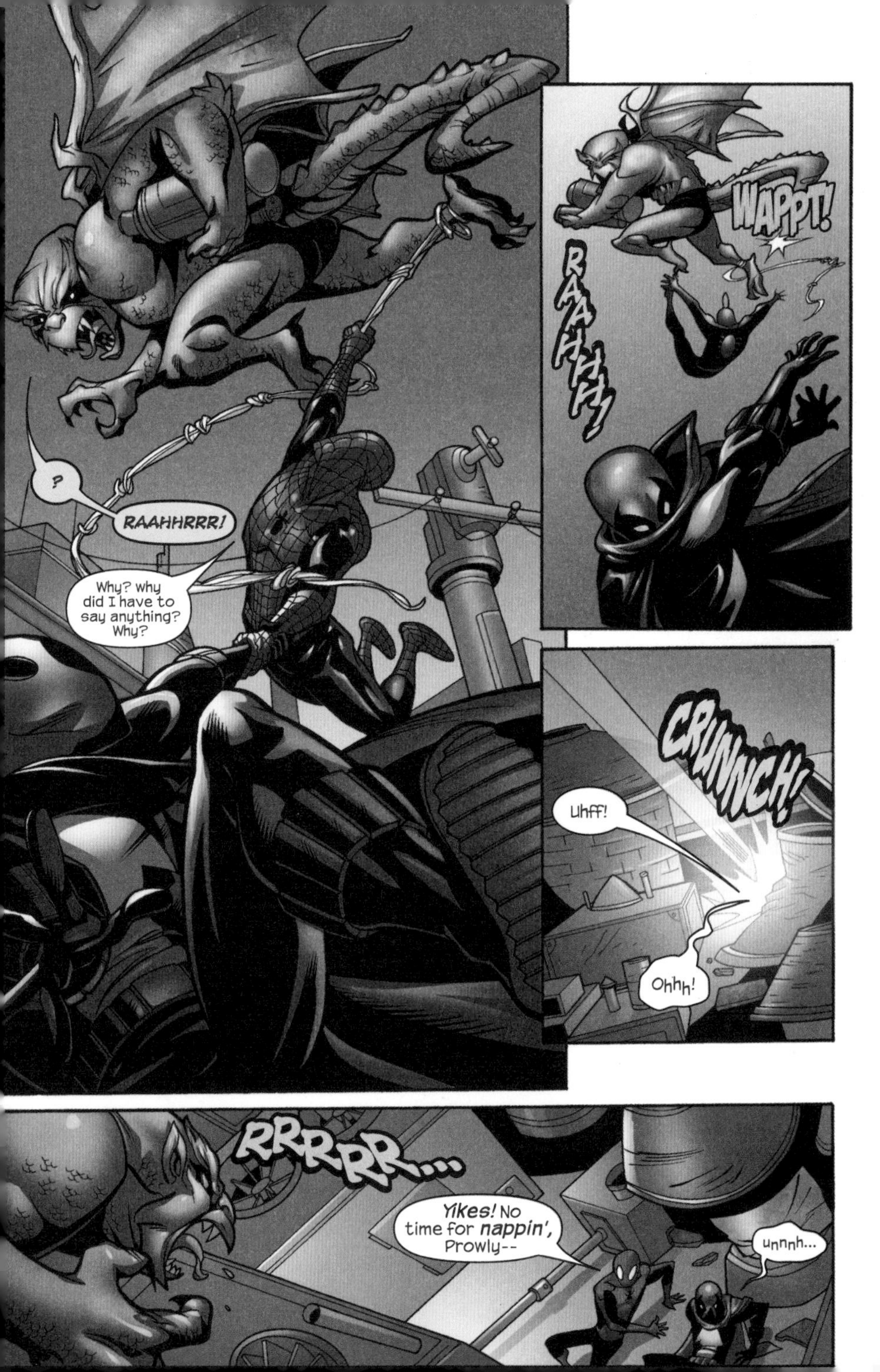
?
RAAHHRRR!
Why? why did I have to say anything? Why?
RAAHHH!
WAPPT!
CRUNNCH!
Uhff!
Ohhh!
RRRRR...
Yikes! No time for nappin', Prowly--
unnnh...

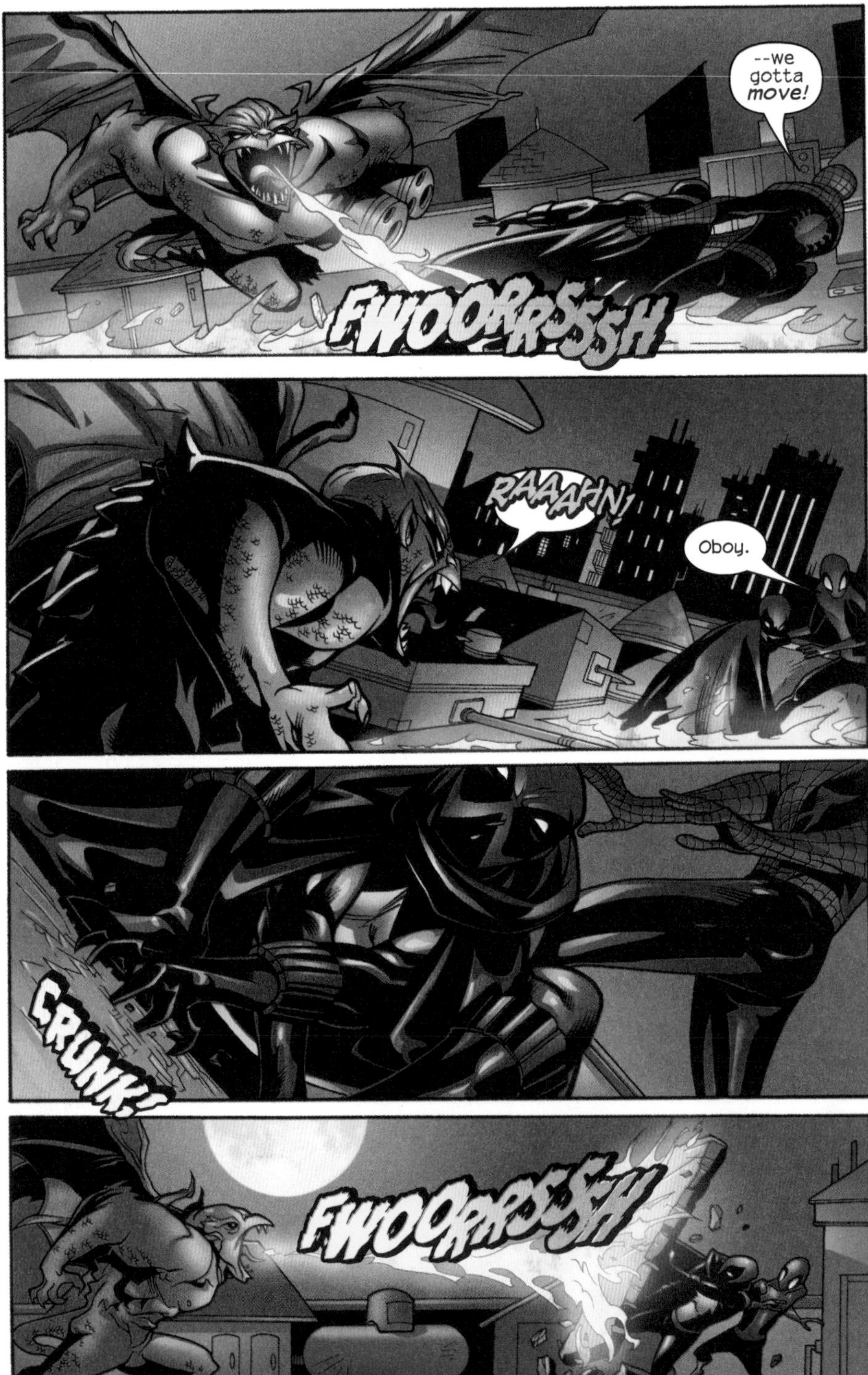
--we gotta move!
FWOORRSSSH
RAAAHN!
Oboy.
CRUNK!!
FWOORRSSSH

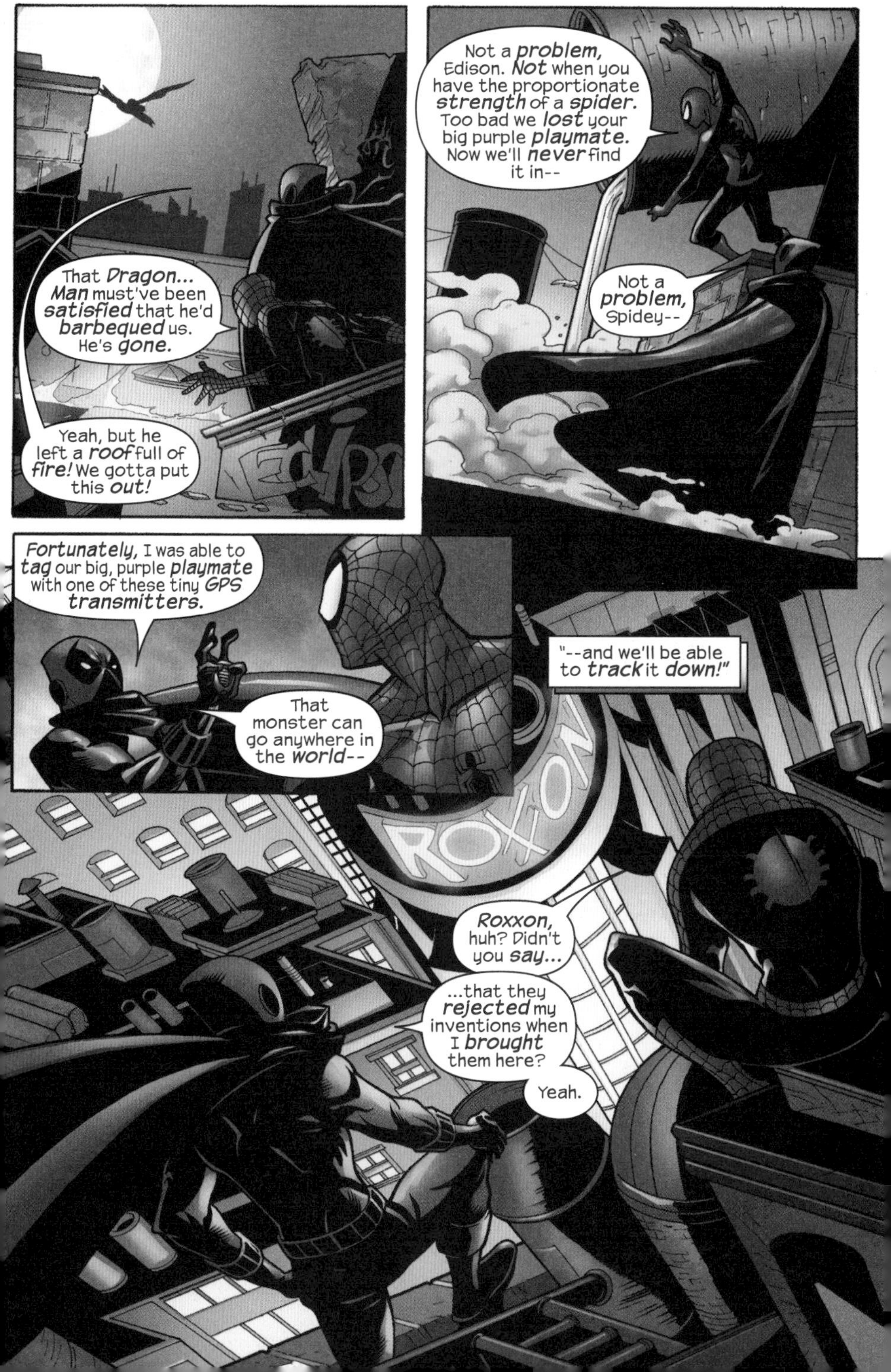
That Dragon... Man must've been satisfied that he'd barbequed us. He's gone.
Yeah, but he left a roof full of fire! We gotta put this out!
Not a problem, Edison. Not when you have the proportionate strength of a spider. Too bad we lost your big purple playmate. Now we'll never find it in--
Not a problem, Spidey--
Fortunately, I was able to tag our big, purple playmate with one of these tiny GPS transmitters.
That monster can go anywhere in the world--
"--and we'll be able to track it down!"
ROXXON
Roxxon, huh? Didn't you say...
...that they rejected my inventions when I brought them here?
Yeah.

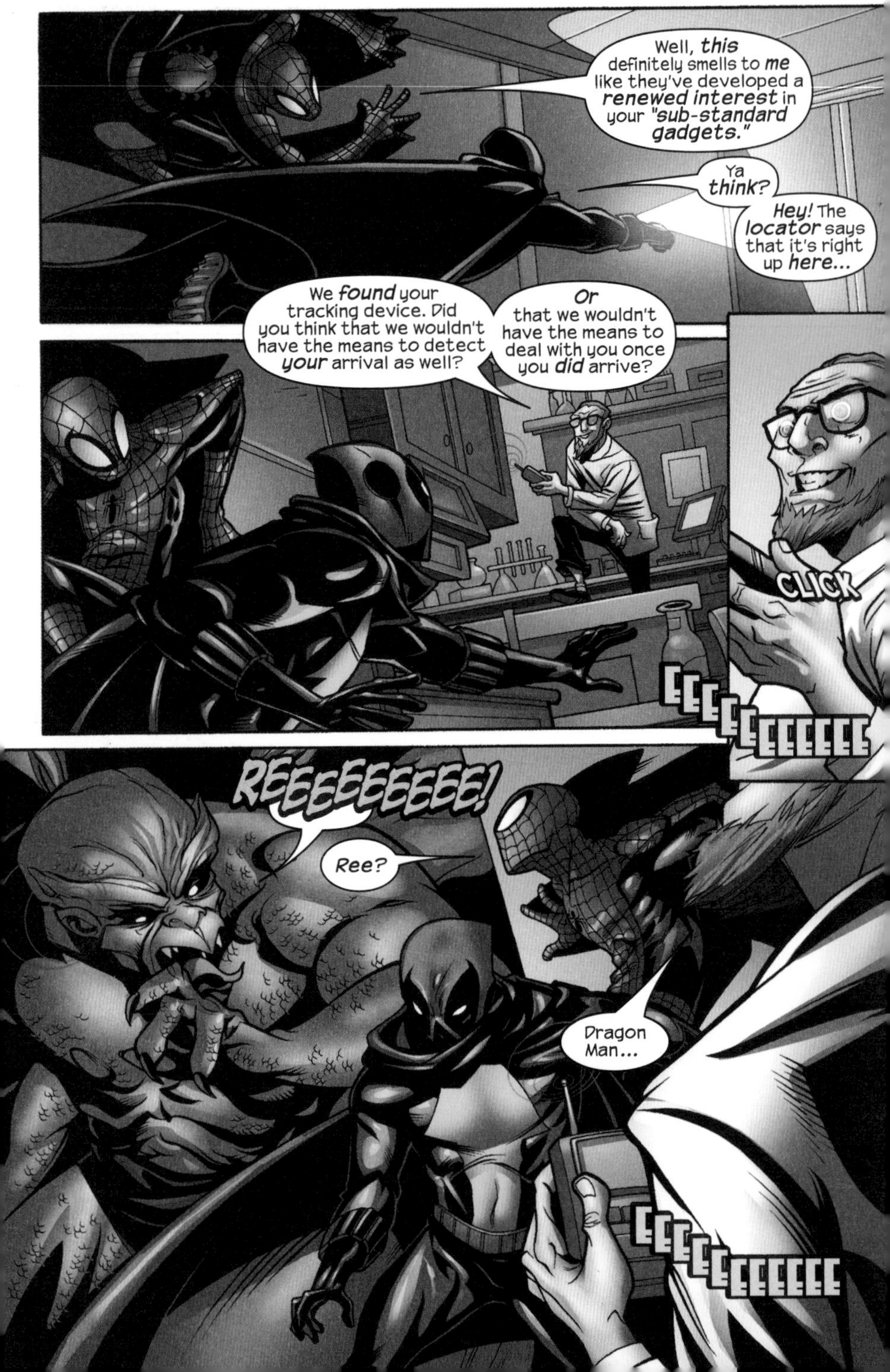

Well, *this* definitely smells to *me* like they've developed a *renewed interest* in your *"sub-standard gadgets."*
Ya *think?*
Hey! The *locator* says that it's right up *here...*
We *found* your tracking device. Did you think that we wouldn't have the means to detect *your* arrival as well?
Or that we wouldn't have the means to deal with you once you *did* arrive?
CLICK
EEEEEEEEEEE
REEEEEEEEEEE!
Ree?
Dragon Man...
EEEEEEEEEEE

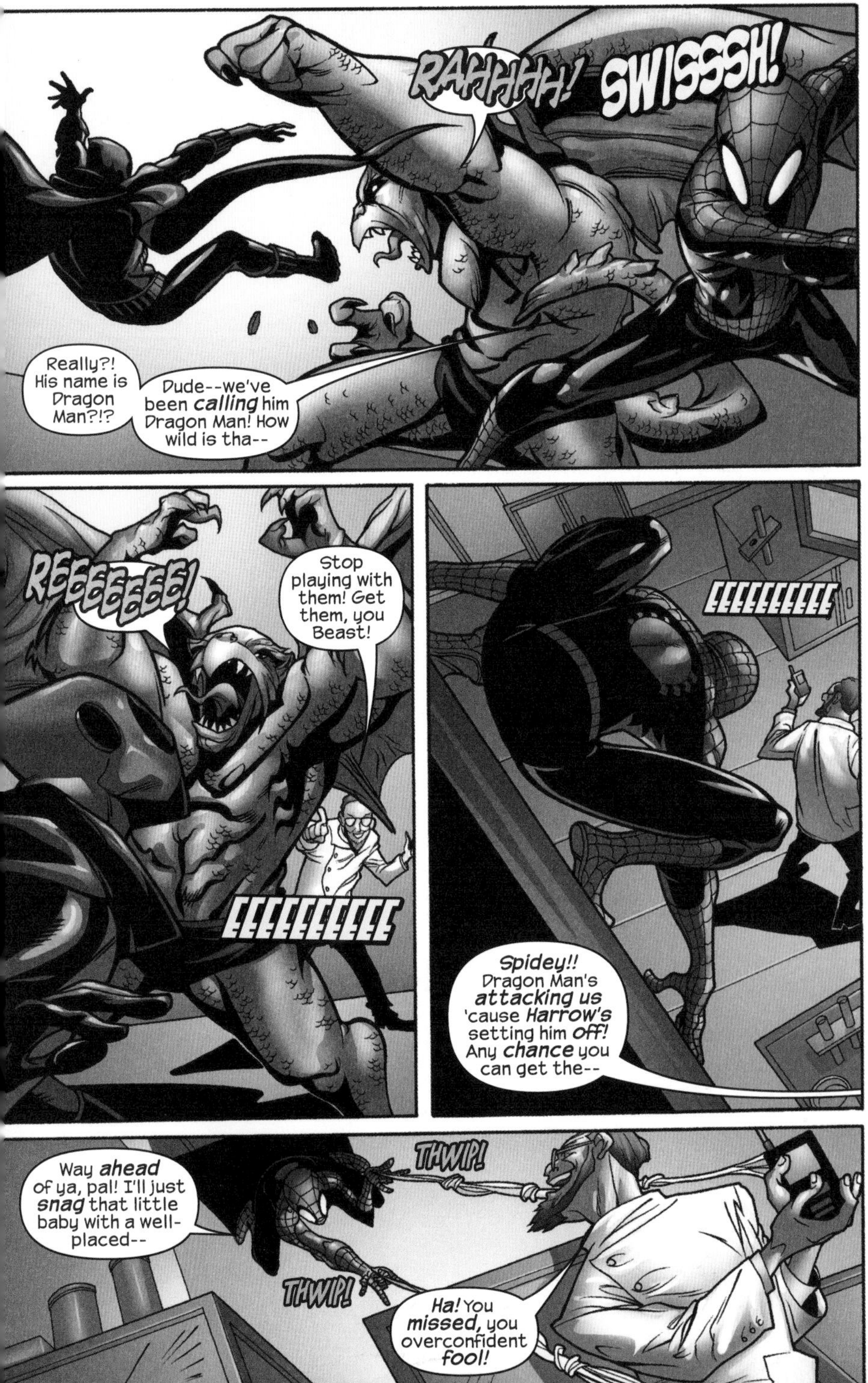
RAHHHH!
SWISSSH!
Really?! His name is Dragon Man?!?
Dude--we've been calling him Dragon Man! How wild is tha--
REEEEEEEE!
Stop playing with them! Get them, you Beast!
EEEEEEEEEE
EEEEEEEEEE
Spidey!! Dragon Man's attacking us 'cause Harrow's setting him off! Any chance you can get the--
Way ahead of ya, pal! I'll just snag that little baby with a well-placed--
THWIP!
THWIP!
Ha! You missed, you overconfident fool!

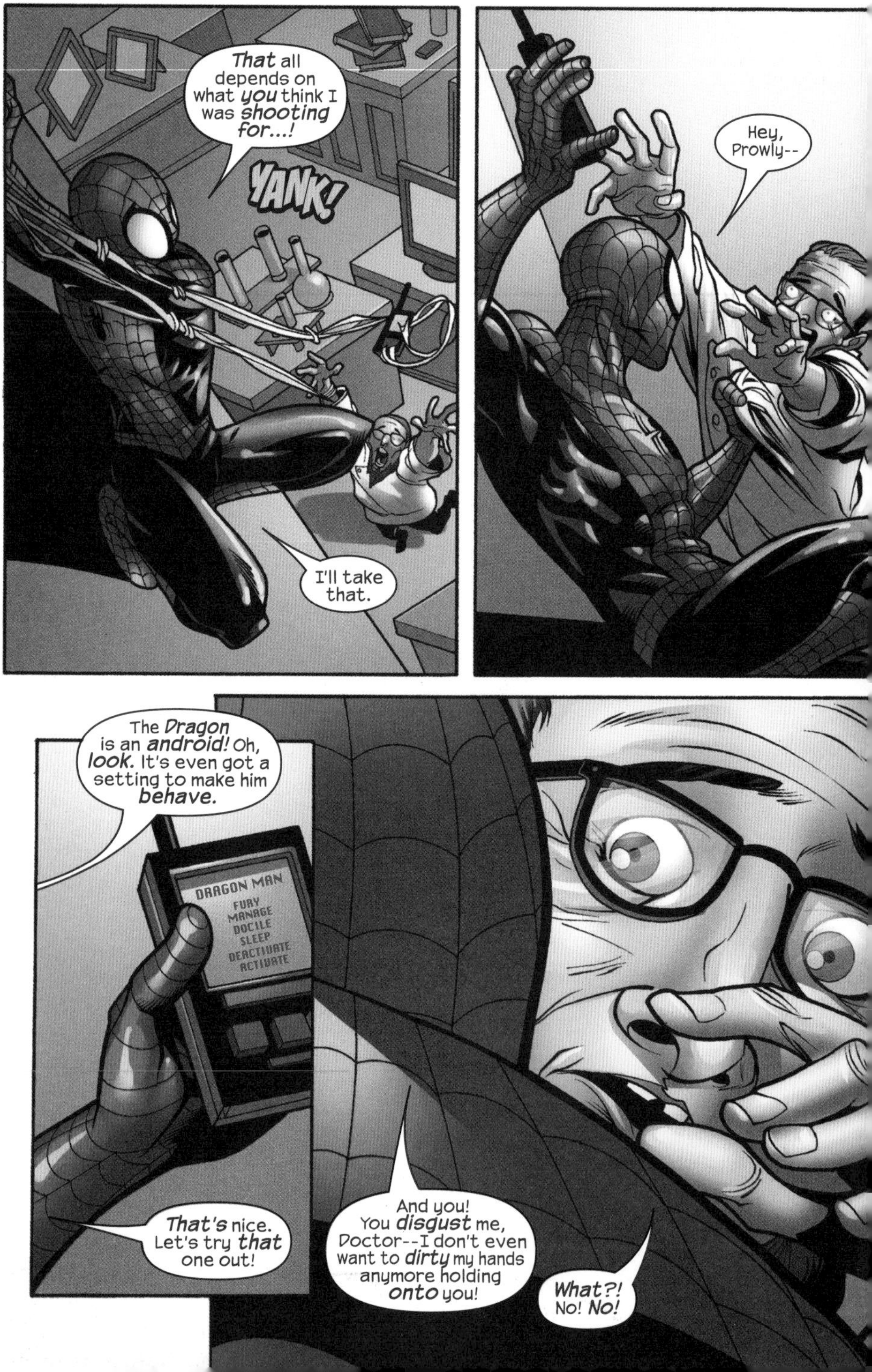

That all depends on what you think I was shooting for...!
YANK!
I'll take that.
Hey, Prowly--
The Dragon is an android! Oh, look. It's even got a setting to make him behave.
DRAGON MAN
FURY
MANAGE
DOCILE
SLEEP
DEACTIVATE
ACTIVATE
That's nice. Let's try that one out!
And you! You disgust me, Doctor--I don't even want to dirty my hands anymore holding onto you!
What?! No! No!

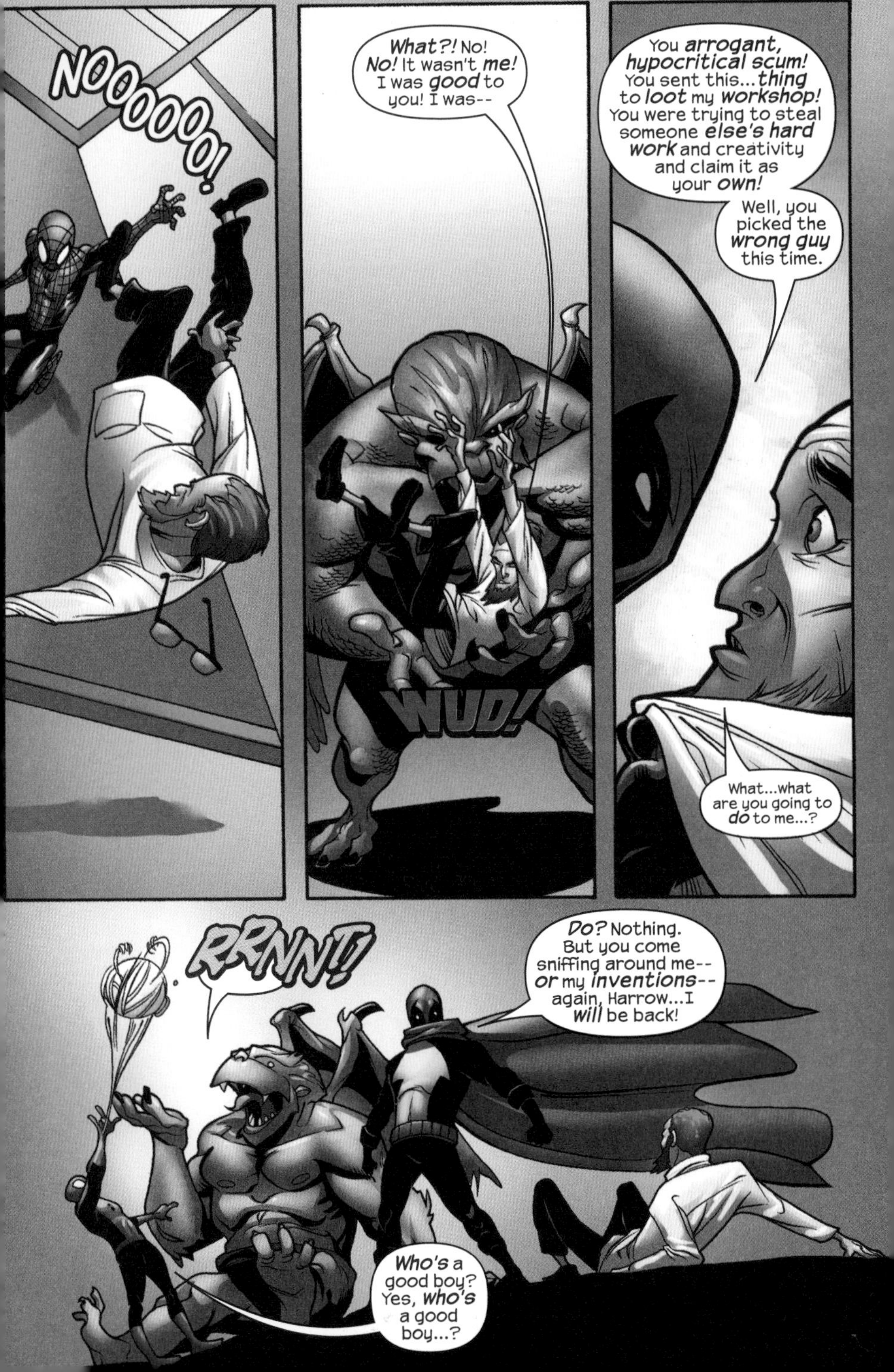
NOOOOOO!
What?! No! No! It wasn't me! I was good to you! I was--
WUD!
You arrogant, hypocritical scum! You sent this...thing to loot my workshop! You were trying to steal someone else's hard work and creativity and claim it as your own!
Well, you picked the wrong guy this time.
What...what are you going to do to me...?
RRNN!!
Do? Nothing. But you come sniffing around me--or my inventions--again, Harrow...I will be back!
Who's a good boy? Yes, who's a good boy...?

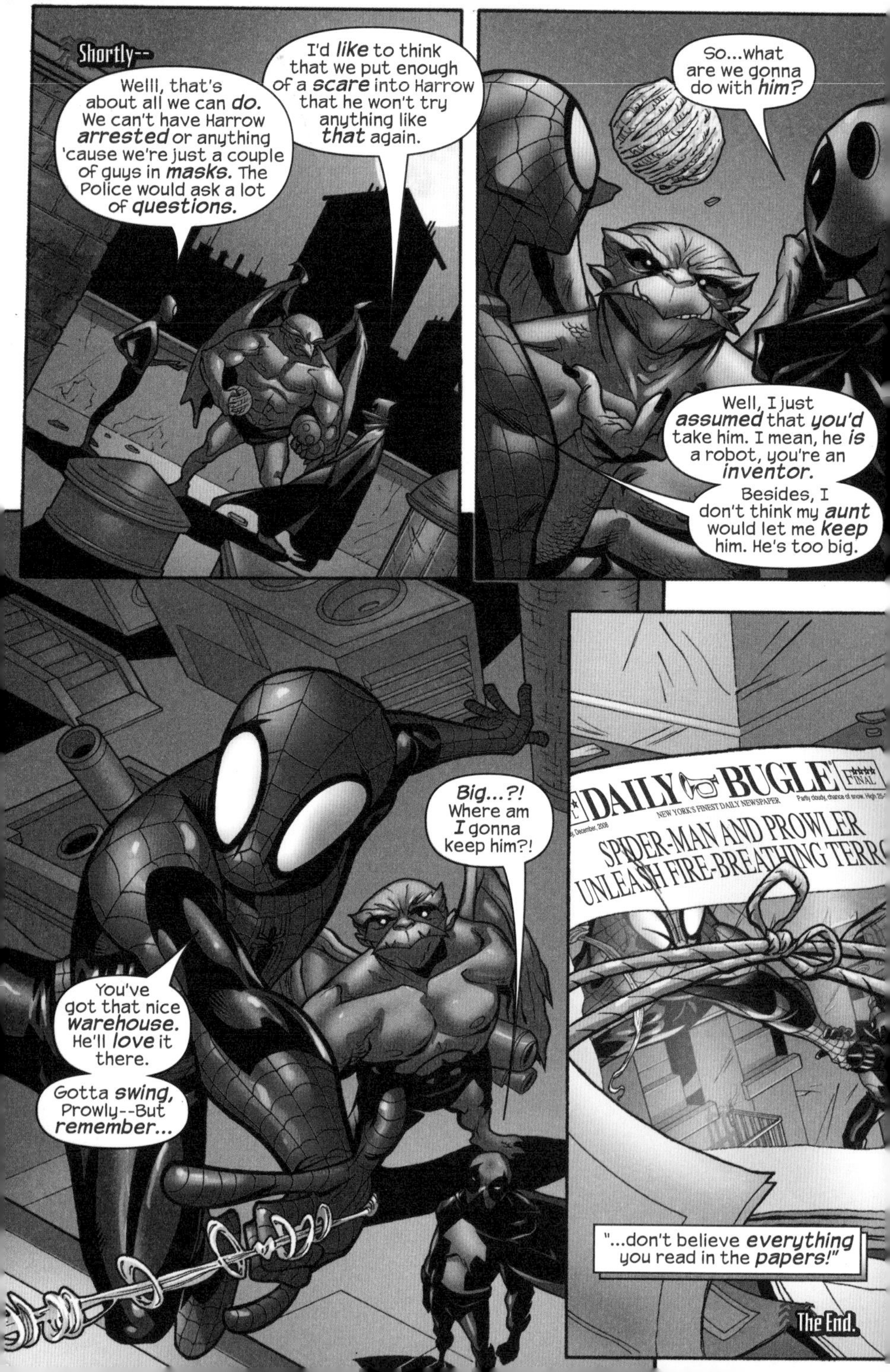

Shortly--
Welll, that's about all we can do. We can't have Harrow arrested or anything 'cause we're just a couple of guys in masks. The Police would ask a lot of questions.
I'd like to think that we put enough of a scare into Harrow that he won't try anything like that again.
So...what are we gonna do with him?
Well, I just assumed that you'd take him. I mean, he is a robot, you're an inventor.
Besides, I don't think my aunt would let me keep him. He's too big.
Big...?! Where am I gonna keep him?!
You've got that nice warehouse. He'll love it there.
Gotta swing, Prowly--But remember...
DAILY BUGLE
FINAL
NEW YORK'S FINEST DAILY NEWSPAPER
SPIDER-MAN AND PROWLER UNLEASH FIRE-BREATHING TERRO
"...don't believe everything you read in the papers!"
The End.

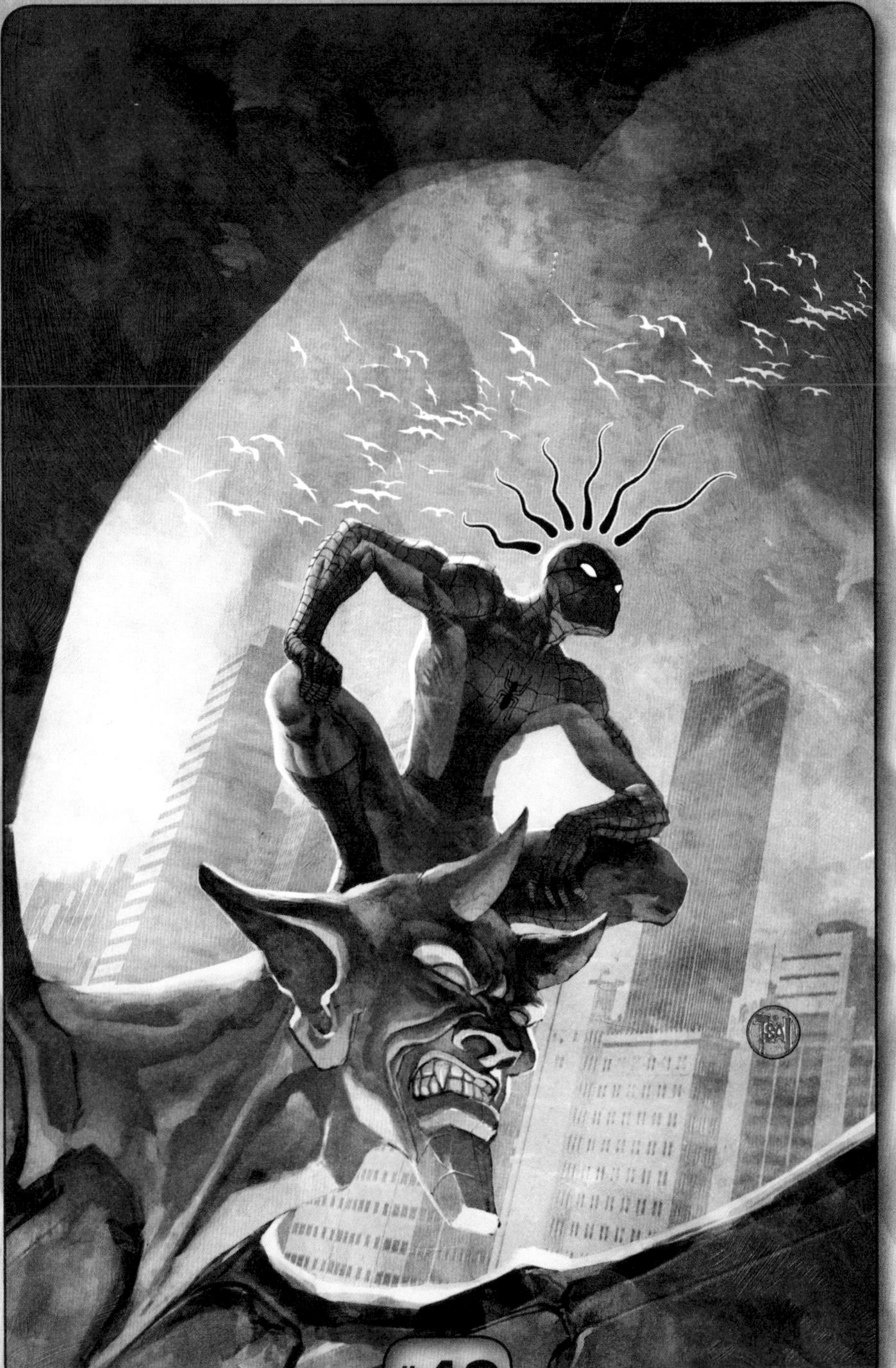

#48

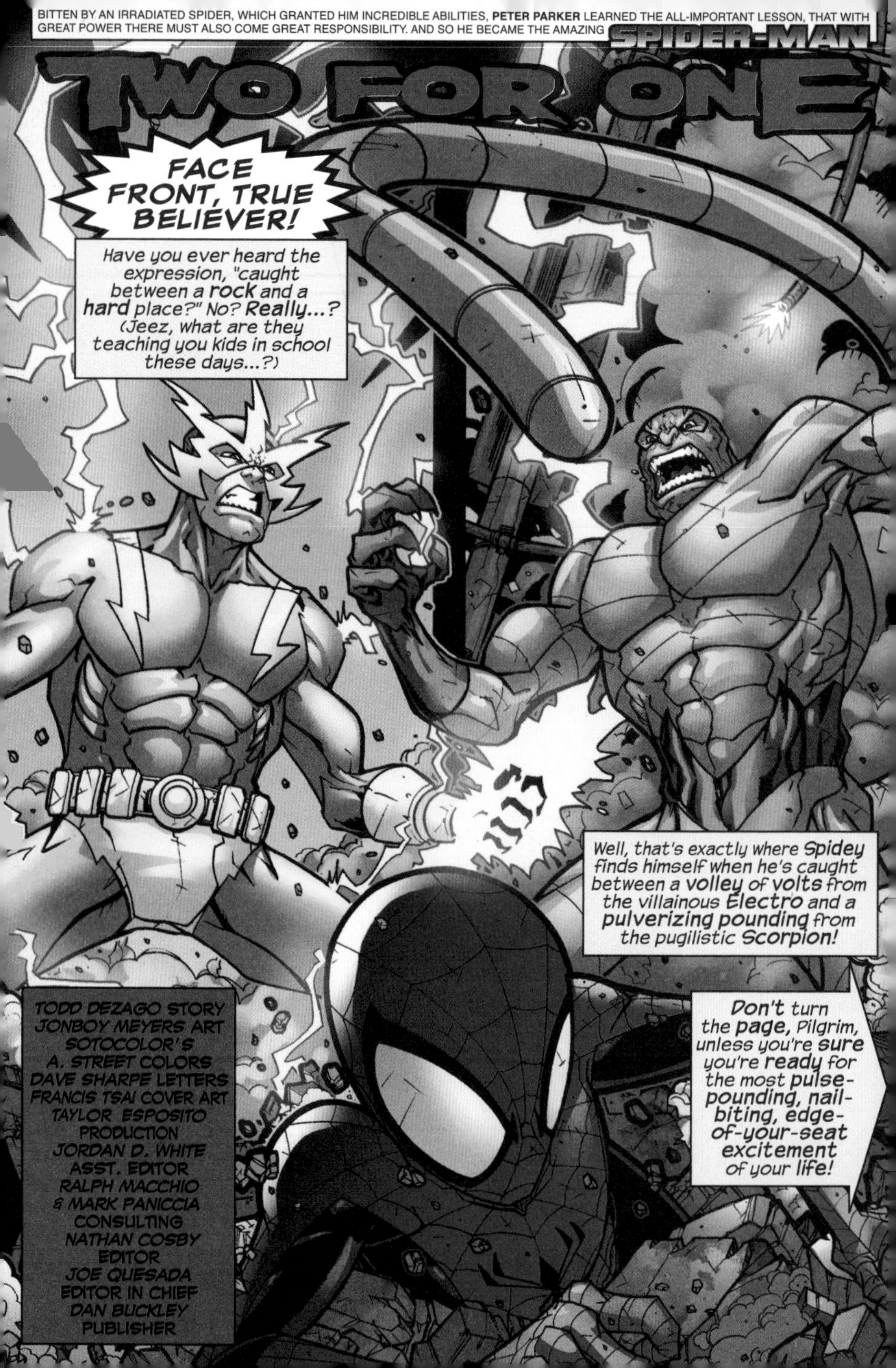
BITTEN BY AN IRRADIATED SPIDER, WHICH GRANTED HIM INCREDIBLE ABILITIES, PETER PARKER LEARNED THE ALL-IMPORTANT LESSON, THAT WITH GREAT POWER THERE MUST ALSO COME GREAT RESPONSIBILITY. AND SO HE BECAME THE AMAZING SPIDER-MAN!
TWO FOR ONE
FACE FRONT, TRUE BELIEVER!
Have you ever heard the expression, "caught between a rock and a hard place?" No? Really...? (Jeez, what are they teaching you kids in school these days...?)
Well, that's exactly where Spidey finds himself when he's caught between a volley of volts from the villainous Electro and a pulverizing pounding from the pugilistic Scorpion!
TODD DEZAGO STORY
JONBOY MEYERS ART
SOTOCOLOR'S A. STREET COLORS
DAVE SHARPE LETTERS
FRANCIS TSAI COVER ART
TAYLOR ESPOSITO PRODUCTION
JORDAN D. WHITE ASST. EDITOR
RALPH MACCHIO & MARK PANICCIA CONSULTING
NATHAN COSBY EDITOR
JOE QUESADA EDITOR IN CHIEF
DAN BUCKLEY PUBLISHER
Don't turn the page, Pilgrim, unless you're sure you're ready for the most pulse-pounding, nail-biting, edge-of-your-seat excitement of your life!

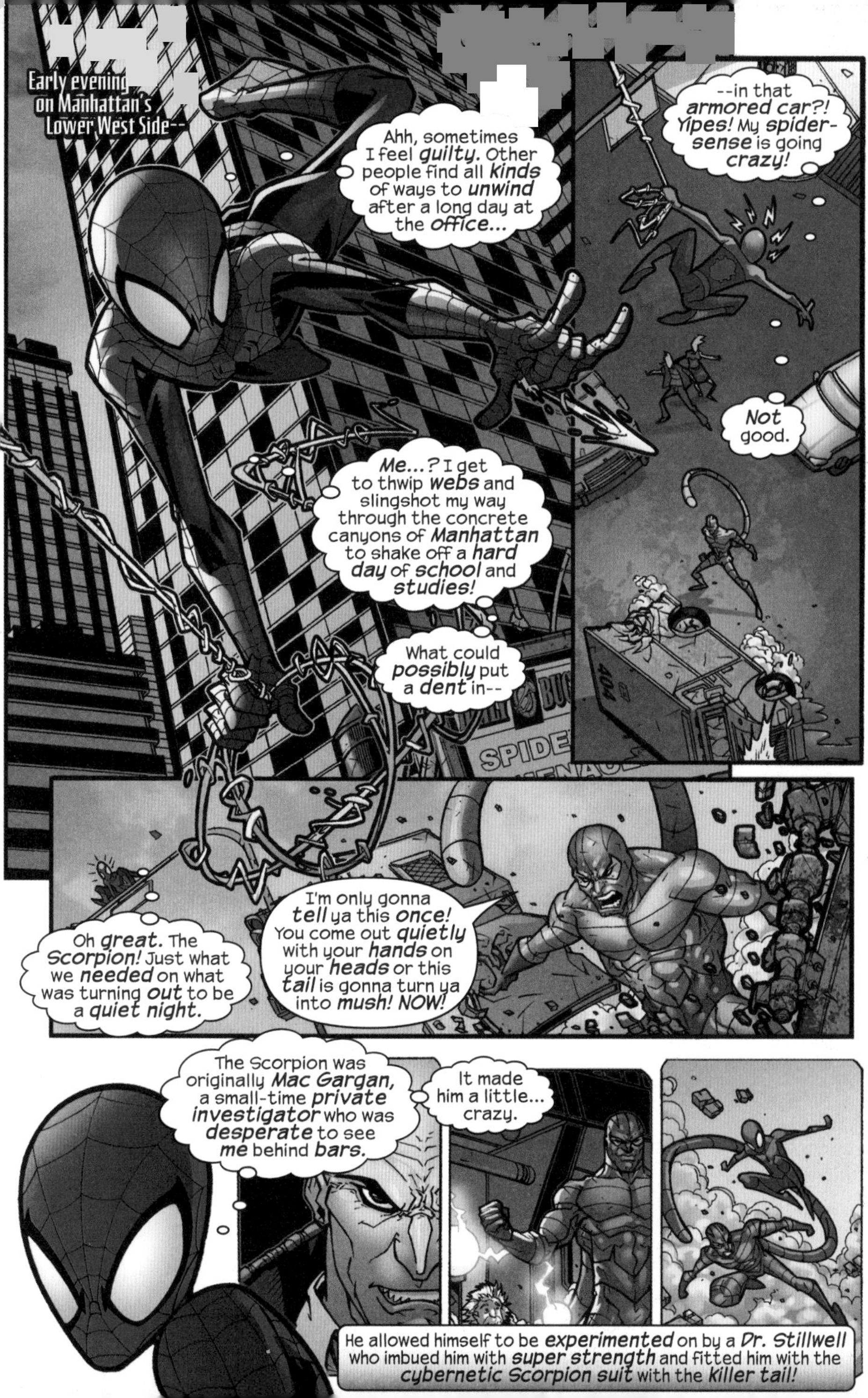

Early evening on Manhattan's Lower West Side--
Ahh, sometimes I feel guilty. Other people find all kinds of ways to unwind after a long day at the office...
Me...? I get to thwip webs and slingshot my way through the concrete canyons of Manhattan to shake off a hard day of school and studies!
What could possibly put a dent in--
--in that armored car?! Yipes! My spider-sense is going crazy!
Not good.
SPIDE
Oh great. The Scorpion! Just what we needed on what was turning out to be a quiet night.
I'm only gonna tell ya this once! You come out quietly with your hands on your heads or this tail is gonna turn ya into mush! NOW!
The Scorpion was originally Mac Gargan, a small-time private investigator who was desperate to see me behind bars.
It made him a little... crazy.
He allowed himself to be experimented on by a Dr. Stillwell who imbued him with super strength and fitted him with the cybernetic Scorpion suit with the killer tail!

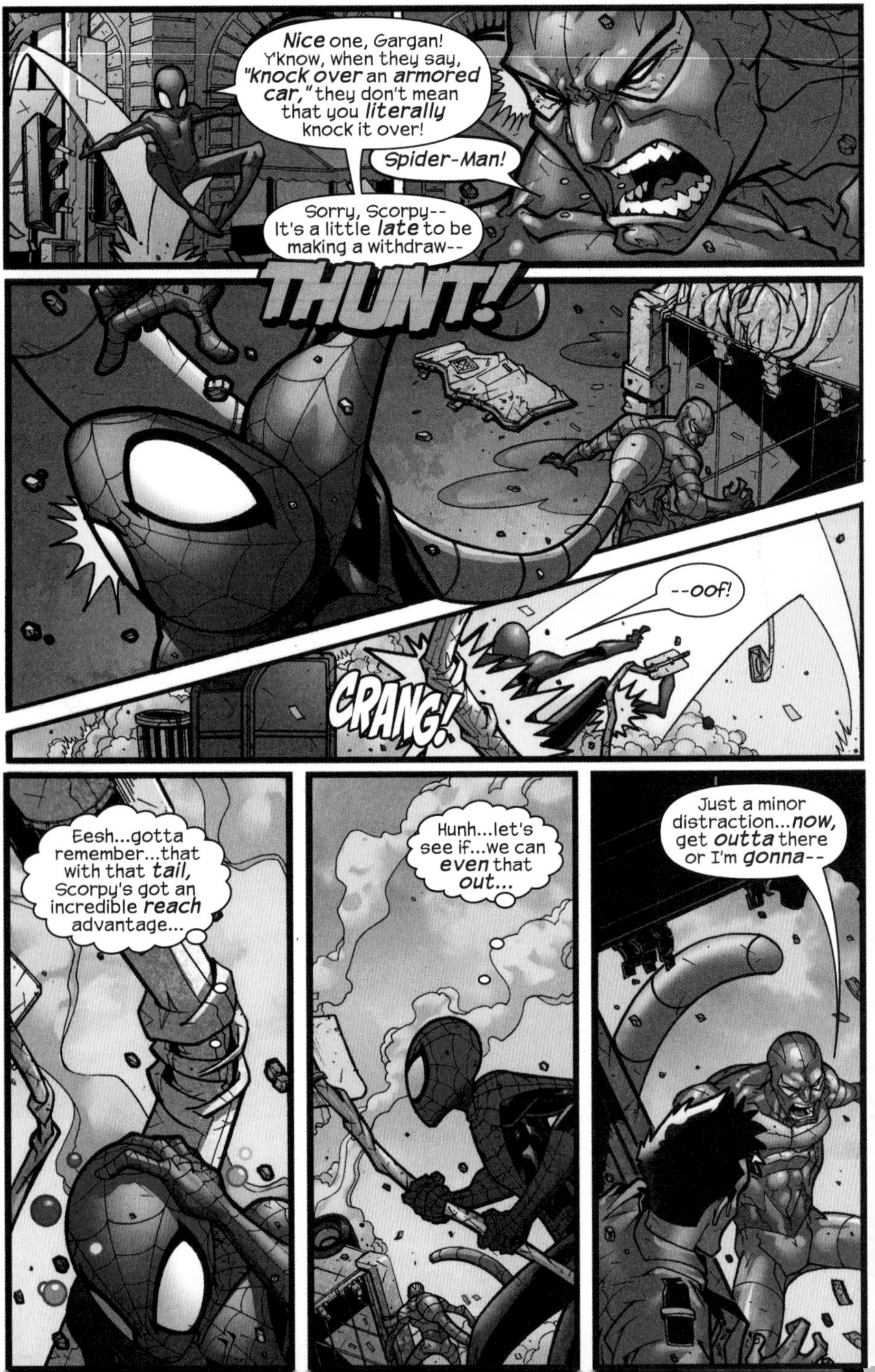
Nice one, Gargan! Y'know, when they say, "knock over an armored car," they don't mean that you literally knock it over!
Spider-Man!
Sorry, Scorpy-- It's a little late to be making a withdraw--
THUNT!
--oof!
CRANG!
Eesh...gotta remember...that with that tail, Scorpy's got an incredible reach advantage...
Hunh...let's see if...we can even that out...
Just a minor distraction...now, get outta there or I'm gonna--

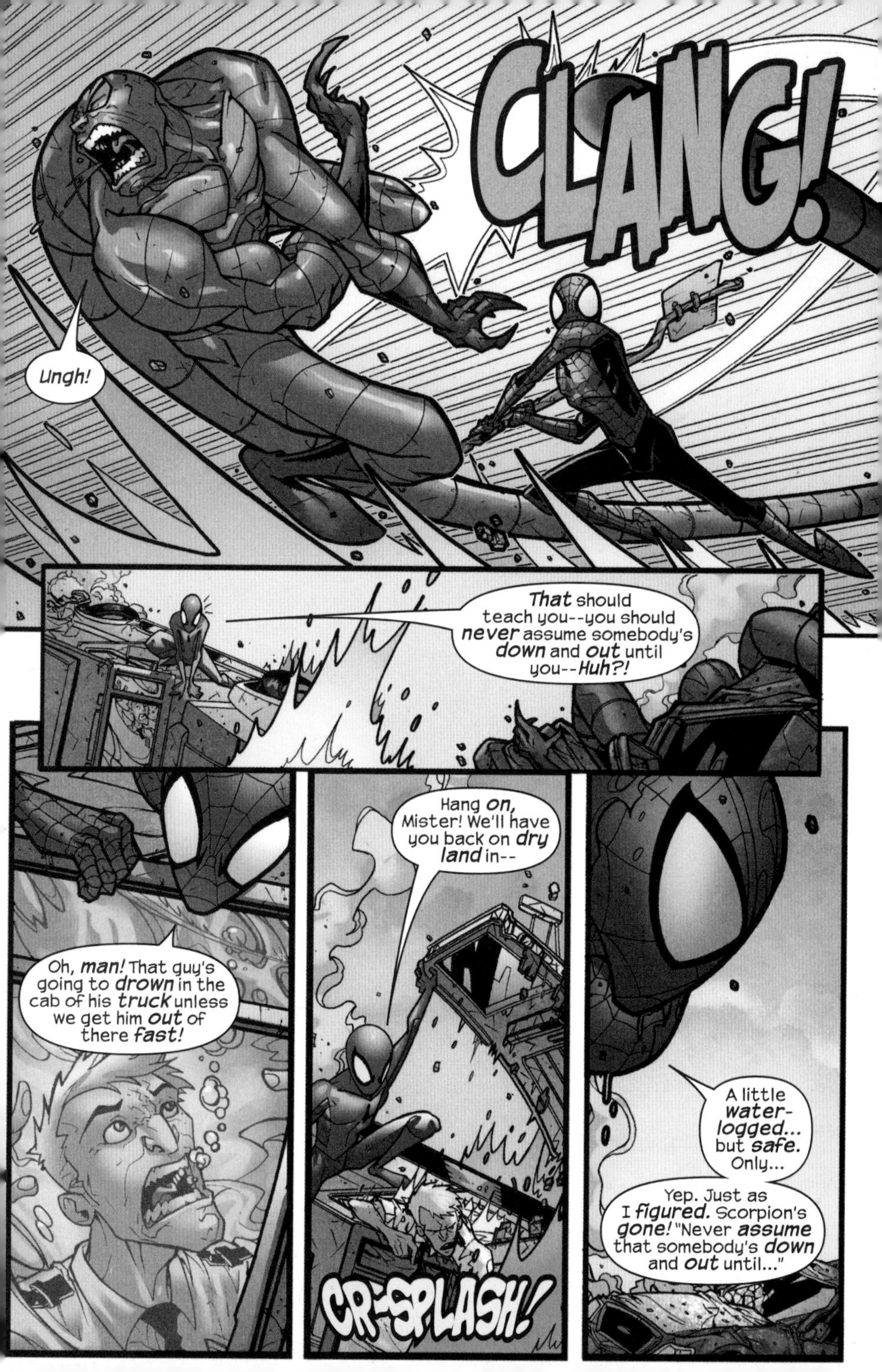

CLANG!
Ungh!
That should teach you--you should never assume somebody's down and out until you--Huh?!
Oh, man! That guy's going to drown in the cab of his truck unless we get him out of there fast!
Hang on, Mister! We'll have you back on dry land in--
CR-SPLASH!
A little water-logged... but safe. Only...
Yep. Just as I figured. Scorpion's gone! "Never assume that somebody's down and out until..."

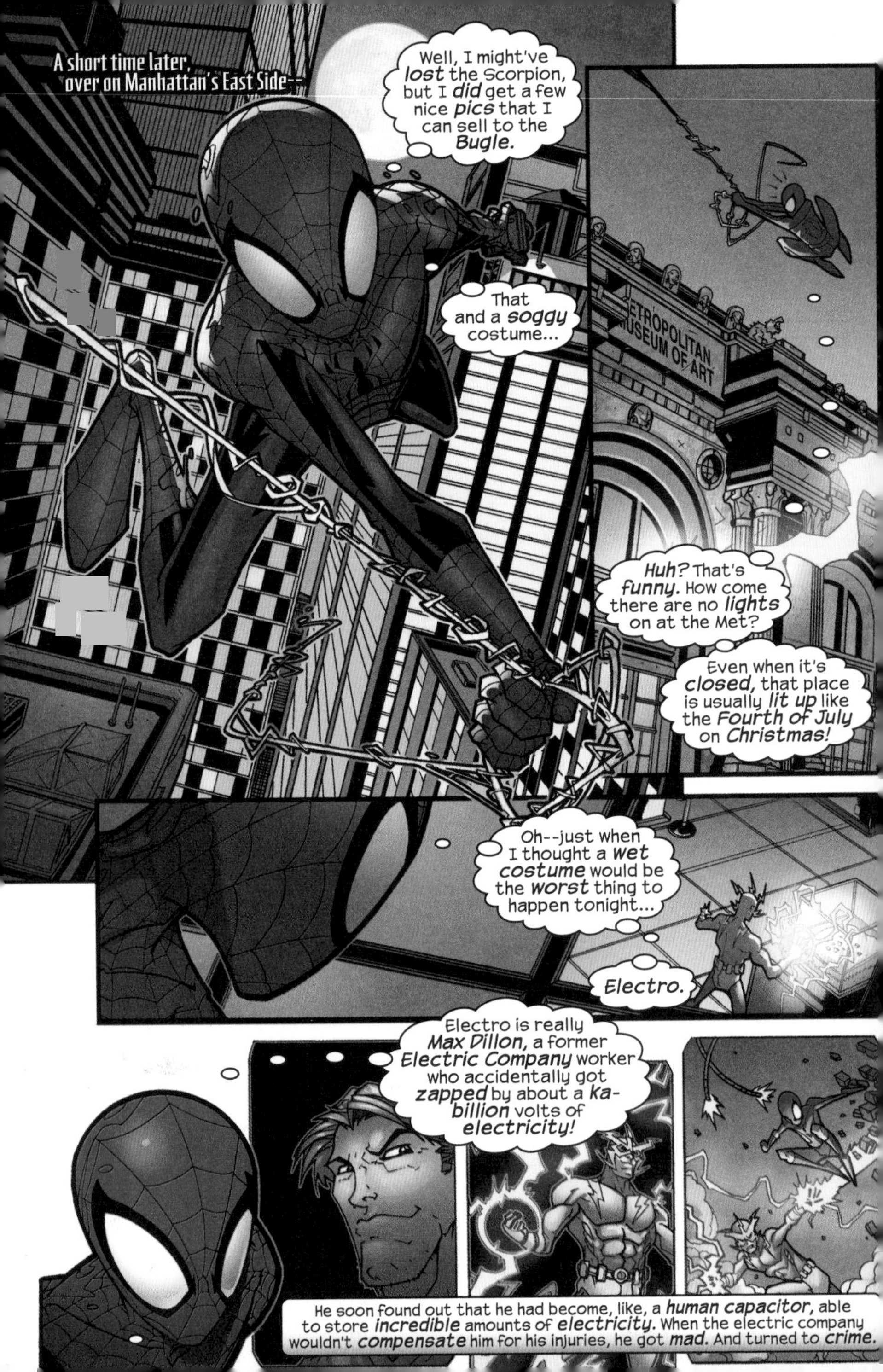
A short time later, over on Manhattan's East Side--
Well, I might've lost the Scorpion, but I did get a few nice pics that I can sell to the Bugle.
That and a soggy costume...
METROPOLITAN MUSEUM OF ART
Huh? That's funny. How come there are no lights on at the Met?
Even when it's closed, that place is usually lit up like the Fourth of July on Christmas!
Oh--just when I thought a wet costume would be the worst thing to happen tonight...
Electro.
Electro is really Max Dillon, a former Electric Company worker who accidentally got zapped by about a ka-billion volts of electricity!
He soon found out that he had become, like, a human capacitor, able to store incredible amounts of electricity. When the electric company wouldn't compensate him for his injuries, he got mad. And turned to crime.

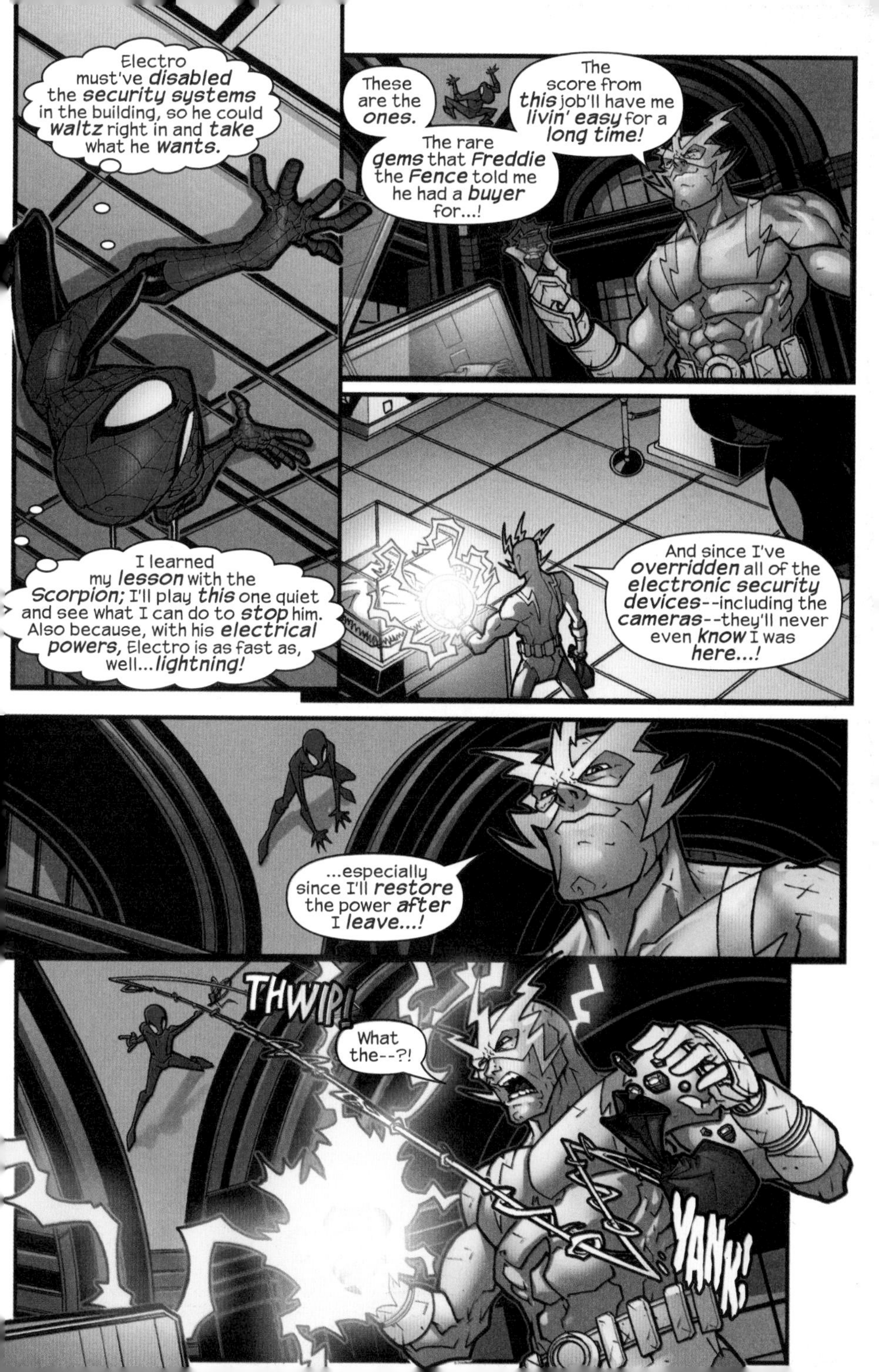

Electro must've disabled the security systems in the building, so he could waltz right in and take what he wants.
These are the ones.
The rare gems that Freddie the Fence told me he had a buyer for...!
The score from this job'll have me livin' easy for a long time!
I learned my lesson with the Scorpion; I'll play this one quiet and see what I can do to stop him. Also because, with his electrical powers, Electro is as fast as, well...lightning!
And since I've overridden all of the electronic security devices--including the cameras--they'll never even know I was here...!
...especially since I'll restore the power after I leave...!
THWIP!
What the--?!
YANK!

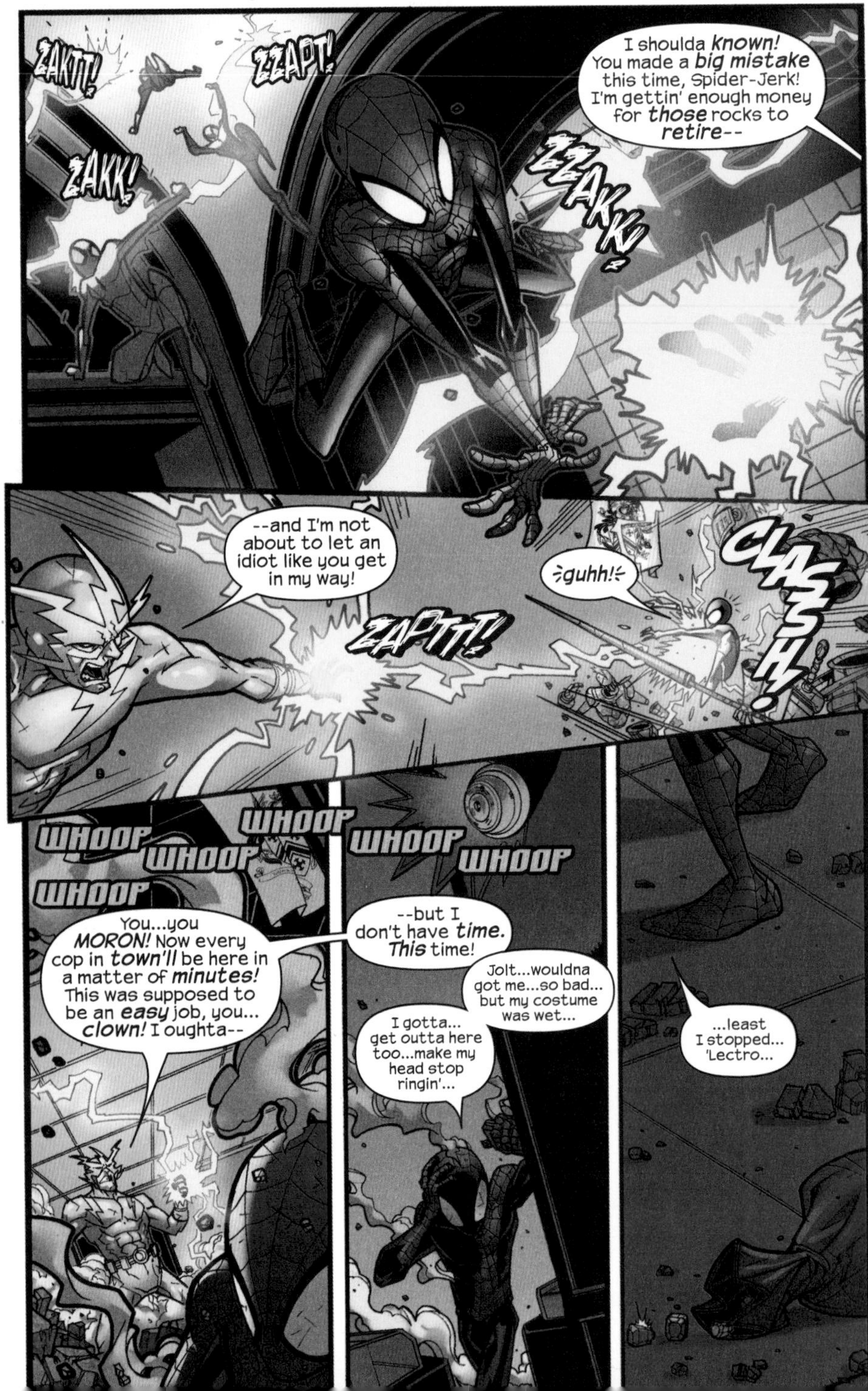
ZAKTT!
ZZAPT!
ZAKK!
I shoulda known! You made a big mistake this time, Spider-Jerk! I'm gettin' enough money for those rocks to retire--
ZZAKK!
--and I'm not about to let an idiot like you get in my way!
ZAPTTT!
guhh!
CLASSH!
WHOOP WHOOP WHOOP WHOOP
You...you MORON! Now every cop in town'll be here in a matter of minutes! This was supposed to be an easy job, you... clown! I oughta--
WHOOP WHOOP
--but I don't have time. This time!
Jolt...wouldna got me...so bad... but my costume was wet...
I gotta... get outta here too...make my head stop ringin'...
...least I stopped... 'Lectro...

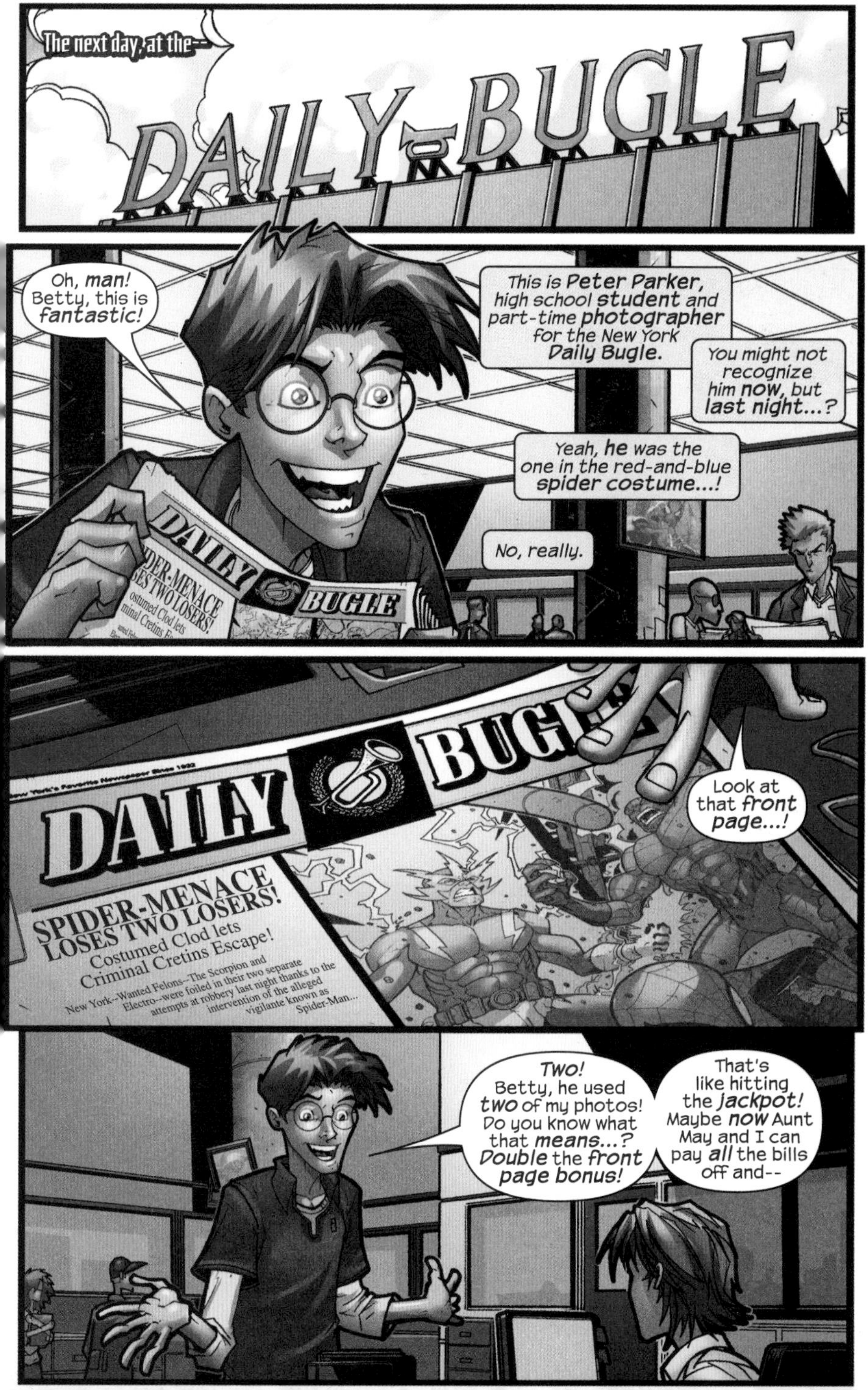

The next day, at the--
DAILY BUGLE
Oh, man! Betty, this is fantastic!
This is Peter Parker, high school student and part-time photographer for the New York Daily Bugle.
You might not recognize him now, but last night...?
Yeah, he was the one in the red-and-blue spider costume...!
No, really.
DAILY BUGLE
SPIDER-MENACE LOSES TWO LOSERS!
Costumed Clod lets Criminal Cretins Escape!
New York--Wanted Felons--The Scorpion and Electro--were foiled in their two separate attempts at robbery last night thanks to the intervention of the alleged vigilante known as Spider-Man...
Look at that front page...!
Two! Betty, he used two of my photos! Do you know what that means...? Double the front page bonus!
That's like hitting the jackpot! Maybe now Aunt May and I can pay all the bills off and--

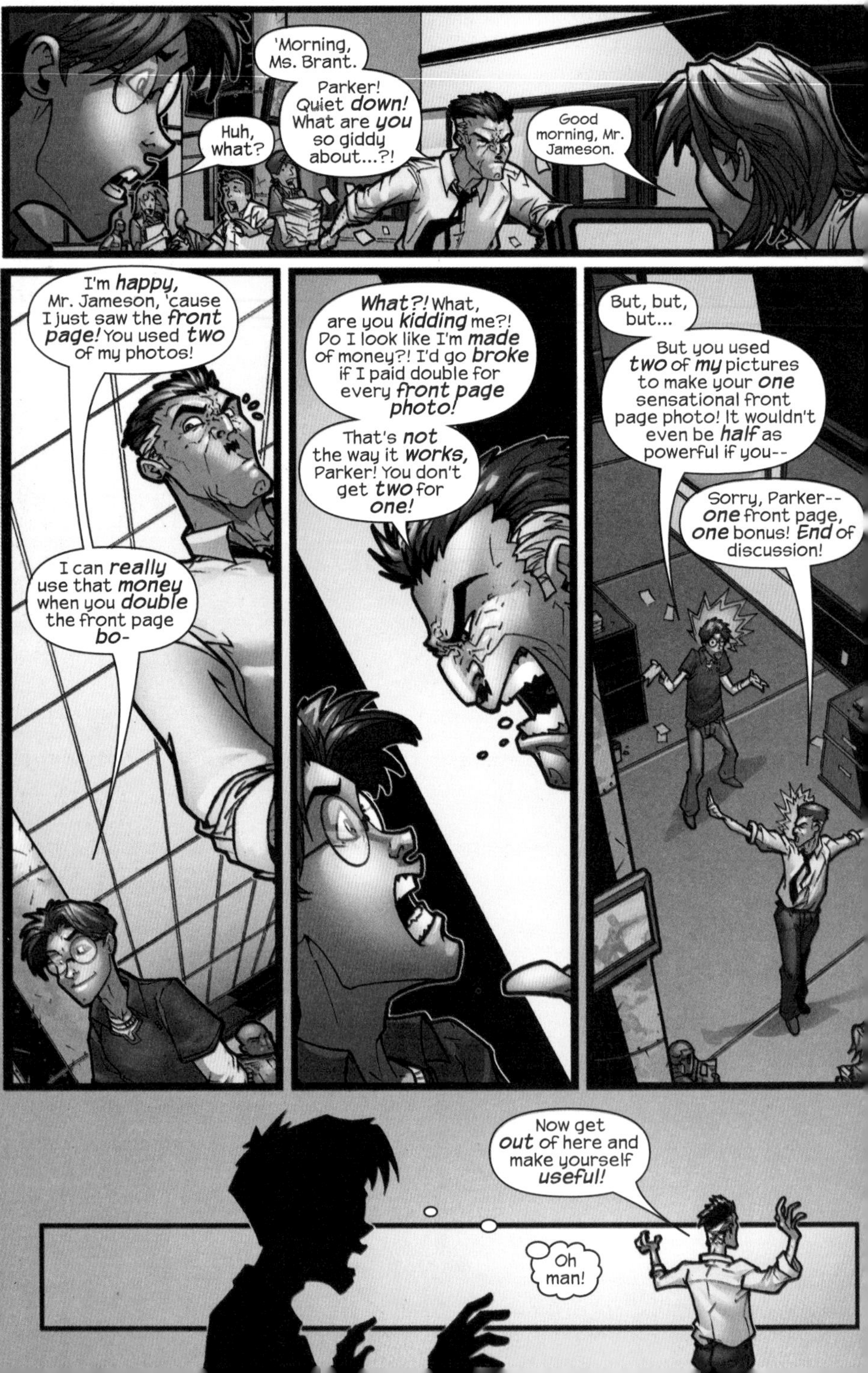

'Morning, Ms. Brant.
Huh, what?
Parker! Quiet down! What are you so giddy about...?!
Good morning, Mr. Jameson.
I'm happy, Mr. Jameson, 'cause I just saw the front page! You used two of my photos!
I can really use that money when you double the front page bo-
What?! What, are you kidding me?! Do I look like I'm made of money?! I'd go broke if I paid double for every front page photo!
That's not the way it works, Parker! You don't get two for one!
But, but, but...
But you used two of my pictures to make your one sensational front page photo! It wouldn't even be half as powerful if you--
Sorry, Parker--one front page, one bonus! End of discussion!
Now get out of here and make yourself useful!
Oh man!

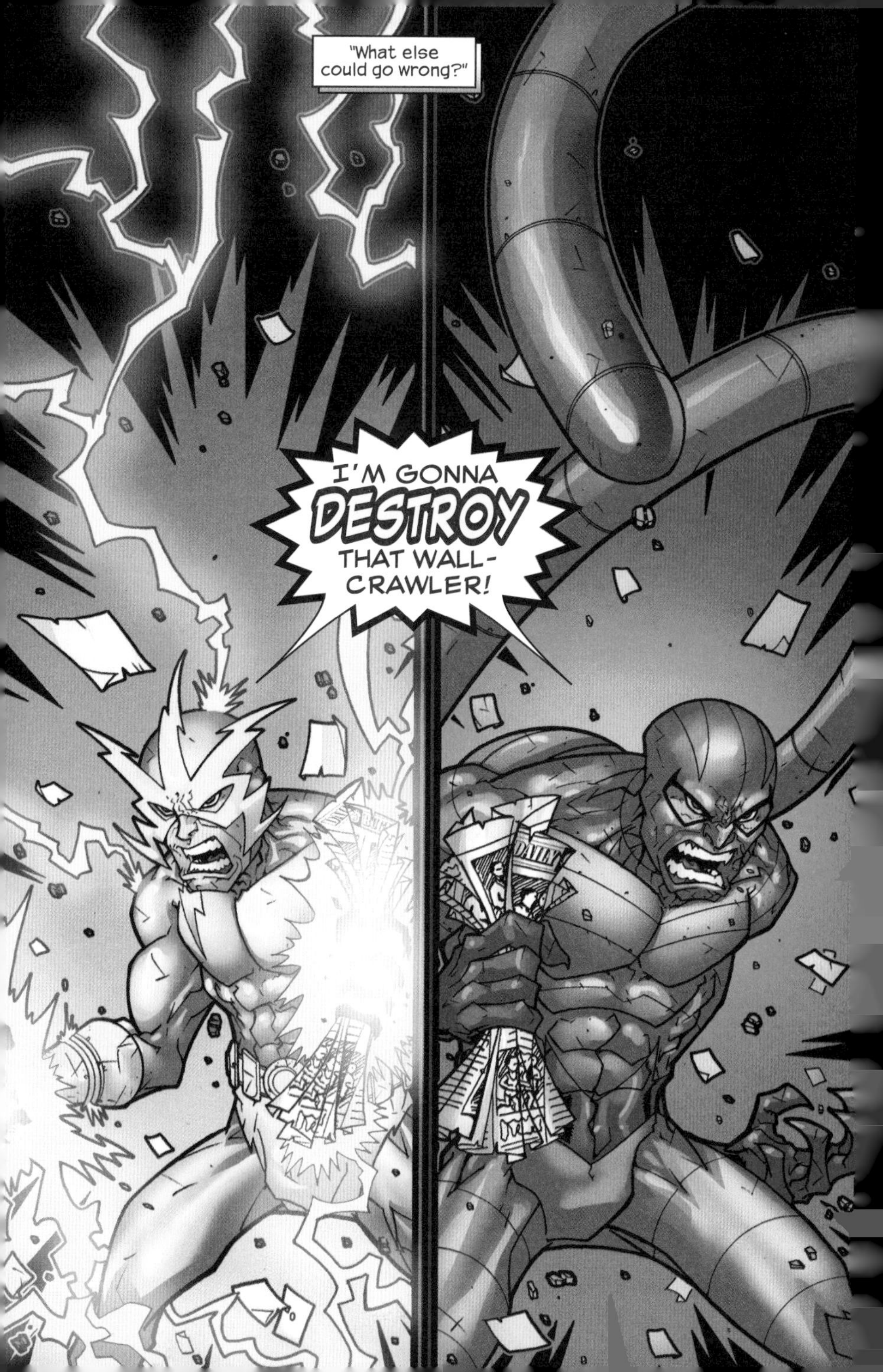
"What else could go wrong?"
I'M GONNA DESTROY THAT WALL-CRAWLER!

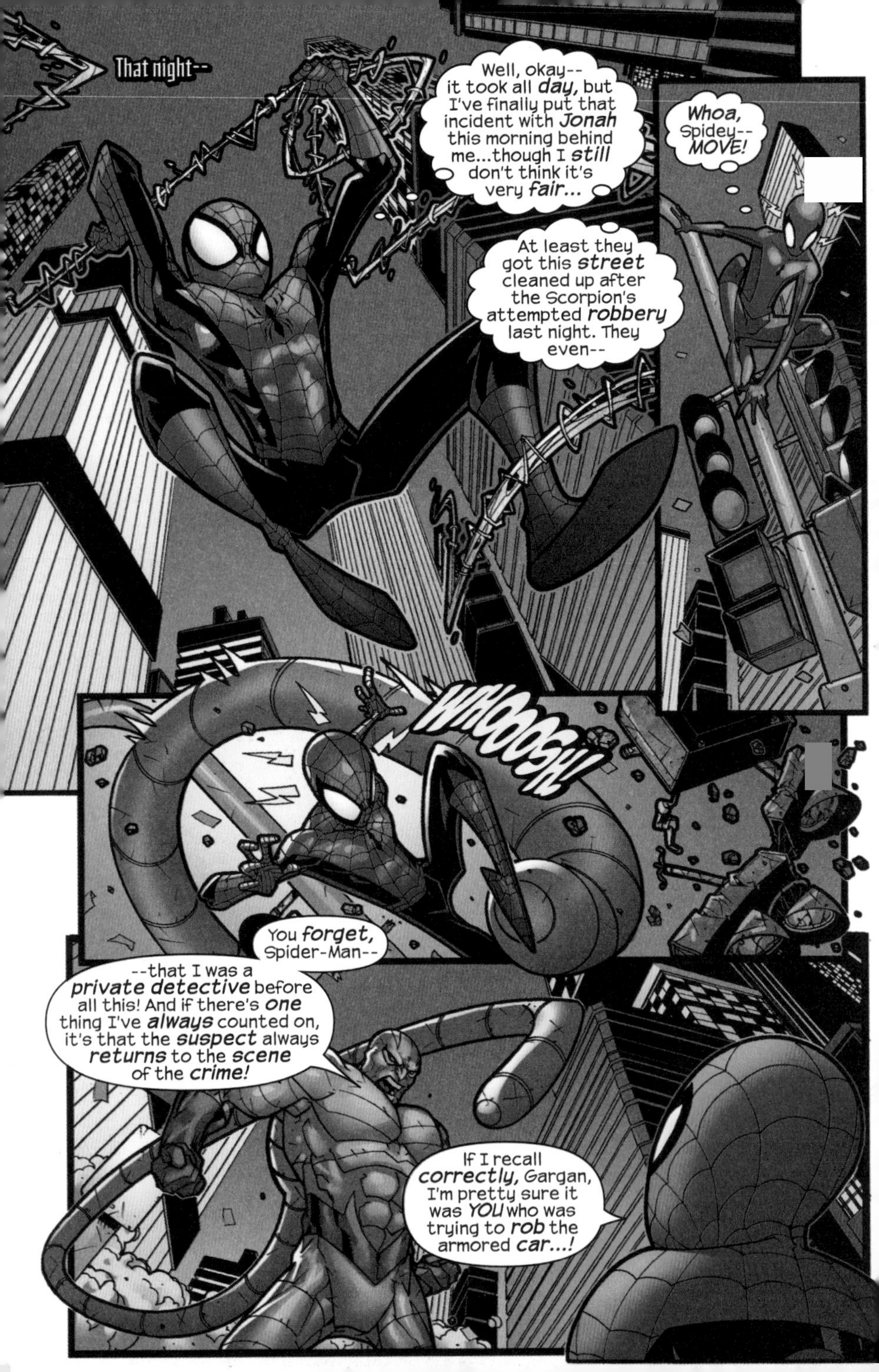

That night--
Well, okay-- it took all day, but I've finally put that incident with Jonah this morning behind me...though I still don't think it's very fair...
At least they got this street cleaned up after the Scorpion's attempted robbery last night. They even--
Whoa, Spidey-- MOVE!
WHOOOSH!
You forget, Spider-Man--
--that I was a private detective before all this! And if there's one thing I've always counted on, it's that the suspect always returns to the scene of the crime!
If I recall correctly, Gargan, I'm pretty sure it was YOU who was trying to rob the armored car...!

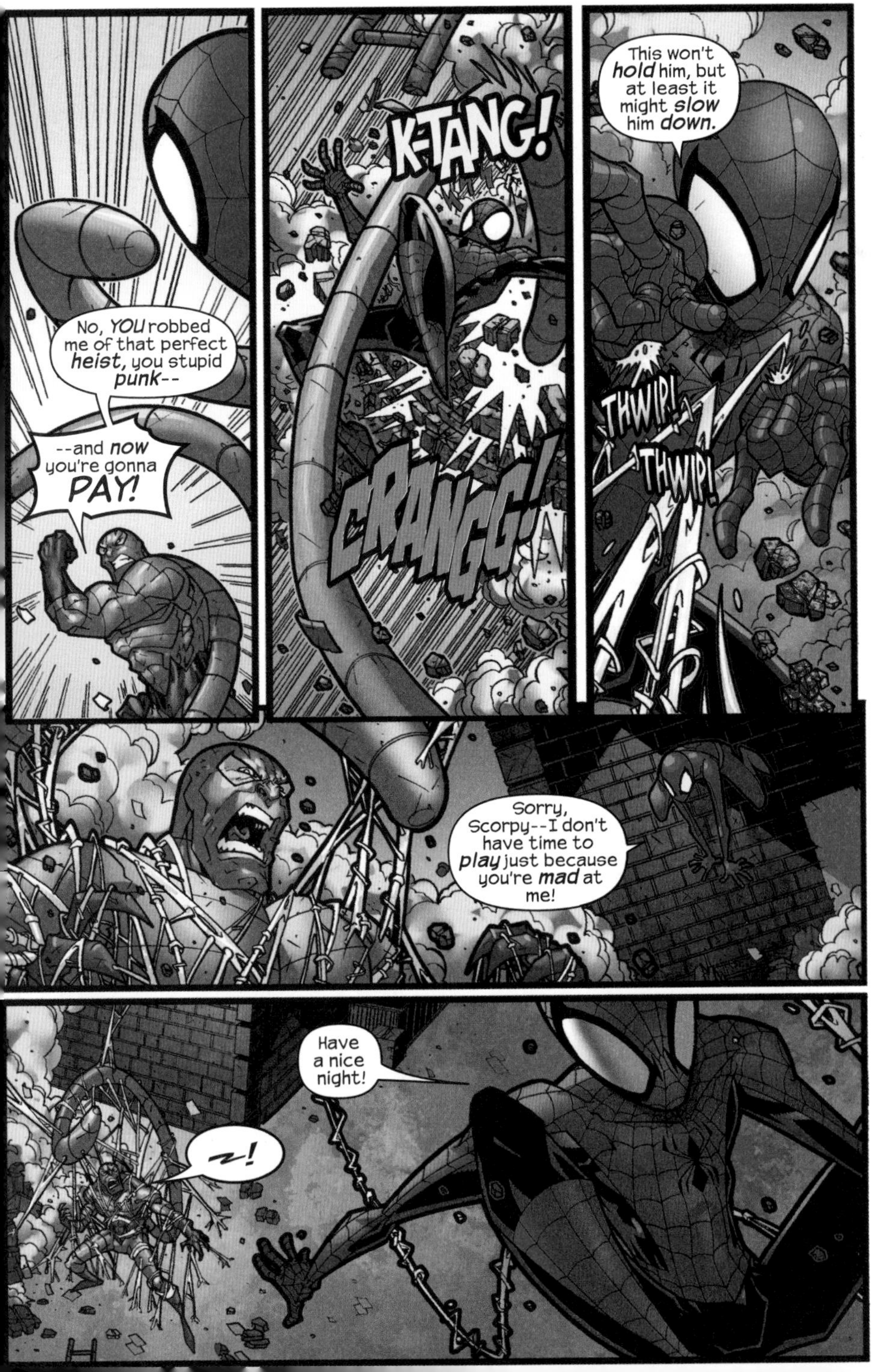
No, YOU robbed me of that perfect heist, you stupid punk--
--and now you're gonna PAY!
K-TANG!
CRANGG!
This won't hold him, but at least it might slow him down.
THWIP!
THWIP!
Sorry, Scorpy--I don't have time to play just because you're mad at me!
Have a nice night!
n!

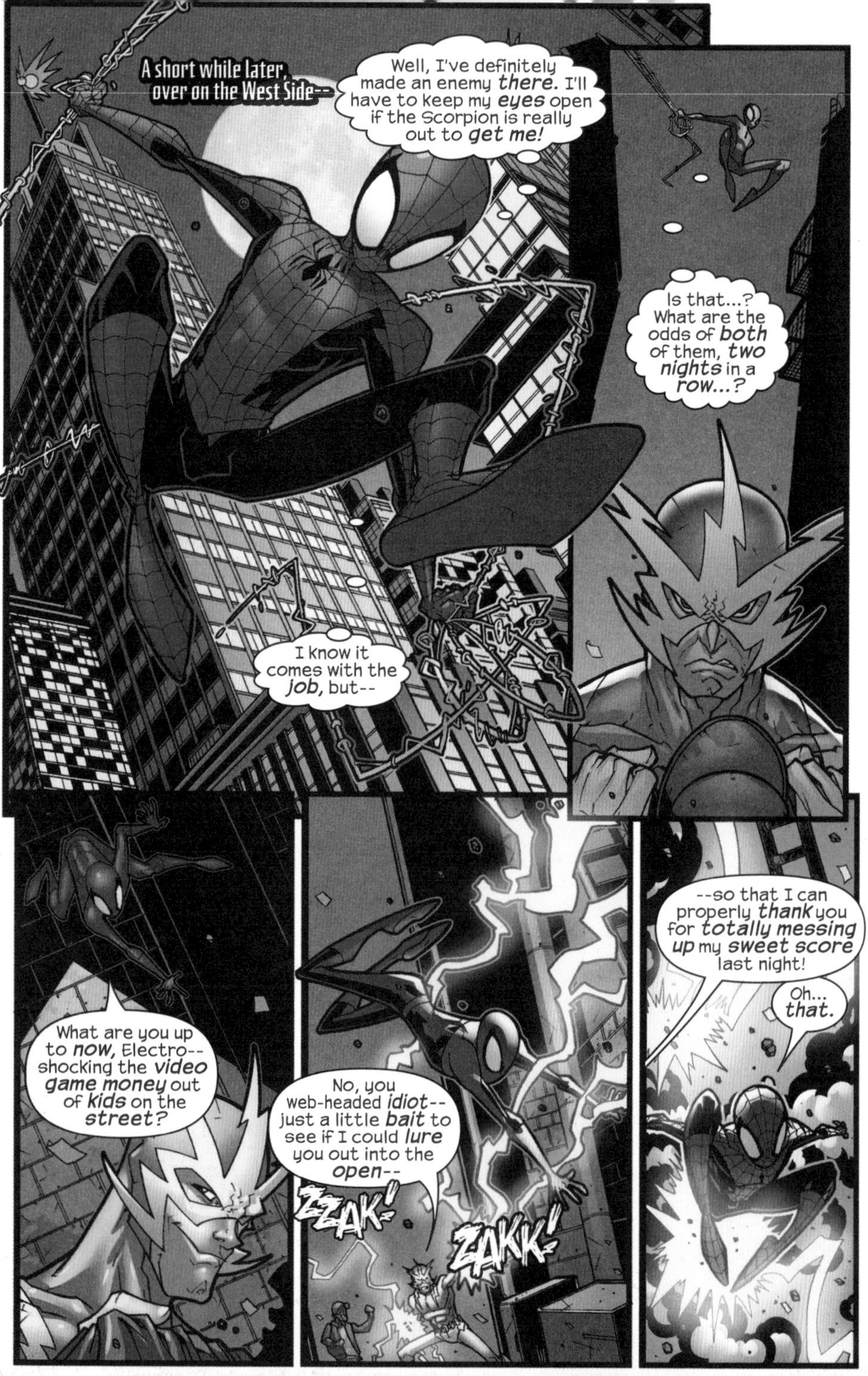

A short while later, over on the West Side--
Well, I've definitely made an enemy there. I'll have to keep my eyes open if the Scorpion is really out to get me!
I know it comes with the job, but--
Is that...? What are the odds of both of them, two nights in a row...?
What are you up to now, Electro-- shocking the video game money out of kids on the street?
No, you web-headed idiot-- just a little bait to see if I could lure you out into the open--
ZZAK!
ZAKK!
--so that I can properly thank you for totally messing up my sweet score last night!
Oh... that.

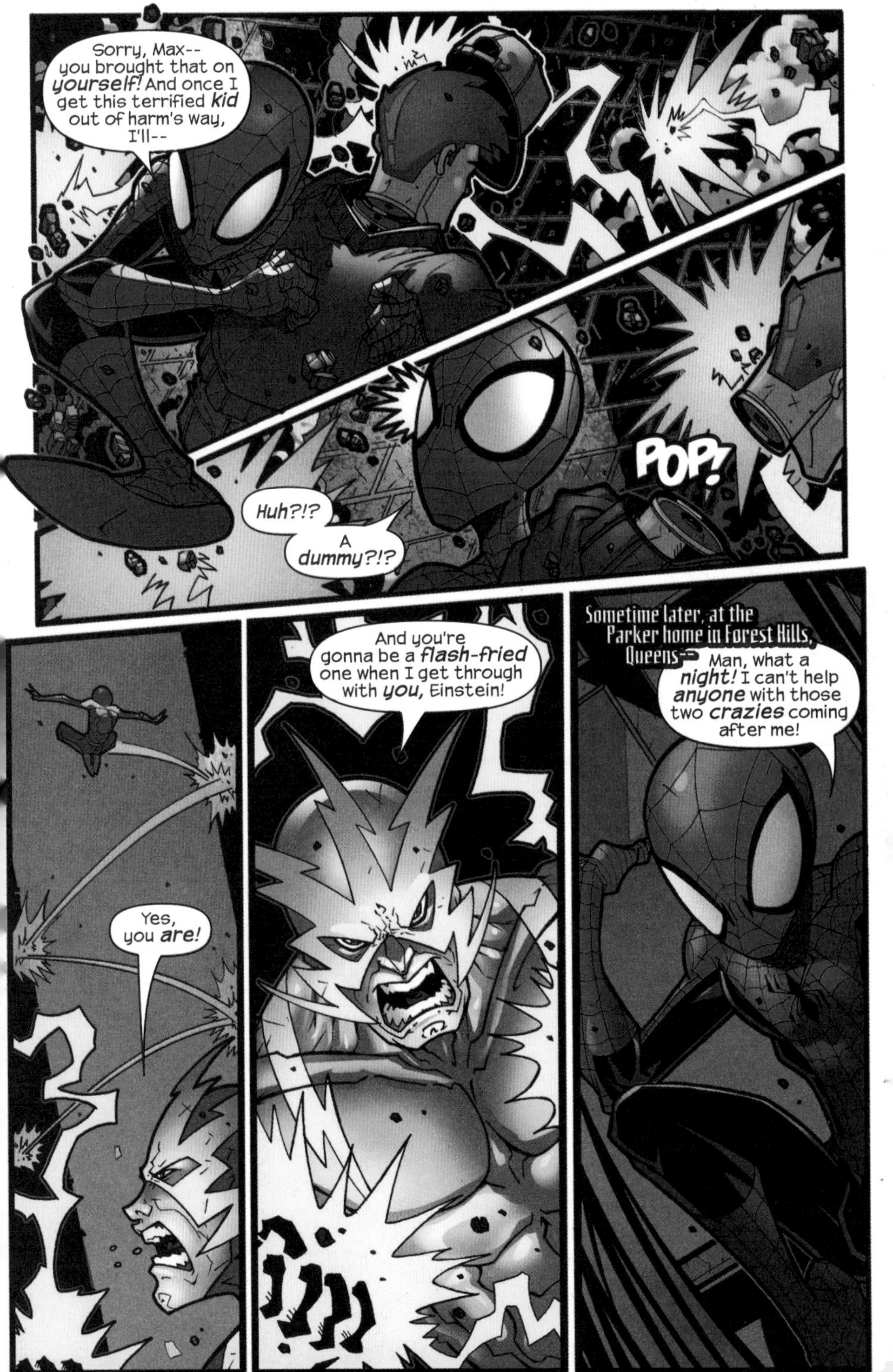
Sorry, Max-- you brought that on yourself! And once I get this terrified kid out of harm's way, I'll--
POP!
Huh?!?
A dummy?!?
Yes, you are!
And you're gonna be a flash-fried one when I get through with you, Einstein!
Sometime later, at the Parker home in Forest Hills, Queens--
Man, what a night! I can't help anyone with those two crazies coming after me!

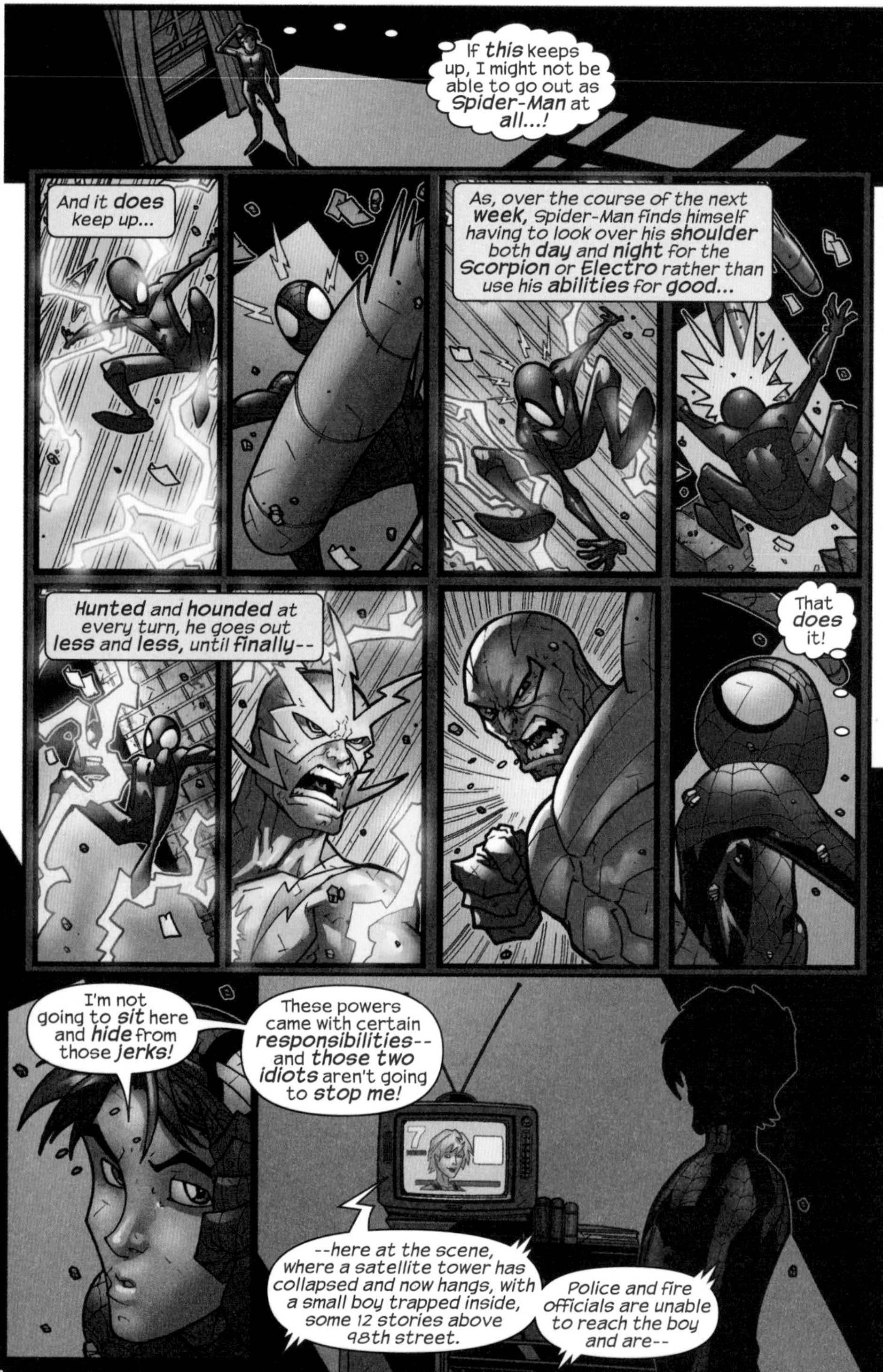

If this keeps up, I might not be able to go out as Spider-Man at all...!
And it does keep up...
As, over the course of the next week, Spider-Man finds himself having to look over his shoulder both day and night for the Scorpion or Electro rather than use his abilities for good...
Hunted and hounded at every turn, he goes out less and less, until finally--
That does it!
I'm not going to sit here and hide from those jerks!
These powers came with certain responsibilities-- and those two idiots aren't going to stop me!
--here at the scene, where a satellite tower has collapsed and now hangs, with a small boy trapped inside, some 12 stories above 98th street.
Police and fire officials are unable to reach the boy and are--

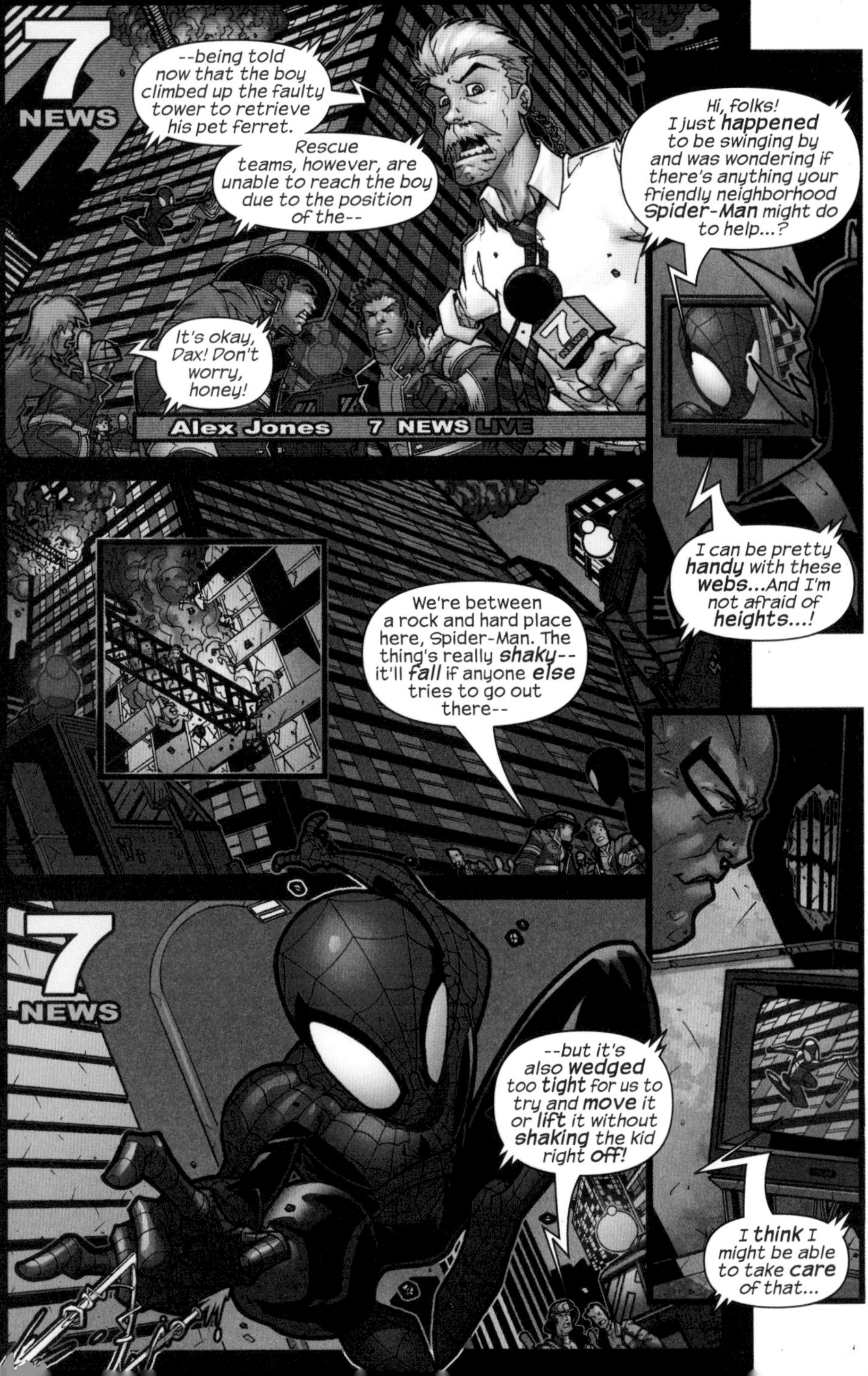
7 NEWS
--being told now that the boy climbed up the faulty tower to retrieve his pet ferret.
Rescue teams, however, are unable to reach the boy due to the position of the--
Hi, folks! I just happened to be swinging by and was wondering if there's anything your friendly neighborhood Spider-Man might do to help...?
It's okay, Dax! Don't worry, honey!
Alex Jones 7 NEWS LIVE
I can be pretty handy with these webs...And I'm not afraid of heights...!
We're between a rock and hard place here, Spider-Man. The thing's really shaky-- it'll fall if anyone else tries to go out there--
7 NEWS
--but it's also wedged too tight for us to try and move it or lift it without shaking the kid right off!
I think I might be able to take care of that...

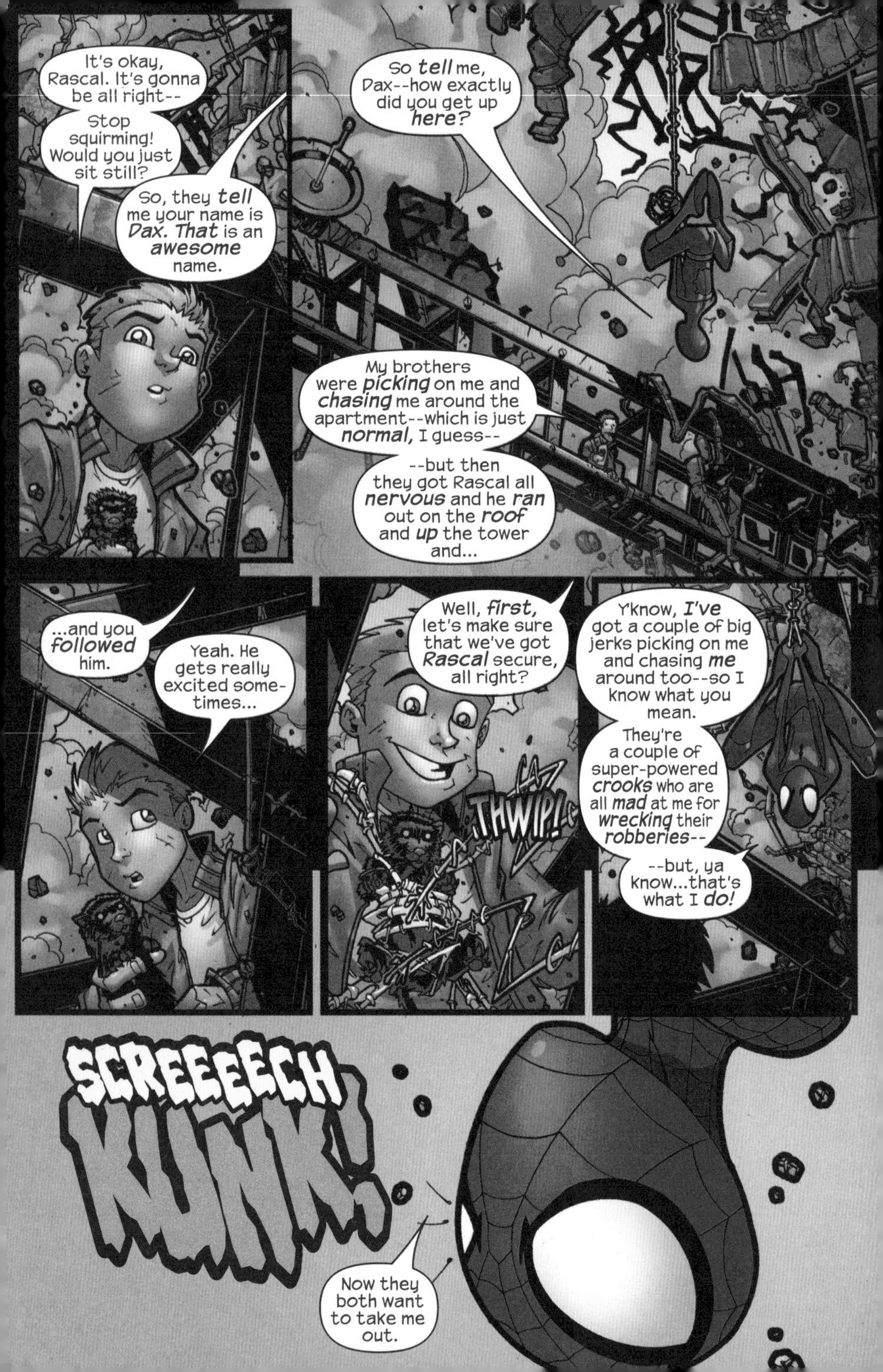
It's okay, Rascal. It's gonna be all right--
Stop squirming! Would you just sit still?
So, they tell me your name is Dax. That is an awesome name.
So tell me, Dax--how exactly did you get up here?
My brothers were picking on me and chasing me around the apartment--which is just normal, I guess--
--but then they got Rascal all nervous and he ran out on the roof and up the tower and...
...and you followed him.
Yeah. He gets really excited some-times...
Well, first, let's make sure that we've got Rascal secure, all right?
THWIP!
Y'know, I've got a couple of big jerks picking on me and chasing me around too--so I know what you mean.
They're a couple of super-powered crooks who are all mad at me for wrecking their robberies--
--but, ya know...that's what I do!
SCREEEECH
KUNK!
Now they both want to take me out.

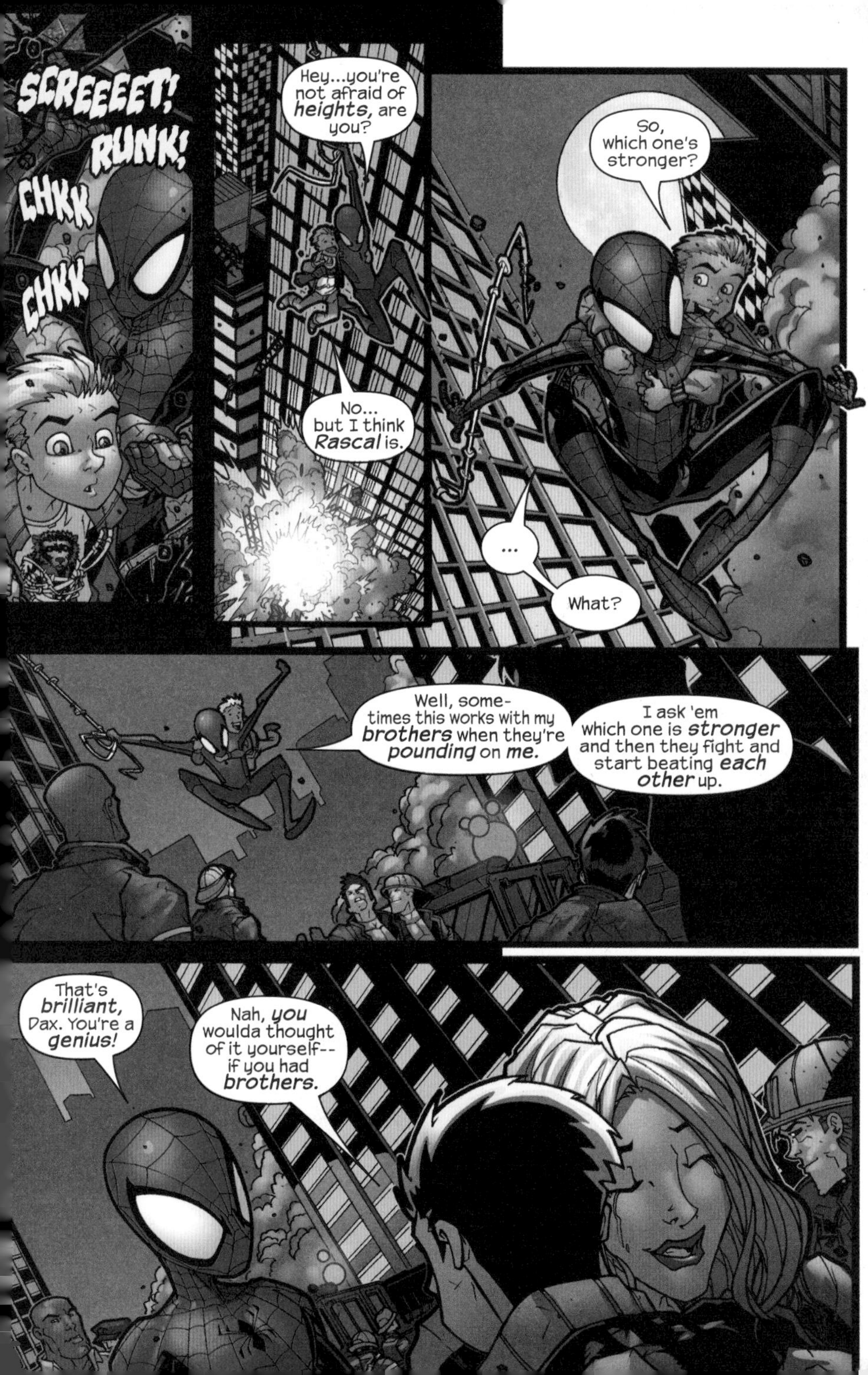
SCREEEET!
RUNK!
CHKK
CHKK
Hey...you're not afraid of heights, are you?
No... but I think Rascal is.
So, which one's stronger?
...
What?
Well, sometimes this works with my brothers when they're pounding on me.
I ask 'em which one is stronger and then they fight and start beating each other up.
That's brilliant, Dax. You're a genius!
Nah, you woulda thought of it yourself--if you had brothers.

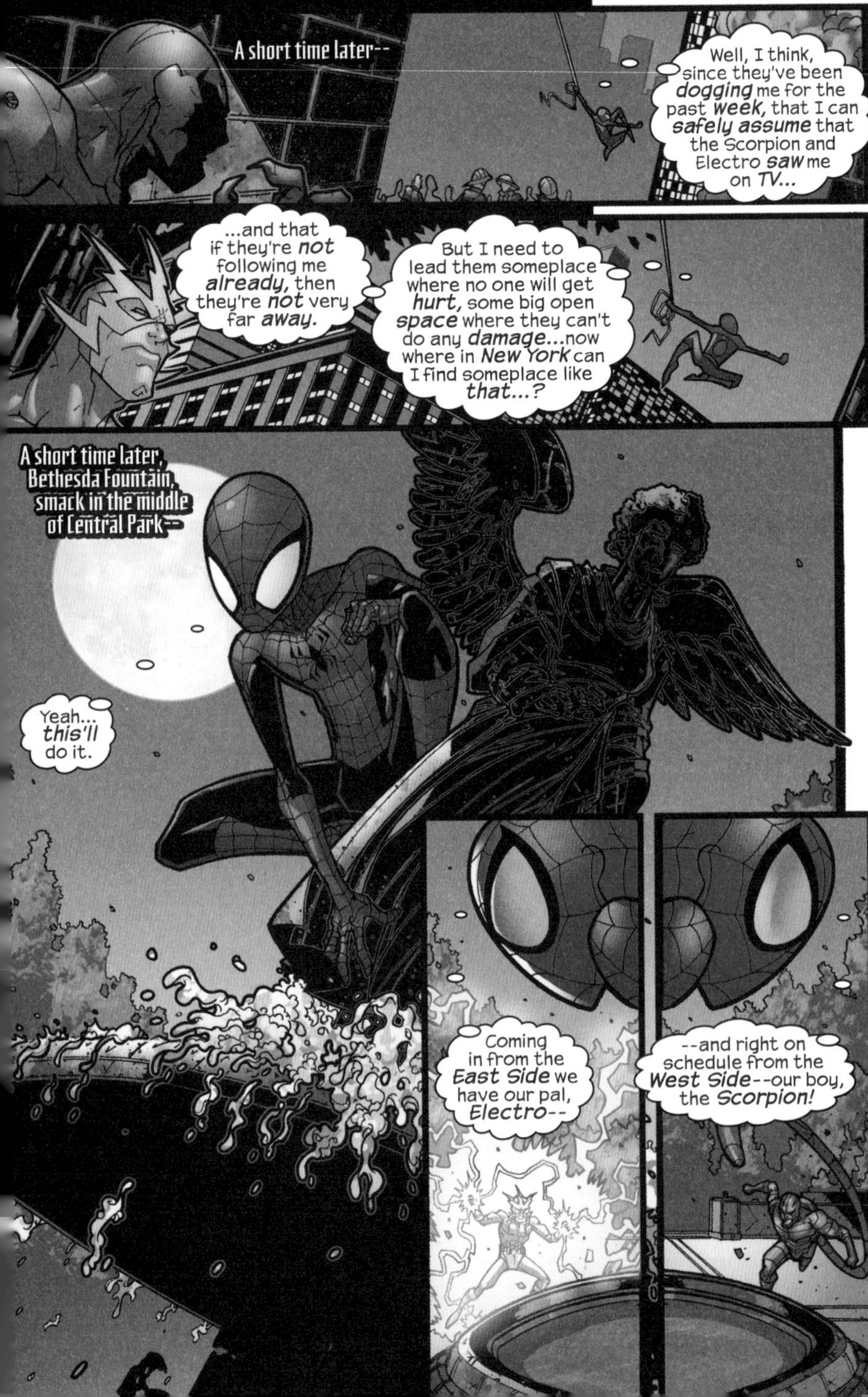
A short time later--
Well, I think, since they've been dogging me for the past week, that I can safely assume that the Scorpion and Electro saw me on TV...
...and that if they're not following me already, then they're not very far away.
But I need to lead them someplace where no one will get hurt, some big open space where they can't do any damage...now where in New York can I find someplace like that...?
A short time later, Bethesda Fountain, smack in the middle of Central Park--
Yeah... this'll do it.
Coming in from the East Side we have our pal, Electro--
--and right on schedule from the West Side--our boy, the Scorpion!

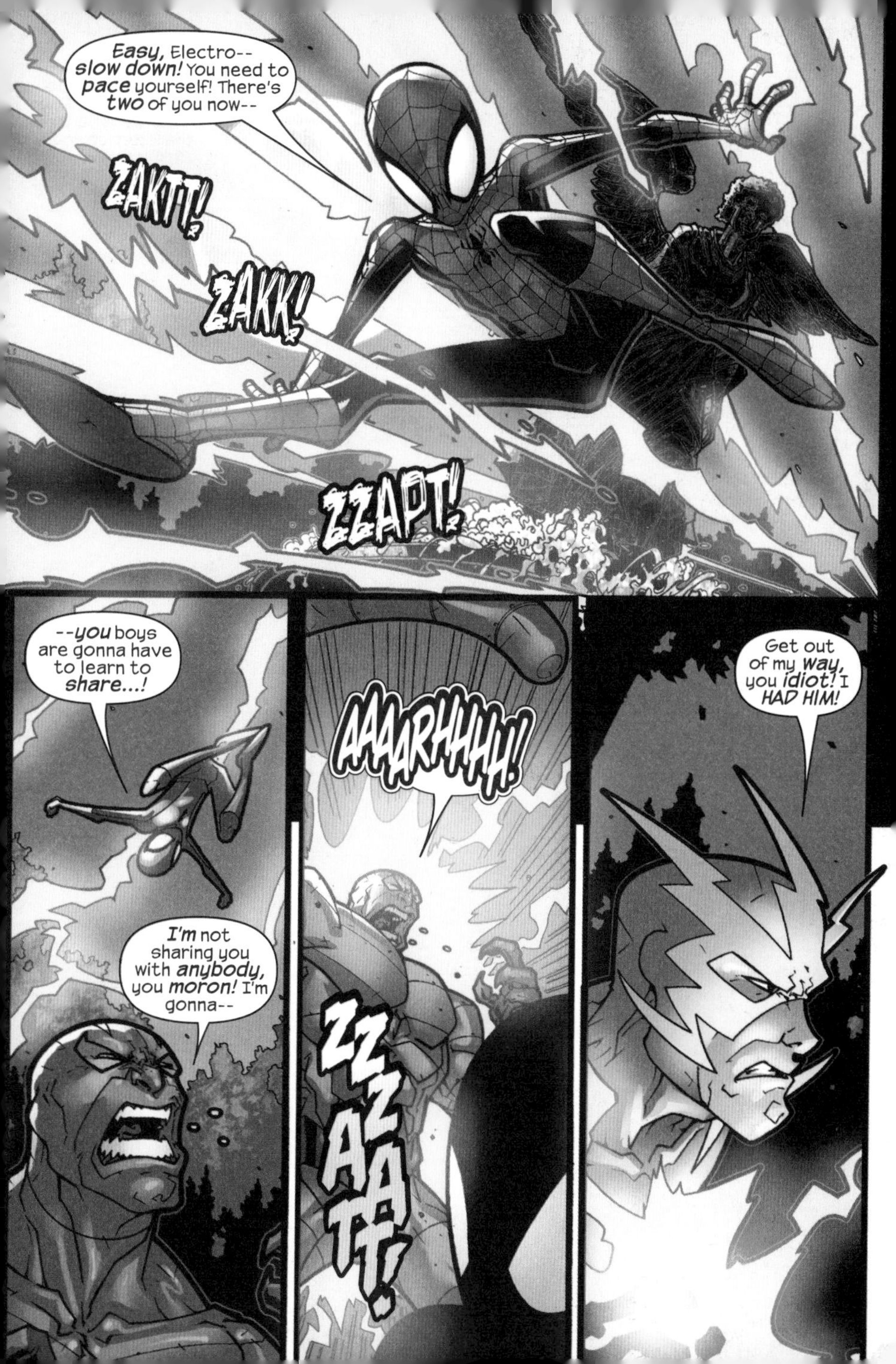

Easy, Electro--slow down! You need to pace yourself! There's two of you now--
ZAKTT!
ZAKK!
ZZAPT!
--you boys are gonna have to learn to share...!
I'm not sharing you with anybody, you moron! I'm gonna--
AAAARHHHH!
ZZZAAATT!
Get out of my way, you idiot! I HAD HIM!

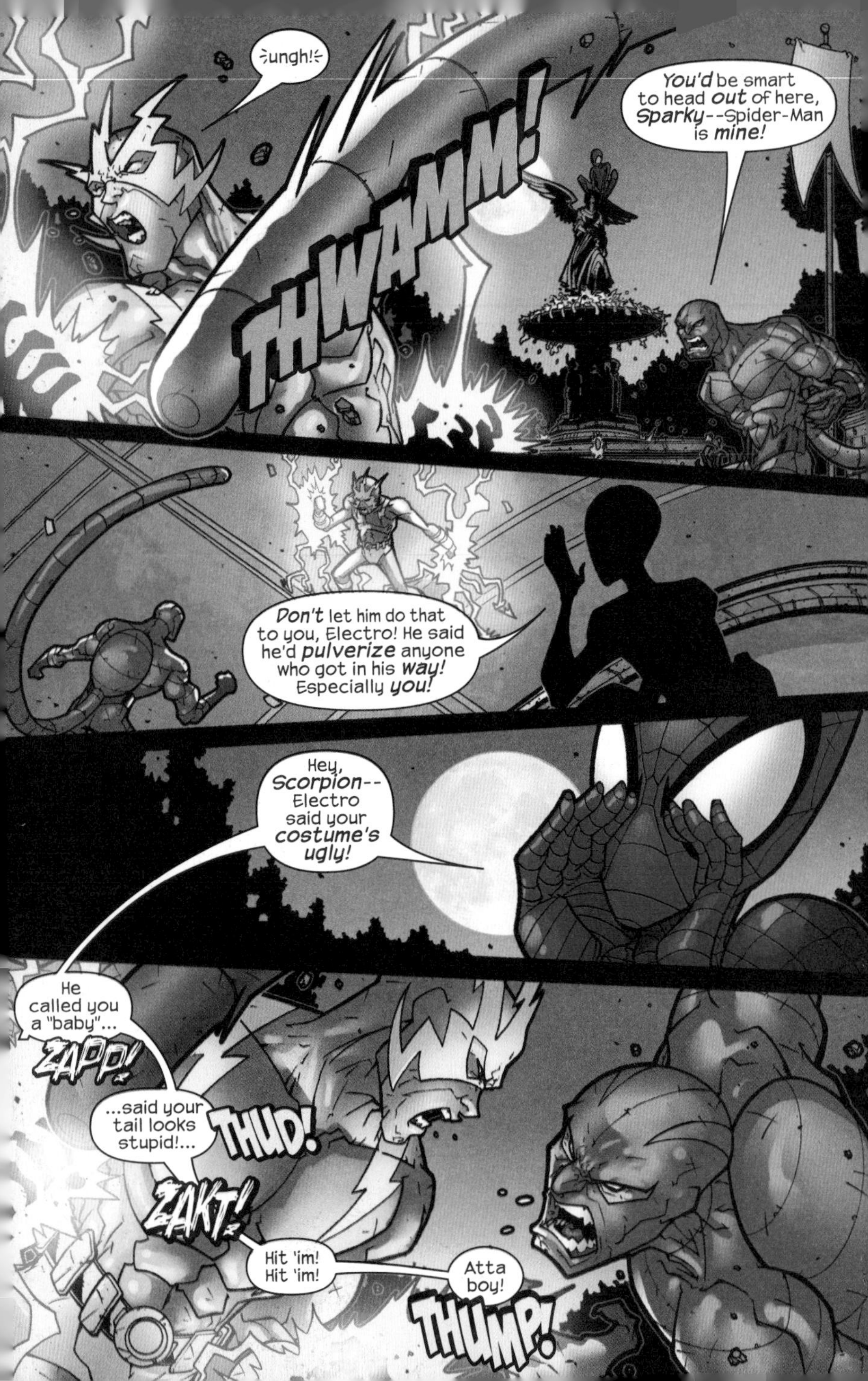
ungh!
THWAMM!
You'd be smart to head out of here, Sparky--Spider-Man is mine!
Don't let him do that to you, Electro! He said he'd pulverize anyone who got in his way! Especially you!
Hey, Scorpion-- Electro said your costume's ugly!
He called you a "baby"...
ZAPP!
...said your tail looks stupid!...
THUD!
ZAKT!
Hit 'im! Hit 'im!
Atta boy!
THUMP!

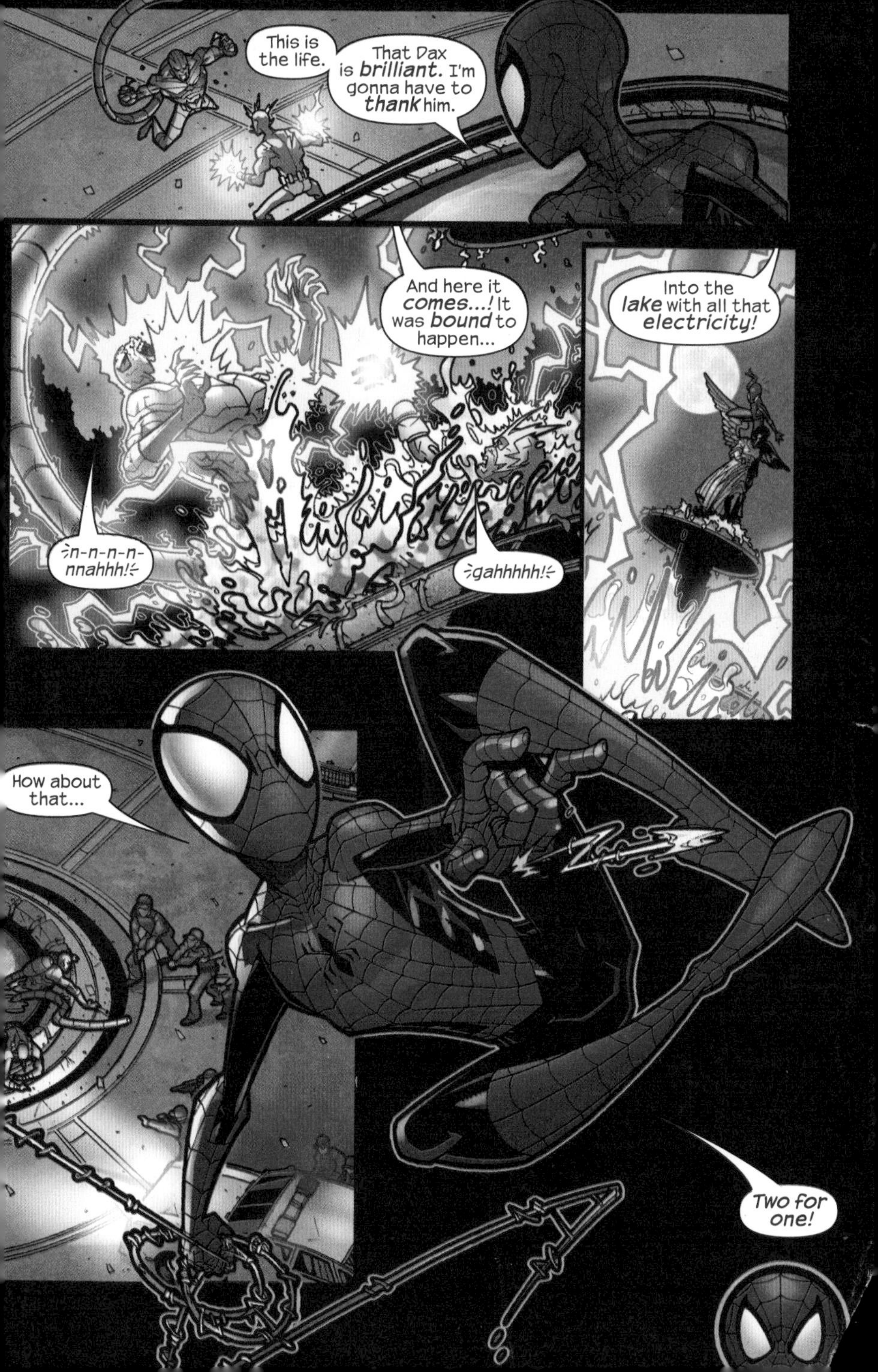
This is the life.
That Dax is brilliant. I'm gonna have to thank him.
And here it comes...! It was bound to happen...
Into the lake with all that electricity!
n-n-n-n-nnahhh!
gahhhhh!
How about that...
Two for one!

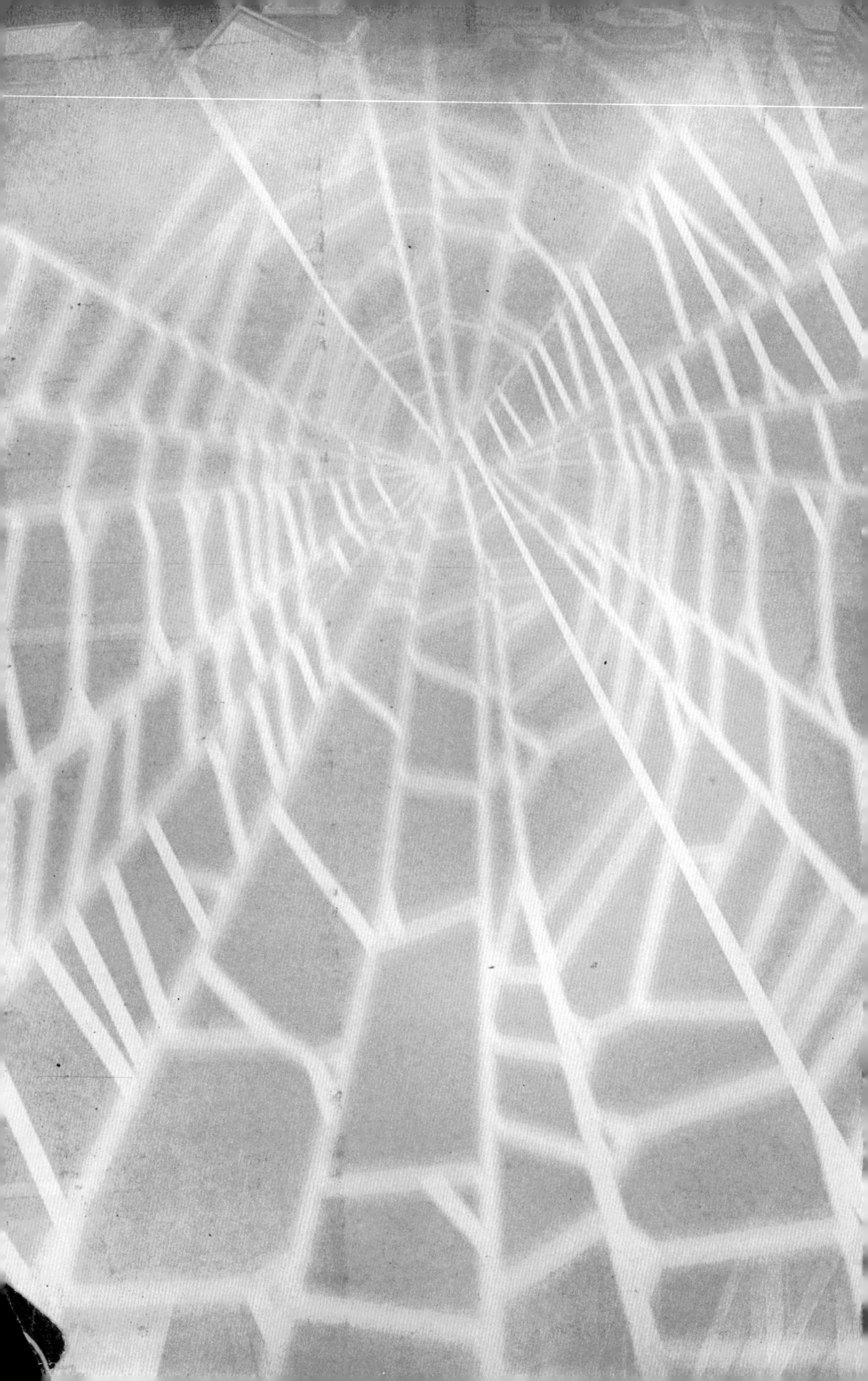